ASAP

Also by Axie Oh

XOXO

The Girl Who Fell Beneath the Sea

Rebel Seoul

Rogue Heart

ASAP

AXIE OH

HARPER TEEN
An Imprint of HarperCollinsPublishers

HarperTeen is an imprint of HarperCollins Publishers.

ASAP

Copyright © 2024 by HarperCollins Publishers

All rights reserved. Printed in the United States of America.

No part of this book may be used or reproduced in any manner whatsoever without written permission except in the case of brief quotations embodied in critical articles and reviews. For information, address HarperCollins Children's Books, a division of HarperCollins Publishers, 195 Broadway, New York, NY 10007.

Library of Congress Control Number: 2023933418

ISBN 978-0-06-329930-6 — ISBN 978-0-06-337098-2 (special edition) — ISBN 978-0-06-338148-3 (international edition)

Typography by Jessie Gang

23 24 25 26 27 LBC 5 4 3 2 1

FIRST EDITION

For all the readers who asked for an encore—this one's for you.

One

My phone buzzes as the cab lets me off at the corner of West 32nd Street and Broadway, where light snow drifts over bright signs in both Hangeul and English. I read the text from Secretary Park: A limousine service will pick you up from your hotel at 11:00 and take you to the airport tomorrow. I'll be waiting when you arrive in Seoul. See you soon.

Okay, thank you, I send back, and sigh at the irony that I communicate more with my mother's secretary than I do her.

Pocketing my phone and pressing my shopping bag to my chest, I look both ways before crossing the street. There's a party arriving at the restaurant door before me, and I wait for them to pass—three guys wearing peacoats and puffy jackets over their NYU hoodies. The last, a dark-skinned boy with glasses, catches sight of me and holds the door open. I hurry forward, smiling at him and bowing out of habit. The boy's ears redden, and when he moves to join his friends, they poke him with their elbows, throwing glances at me over their shoulders.

As I slip off my coat, a few people seated by a bar area turn to stare. Along with my booted heels and custom handbag, I'm wearing a bodysuit with high-waisted jeans. I would have changed after the show—the last of the events I was invited to for New York Fashion Week—but that would have taken time, and I didn't want to waste any more. Not tonight.

I scan the restaurant, searching for a familiar face. The place is packed with foreigners, *Americans*, speaking English so fast it makes my head spin. The hostess, who'd been seating the group of university students, returns to the podium. "Eoseo oseyo," she says. She must have picked up on my nerves, because she's switched from English to Korean. I'm immediately put at ease. "How many?"

"I'm meeting someone," I tell her. "She's around my age and height, probably wearing a baseball cap." She's hardly ever without it.

"Ah." The hostess nods. "Your friend arrived a few minutes ago. Follow me. I'll bring you to the table."

She leads me through a side door and up a stairwell strung with Christmas lights, though it's February. We move aside to let a group of girls and boys walk down the stairs. They're dressed as if going to a concert, in stylish clothes and heavy makeup, which is similar to how I'm dressed having come from a runway show. A few hold signs with messages printed in English.

XOXO's #1 Fan

Sun-oppa, marry me!

Bae Jaewoo, I love you!

"It's always more crowded when an idol group is in the city," the hostess explains to me. "I think some fans not-so-secretly hope to run into one of their favorite idols at one of the restaurants in Koreatown." I glance at her face, but she doesn't appear to be speaking in judgment, just stating a fact. "It's good for business."

"Have you had many idols in the restaurant?" I ask.

"The owner keeps celebrity autographs above the checkout counter. I've never seated an idol, but my boss said last month Jun from 95D was here with a few friends."

Jun-oppa! She catches sight of my expression and smiles knowingly. "A fan?"

"I have a poster of him on my bedroom wall."

"Then you should be pleased to know that he's a good tipper."

We proceed up the steps to the second floor. The room here is narrower but just as crowded. Designed to replicate a pojang-macha, the circular metal tables are surrounded by seats that look like upside-down trash cans. Servers wind through the tables carrying trays of Korean street foods served on bright green plastic plates. Several large screen monitors around the room play the same music video; currently it's BTS's catchy "Anpanman."

Spotting my friend at a table at the back of the restaurant, I tap the hostess on the shoulder. "I see her," I say, and the hostess nods, leaving me to make the rest of the way alone.

My best friend, Jenny Go, leans with her back against the wall, scrolling through her phone, her Dodgers ball cap—a gift from her father—pulled low over her eyes.

"Jenny!" I yell when I'm practically standing over her.

She looks up, startled. "Sori!" Jenny leaps from her seated position and flings herself so hard into my arms that we almost topple over.

The last time we saw each other was this past summer, when she came to visit her boyfriend in Seoul. We text every day, but it's not the same. The few months she spent as my roommate, during my final year of high school at Seoul Arts Academy, were possibly

3

the best of my life. I'd always dreamed of hanging out with friends between classes and after school, of having a best friend I could bare my soul to. That all came true when I met her. I'm horrified to find tears pricking the corners of my eyes.

"Oh no, Sori!" Jenny cries. "Your makeup!"

She grabs a menu and fans me as I blink upward until the tears dry.

When I've recovered, she takes my hands in hers, squeezing.

"You're gorgeous!" she exclaims. At the same time, I say, "You look healthy."

She laughs.

I love how I make her laugh. Everything I do seems to amuse her. When we first met, I thought she was laughing *at* me, but I soon realized it's that she truly adores me.

My whole life I've had people pursue me because of my money or my family connections, but Jenny wanted to be my friend not knowing anything of my background. She would say it was because of my stellar personality. Which would only be half true. Even I can admit, I'm a bit prickly.

"Sori," she says, "did you dress up just for me?"

"Jenny," I say dryly, "I dress up every time I go out."

She's dressed comfortably in a sweatshirt and sweatpants, both printed with the name of the music conservatory where she studies: the Manhattan School of Music.

I place the shopping bag I've been carrying all over the city onto the table, taking the seat opposite. "I got you a few gifts."

"Chanel!"

I rest my chin on my hand as I watch her exclaim over each

item. They're mostly samples I picked up at shows, plus a few Korean brands that I know Jenny likes. She takes out a cylinder of lip gloss. Uncapping the top and using the obsidian walls of the restaurant as a reflective surface, she sweeps it across her lips.

I pick up a corn chip from a bowl on the table, examining it between my nails before popping it into my mouth. "How was the concert last night?" She'd told me she was going to see XOXO a few months ago, when the group had announced the US stops for their world tour. "Did you sit in a VIP box?" I tease.

The many XOXO fans in the restaurant would be eager to know that my best friend is dating the group's main vocalist, Bae Jaewoo. They'd made it official when they were classmates at SAA, with me and Jaewoo's other bandmates—except for Sun, who had graduated by the time Jenny enrolled.

"Manager Nam got me the tickets," Jenny says, naming XOXO's manager, Nam Ji Seok.

"Ah." She doesn't have to explain further. Ji Seok would *never* put a girlfriend in a VIP box, where she'd be too visible. While idols *do* date, it's considered bad publicity to flaunt it, let alone publicly admit to it.

"They were good seats though," she says. "I took Uncle Jay, and he kept on striking up conversations with random fans. It was super embarrassing."

Even as she says the words, there's a glow to her cheeks, and I know that she not-so-secretly loved it. Her "uncle" Jay was her dad's best friend before he passed away.

"Have you seen Jaewoo?" I ask, picking up another corn chip. "Besides at the concert."

She shakes her head. "Our schedules haven't worked out, but we have plans to spend the day together tomorrow. He wants to go to a baseball game."

"That sounds nice." And like something Jaewoo would want to do. I've known him since we were in middle school, and he's always been absolutely wild for baseball. In fact, the one and only time I'd been to New York before this trip, I'd gone to see a baseball game with him and another of our friends, Nathaniel. It was the summer between middle and high school. I'd never been interested in the sport, but watching them get so excited, cheering and hugging each other after a particularly daring play, I'd felt a slice of their joy. I still remember that warm feeling.

"You want to come?" Jenny asks, drawing me back to the present.

I lift an eyebrow. Jenny *would* invite me to hang out with her and her boyfriend.

"I have a flight back to Seoul tomorrow," I tell her and make a mental note to let Jaewoo know that he owes me one.

"I wish we could've spent more time together," she says. Then she seems to remember something, because she leans forward excitedly. "Oh, wait! I forgot to tell you. Remember that quartet I was telling you about, the one with the residency in Tokyo? I've decided to go for it."

"Really?" My heart leaps at the thought of her being so close. From Gimpo Airport, the flight to Tokyo is only two hours. Much shorter than the sixteen-hour flight from New York to Incheon.

She'd told me about the opportunity a few weeks ago, that her

6

school was auditioning a cellist for a string quartet that would tour Asia. If she gets the spot, she'll be in Japan for six months.

"It's still a long shot," she says nervously, pulling at the brim of her ball cap. "Most of the cellists auditioning are older than me, and maybe more deserving . . ."

"Stop that." She looks up, and I hold her gaze. "You work so hard, and you're talented. You are as deserving of this chance as anyone. I'm proud of you."

"Yes, okay." She blushes, then nods. "You're right. Thanks, Sori."

"We need to celebrate," I say firmly. "I'll buy you a drink."

I press the call button on the side of the table and a bell sound pings overhead. A server appears within seconds.

"Two ciders, please," I order.

When our cans of ice-cold Chilsung Cider arrive, we pop open the tabs and clink the cans together. "Geonbae!" we shout together.

The cider is sweet and bubbly and leaves a tingling sensation in my mouth and throat.

"What about you?" Jenny says. "I want to know everything you've been up to. Has your mom finally decided to debut a girl group?"

My mom is none other than Seo Min Hee, CEO of Joah Entertainment, the record label XOXO is signed to, and one of Korea's "Top Most Influential Women of the Decade." The tight feeling in my chest, which started a few months ago and has only gotten worse in the past few weeks, returns at the thought of my mother.

"Sori?" Jenny frowns. "Is everything okay?"

"I don't want to debut anymore." It's the first time I've spoken the words aloud. "I've been feeling this way for a while now."

Jenny's brow furrows, but she doesn't interrupt me.

"I was hoping it would pass, that it was just fatigue from having been a trainee for so long . . ." I'd been working with the goal of becoming an idol since graduation, even before then. When I was in high school, I would wake up three hours before school every day just to practice my dancing. In middle school, I would spend hours studying choreography. It's *always* been my goal, my dream. "But the closer it came to becoming a reality, the more I dreaded the idea of it, of having to live my life entirely at the whim of others and be judged for every action." Memories from middle school stir in the back of my mind: whispers following me in the halls, the shuttering click of a camera as one of my classmates snapped a photo of me.

"Even then," I say, drawing in a breath, "if I loved performing enough, if I was passionate about the music, then it would be worth it, but I'm not."

What kind of trainee isn't passionate about music? But that's *why* I don't think it's right for me. I love dancing, but I don't know if that's enough anymore.

I study Jenny's face, which has remained expressionless the whole time. What is she thinking? Music has always been her passion; it's what brought her and Jaewoo together in the first place, it's what brought *us* together when we both attended SAA. Does she think I'm making a mistake?

"That's fair," Jenny says. "You of all people would know what it's like to grow up in the public eye. I could see why you'd choose to stay out of it."

Heat stirs the back of my eyes, but I refuse to cry for a second time tonight.

"There's nothing wrong with changing your mind," Jenny continues gently. "It's never too late to try something new. You'll find something else that you're more passionate about."

If only my mom thought the same. For many reasons, some of which I don't even know if I *can* explain to Jenny, she'll be the most disappointed that I've changed my mind. But that's for me to worry about when I return to Korea.

"Thanks, Jenny. I needed to hear that." I pick up the menu and—surreptitiously—fan my face. "After not seeing each other for over six months, are we really giving each other pep talks?"

She laughs. "What are best friends for? But seriously, Sori, let's not wait another six months to have a heart-to-heart."

I flip over the menu. "You're right, and I'm starving. Should we order some food?"

She grins. "I thought you'd never ask."

An hour flies by, then two, as she tells me about her classes and family, and I tell her about our friends in Seoul, as well as my most recent modeling job in Singapore, all while devouring our favorite foods we used to have while at school. Tteokbokki, the sweet and spicy rice cakes covered in melted mozzarella cheese. Garlic fried chicken, deep fried and coated in a sweet and sticky soy garlic sauce. And thick rolls of gimbap stuffed with seasoned vegetables and sliced into pieces.

The crowd in the restaurant gets rowdier as the night goes on. In the middle of the room, a group of businessmen are playing drinking games, dumping their shot glasses into pints of beer.

"We should go!" I shout over their loud cheers.

"Let me use the restroom first!" Jenny hops up from her seat, weaving around the tables. Once she's disappeared into the stair-well, I call over our server to pay the bill. Jenny will be upset when she gets back, but what's the use of having money if you can't spoil the people you love?

For a moment, the noise level in the bar dies down as the cur-rent music video ends. Then a small cheer erupts as the logo for Joah Entertainment appears on all three monitors.

"Didn't you try to get tickets for their concert tonight?" the girl at the next table over asks her friend.

"I did, but they've become so popular, it was impossible." They're speaking in Korean, their voices carrying over the open-ing bars of XOXO's newest single.

The song opens on a rap shared by XOXO's two rappers, Sun and Youngmin, their voices complementing each other's. Then it leads into the pre-chorus, sung by Jaewoo alone, his vocals smooth and powerful.

The girl across from me sighs dreamily. "Bae Jaewoo is so hand-some in this comeback."

I smile, wondering what Jenny would think of these girls swoon-ing over her boyfriend. Though she's probably used to it by now.

The music video changes to a different set for the chorus and my eyes stray to the monitors. The concept for their comeback is a nightmarish wonderland, where each member offers a temptation.

"It's Lee Jihyuk for me," the other girl says, calling Nathaniel, XOXO's other vocalist, by his Korean name. "The way he moves his body is downright sinful."

I'm only half listening to her words, unable to tear my eyes

10

from the screen. Nathaniel is at the front of the formation, as he always is in any of their more difficult choreography. As I watch him, I'm struck with a series of memories, of when we were in middle school and he chased me around the schoolyard with a frog in his hand, and then later, in high school, watching him play soccer on the field, his eyes that found mine when he made a goal, and then *later*, his hand sliding down my waist, the other moving back my hair as his lips pressed against the curve of my neck.

Jenny slides into her seat.

"Sorry I took so long," she says. "Jaewoo called."

"Oh?" I pick up the menu again, which has far surpassed its original intended use, as I fan myself for the third time tonight. I glance at the clock on my phone. XOXO's concert must have ended.

Jenny fidgets with her ball cap, and I raise an eyebrow. "What's wrong?"

All in one breath, she says, "The members were scheduled to go back to the hotel after the concert, but they decided last minute to go to a restaurant. It's down the street. Jaewoo invited me over.

"He invited you too," she adds hurriedly. "I told him we were together."

I feel my heart racing in my chest, a feeling I haven't felt in such a long time that I can't exactly place it. Is it nerves?

"All of the members are there," I say, not a question, more a seeking of confirmation. Sun, the oldest, lead rapper, and leader of the group; Youngmin, the youngest and main rapper; Jaewoo, the main vocalist . . .

11

"All of them," she confirms.

Or is it . . . excitement?

"You know what?" Jenny says. "This is our night. I'll text Jaewoo that we can't make it."

I reach out and place my hand over hers, my heart filling with warmth. She wants to see Jaewoo, but she's thinking of me. For her, I'd do anything, even face Nathaniel—lead vocalist, main dancer of XOXO, and my ex-boyfriend.

Two

The street is somehow more crowded than two hours earlier, though it must be close to eleven. Jenny and I hook arms as we weave in and around standstill traffic. The address Jaewoo sent is for a restaurant down the street. A glance at the menu behind the window shows that it serves mainly hansik, traditional Korean food.

Two blocks down, a large crowd of people gather outside another restaurant, though they don't appear to be waiting to go inside. Then I spot the van parked at the curb. XOXO's crew and backup dancers must be eating at that restaurant to divert attention away from the actual location of the members.

A few fans look over, passing over Jenny and lingering on me. I pull my coat tighter around me.

"Jaewoo says there's a side entrance to the restaurant," Jenny says. We round the building into a short alley with a single dumpster. There's a mildly distressing streak across the wall that could be either old paint or blood.

"As far as New York City alleys go, this isn't that bad," Jenny says.

"Well, as long as we're murdered in a 'not that bad' alley." I raise my bag in front of me, the clasp facing out.

"I hope this is the right door." It doesn't budge when Jenny tries the handle. Stepping back, she brings her phone to her ear. "I'm outside," she says.

From inside there comes the sound of rushing steps, then the door bursts open.

"Jenny!" Jaewoo says, breathless. His hair is longer for this comeback and it slips rakishly over his eyes. He slowly lowers his phone from his ear, his gaze never leaving Jenny.

I wait for her to rush forward, but she remains unmoving. A glance at her face shows she's . . . blushing. Is she being shy? How annoying. I shove her from behind and she stumbles into Jaewoo's arms.

While they're canoodling, I check the alley to make sure we haven't been followed, then step through the door, shutting it behind me.

We're in a service stairwell, with crates stacked against the wall to the right. On the left, concrete stairs lead upward. I catch sight of Ji Seok at the top. He nods to me before turning his face away, respectful of the couple's privacy. I sigh. What have I become that I relate most to XOXO's manager?

"Min Sori, it's been a while." Jaewoo holds out an arm and I step into his embrace. It seems not that long ago we were the same height, and now he's tall enough to rest his head briefly on the top of mine before releasing me.

"Tonight was supposed to be *my* night with Jenny," I say, stepping back. "I'll never forgive you." I'm only half joking.

He matches my serious tone. "I owe you a life debt." Then he breaks into that boyish grin that has set aflutter the hearts of fans the world over. "Are you two hungry? Let's go to the room." He herds us up the stairs, where Ji Seok bows to Jenny and me.

"Look at what Sori got me," Jenny says, showing Jaewoo the contents of the shopping bag.

"I'm surprised she didn't get you a stuffed animal." He laughs.

"I knew you were in New York City," Ji Seok says from where he walks beside me, "but I didn't think we'd see you."

Though the XOXO members and I are contracted to the same company, there's no reason for our schedules to overlap. Our lives are entirely separate. I wonder, briefly, if he'll tell my mother about this meeting but quickly dismiss the thought—Ji Seok might be employed by Joah, but his loyalty is to the members.

Through a side door, we enter a long hallway lined on either side with private rooms. As we approach the largest one at the end, my palms start to sweat. I bury them deep into the pockets of my coat.

Because of the tour, and the time I spent in Singapore, it's been the longest I've gone without seeing Nathaniel since we graduated from the academy. The months immediately following the breakup had been . . . difficult. We'd started dating in secret when we were both sixteen, before Nathaniel had debuted. But soon after, a photo of us was leaked to the public, leading to a scandal that almost ruined the boys' careers. With the insistence of the higher ups, my mother included, we mutually decided to break it off.

It was clearly the right decision. XOXO went on to become one of the biggest idol groups in the world, and even if I'm not quite at that level, I have a future in the industry, should I choose to pursue one, which wouldn't have been the case had Nathaniel and I stayed together.

As we approach the door to the room, I take a deep breath. Though those first few months after the breakup were hard, we did manage to graduate high school as friends. After all, we were friends *before* we got together.

There's no reason to be nervous now. Nerves suggest there are still feelings there and *that* can't be possible. Because if I'm still in love with Nathaniel Lee of XOXO, then breaking up with him might possibly have been the worst decision of my life.

Jaewoo slides the door open. I register a room with a wooden dining table inset with charcoal grills. It's bordered by upholstered chairs on one side and a booth on the other.

"Min Sori?" The deep voice draws my attention to the corner of the booth where Sun, XOXO's leader, leans casually against the wall. "This is unexpected."

He's dressed in a loose shirt, his long hair pulled back from his striking face. Jenny says Sun looks like a supervillain in a video game, but I always thought he looked more like someone who should have been a prince during the Joseon dynasty.

"Sun-oppa," I say. While Jaewoo, Nathaniel, and I trained together at Joah, I've known Sun the longest. As the grandson of the president of TK Group, we've been thrown together at enough banquets to last a lifetime. "I was having dinner with Jenny when Jaewoo called."

"I see," he says. I feel more at ease after this short interaction with Sun. I've known all of the members since we were in middle school. Yes, we're all older *now*, but there's no reason to treat any of them differently.

Sun's gaze shifts to someone behind me, and the back of my neck prickles, like a spark of electricity against my skin.

"Sori." *His voice.* "Why does it take crossing the whole world to see you?"

I school my features before turning around.

When I lift my eyes to meet Nathaniel's dark-eyed gaze, my stomach flutters.

I know that it's close to midnight and he's coming off two nights of concerts in New York City, but he looks *indecent*, as if he'd just stumbled out of bed. His hair is dyed a dark blue for this cycle of promotions, and strands of it fall across his brow.

"You can see me any time," I say, tucking my hair behind one ear. It's a nervous tic of mine, but I need to do something with my hands. "We live in the same city."

His eyes move from my ear—where he'd followed the movement—before returning to my face, an odd expression flitting over his features.

It's gone in a flash as his attention shifts to Jenny, who's finished greeting Sun. "Yo, Jenny Go." His whole demeanor changes, that famous dimple of his deepening. "Have you no shame? Crashing our dinner outing."

"Of all the cuisines to choose from in New York City, you go to a Korean restaurant." She matches his teasing tone. "Aren't you flying back to Seoul in a few days?"

"What can I say?" He lifts his hands in a helpless gesture. "Koreans will always find a Korean restaurant, no matter what country we're in."

17

"I like the hair."

"The concept was classy gangster. An oxymoron, don't you think?"

"Not if you're Won Bin," she says, referencing *Ajeossi,* her favorite film of all time.

"His character wasn't a gangster, Jenny," Nathaniel drawls. "He was ex–special forces."

"Same thing." Jenny shrugs.

"No, it's not!"

My head has been whipping back and forth between them as they've been speaking in rapid-fire English, my chest tightening with every second that goes by.

Jaewoo inserts his body between them, grabbing Jenny's hand. "Let's not remind Jenny of her celebrity crushes."

She slides into the booth next to Jaewoo, while Nathaniel falls easily into the seat opposite her. "Do you count?" he quips.

Ji Seok sits across from Sun, which leaves me the middle seat, beside Nathaniel.

"Where's Choi Youngmin?" I switch the conversation back to Korean. Jenny had said all the members would be here, and yet there's no sign of XOXO's maknae.

"He has schoolwork, so he went back to the hotel," Jaewoo answers. I'd forgotten that XOXO's youngest member was still in high school.

"That'll be you soon," Sun says, picking up the glass of beer in front of him. I'm surprised to see him drinking, since we're in the United States, before I remember that he recently turned twenty-one. Then I realize who he's speaking to.

18

I turn toward Nathaniel. "You're taking a class?"

"You sound surprised."

I always thought that if any of the XOXO members pursued a higher education, it would be Jaewoo, who had the best grades in high school.

"It's unexpected," I say. Nathaniel—who'd been reaching his hand out toward his water glass—goes still. I realize, too late, how this must sound, that my expectations of him are so low, I'd find it completely shocking that he'd take university courses. "You never liked studying," I finish softly.

He continues forward and picks up the glass. "People change." Bringing it to his lips, he takes a long drink of water.

I've upset him. I know I have, without him having to say it, his shoulders hunched slightly forward. I want to ask him what he's studying but I feel like I lost the right. With my chopsticks, I pick up a single black bean, plopping it into my mouth.

"So you're here for fashion week?" Ji Seok asks, oblivious to the awkwardness between Nathaniel and me. "Have you explored the city at all? It's your first time here, right?"

At this, Jaewoo lifts his head, glancing at me from across the table. Ji Seok became the boys' manager *after* that summer I spent in New York with Jaewoo and Nathaniel.

"I've been busy with shows. I haven't had time to do anything else," I say, answering his first two questions.

"Sori's not impulsive," Nathaniel says. "Not like Jenny."

My cheeks, which were already warm from the previous inter-action, grow even hotter. What is *that* supposed to mean?

Jenny frowns. "How am I impulsive?"

"You moved to Korea to chase after Jaewoo."

"Wow," Jenny says dryly, "I can't even begin to wrap my head around how untrue that statement is."

A knock at the door interrupts them. A woman I've never seen before walks into the room.

Ji Seok transforms into manager mode, standing up from his chair to block the woman. "Can I help you?"

She moves to peer around him. "I was in the VIP box earlier. My name is Jeon Sojin. I'm the daughter of CEO Jeon of Hankook Electric." She doesn't have to explain herself further. Hankook Electric is a major shareholder of Joah Entertainment.

Ji Seok hesitates—and in that short second, it's like I can see a half dozen thoughts flit through his head—then he bows. Sun's gaze meets mine, both of us registering an irrefutable truth. XOXO can't afford to offend CEO Jeon's daughter.

Rising to his feet, Sun bows to her. "Please, won't you join us?"

The other members of XOXO take their cues from their leader, standing to bow as well. Jenny frowns, probably confused as to why we're indulging this rude woman who'd interrupted our dinner. But situations like this happen all the time in our industry. We have to please people with power, whose influence could benefit the company, or, if they take offense, prove catastrophic.

Sojin gestures for a server to pull up a chair beside Nathaniel, then accepts a bottle of soju and two shot glasses from another, having apparently ordered the alcohol beforehand. "You're a hard one to get a hold of. I sent gifts to your company, *expensive* gifts, and you've never worn them or replied with a message." It's clear

20

she's not a fan of XOXO so much as inappropriately interested in Nathaniel. "Don't I merit a bit of gratitude?"

"Thanks," Nathaniel deadpans. Beside me, Ji Seok winces at his tone, which isn't exactly friendly. Nathaniel also never received those gifts—it's against company policy to accept anything other than letters from fans.

Sojin's lips purse. However she imagined this scenario playing out, it probably wasn't like this, with Nathaniel coldly rejecting her advances.

"Jihyuk-ssi." Sojin rallies, sliding the bottle and one of the glasses toward Nathaniel. "Let's share a drink."

"He's not old enough," Ji Seok protests.

"Oh, shush." She clicks her tongue. "He's old enough in Korea."

There's a loud snort of derision. Everyone freezes, and then all our gazes land on Jenny.

"How dare—?" Sojin bristles, then cuts off.

I realize immediately what Sojin has noticed. Jenny's sitting close enough to Jaewoo that their shoulders touch. She quickly moves away, but it's too late. Sojin's lips peel back in a smirk.

"You go to the Manhattan School of Music?" she asks. It's an easy deduction to make—the school's name is emblazoned across the front of Jenny's hoodie.

"Yes," Jenny says quietly, her voice unsure. It's so unlike Jenny that I feel my pulse jump.

"What instrument do you play?" Sojin pries. "I feel like I've seen you before. What's your name?"

Jenny pulls her ball cap lower, hunching her shoulders. Jaewoo's hand curls into a fist on the table, his eyes narrowing, and I *know* he's about to say something he shouldn't.

"What brings you to New York City?" Nathaniel attempts to draw Sojin's attention back to him, but she's zeroed in on Jenny, clearly enjoying how uncomfortable she's making her.

"You know," she sneers, "girls like you shouldn't act so brazen, flaunting yourselves. It's shameless."

Something snaps within me, like a firecracker popping off. Jeon Sojin, you want to see shameless?

Shifting straight in my chair, I remove my coat, something I've avoided doing until this moment so as not to draw too much attention. That's not the case now. Sojin's eyes lock on me, or more specifically, on my bodysuit, which clings to my shoulders and chest. Slowly, I glide my hand across the back of Nathaniel's chair, letting the very edge of my fingers touch his back. As he turns, his eyes widen slightly.

"You haven't paid any attention to me all night." I pout, letting more breath into my voice. Though I never studied seriously to be an actor, I did take acting classes as a trainee. I lower my eyelashes before raising my eyes to meet his. "It's like I'm not even here."

Nathaniel, for his part, recovers quickly, taking my cue. His dark eyes never break contact with mine as he says, "I could never forget that you're here."

My heart stutters, and I almost lose focus. He's *good* at this.

I try to concentrate, hoping that I've read Sojin correctly and that her own insecurities, and jealousy, will flare up with how uncomfortable *I'm* making *her* feel.

"I've missed you," I whisper, moving my other hand toward his on the table. He doesn't hesitate, shifting his palm so that it's facing up. When I place mine over it, he closes his fingers around me, and I feel the warmth of his hand down to my stomach.

I'm glad that it's him. Here, with me. There's no one I trust more to pull this off, no one I'd even feel safe enough to try this with. No matter what we are to each other now, we still make a great team.

"I've missed you too," Nathaniel says, but he's no longer looking at me.

Abruptly, Sojin stands, knocking over the soju bottle. Nathaniel releases my hand to catch it before it spills over the side of the table. "I forgot I have an important business meeting in the morning." She won't meet anyone's eyes. "I'll excuse myself first." Before the others can stand to bow, she's out the door.

I remove my arm the moment she's gone, slumping in my chair with relief.

"Did you really just intimidate her into leaving?" Jenny says, her voice filled with awe. "Gi Taek would be so proud."

I laugh. Our classmate from Seoul Arts Academy, Hong Gi Taek, *would* support my pettier side.

"Very cool, Min Sori," Jaewoo says, and Sun gives me a thumbs up from the corner.

I'm startled by a sliding sound as Nathaniel pushes back his chair. "I think some of that soju got on me," he says.

No one seems to notice him leaving, Sun and Jaewoo wondering how Jeon Sojin had found them at the restaurant, and Ji Seok apologizing profusely to Jenny.

When Nathaniel returns, the night continues as if we were never interrupted. Afterward, we exit through the back alley in pairs, with Sun and Ji Seok ahead of Jenny and me, and Jaewoo and Nathaniel bringing up the rear. They're all decked out in large coats, hats, and masks that would be comical if it wasn't snowing outside.

I'm hugging Jenny goodbye—I don't know the next time I'll see her—when I hear Nathaniel call my name from the street. "Sori."

He's flagged down a taxi, holding open the back door. I hurry over. There's black ice on the curb and I take his outstretched hand. I have the brief impression of his fingers lightly squeezing mine and his voice close to my ear—"Text Jenny when you get to the hotel"—before the door's shutting and there's a loud thunk as he hits the top of the taxi. As it moves away from the curb, I turn around in my seat to watch him through the blurry window until he's swallowed by the lights.

Three

Thanks for texting that you got back to the hotel safely. I read Jenny's response after stepping out from the shower, wrapped in a fluffy white robe.

I jump onto the bed and kick off my hotel slippers before texting back. We exchange a few more messages before she stops responding and I know she's fallen asleep.

I wait for my body and mind to relax, but same as the last couple of nights, I remain stubbornly awake. Even though it's well past midnight in New York City, my body seems to think it's late afternoon in Seoul.

I pick up my phone again. Below the texts from Jenny is the message Secretary Park sent me about tomorrow's flight, and below *that* is a message from Secretary Lee, my father's secretary, scheduling an appointment to see my paternal grandmother at her home in two weeks' time. I take a screenshot of the text and scroll to my last text exchange with my mother—over a month ago— and drop it into the message box. We used to always laugh together at some of the antics of the paternal side of my family—my aunt makes Jeon Sojin seem like an angel. As I hover over the Send icon, I hesitate.

Lately, the relationship between my mother and her in-laws has become more . . . tense. Maybe a message like this would only remind her that they've essentially cut her out of their lives.

Regardless that it's my father who's the reason for my parents' separation, his family will always blame my mother.

I delete the screenshot and, instead, text Secretary Lee that I'll be there at the appointed time.

I throw my phone across the four-poster and press my face into the pillow. Maybe if I stay like this long enough, I'll trick my mind into thinking I've fallen asleep. But it seems to have the opposite effect. In the darkness, all I see are memories from the last time I was in New York City. It wasn't winter then but summer. Walking with sandals on the boardwalk, sugar on my fingers. Watching Nathaniel as he raced toward me with a bright, triumphant smile, a stuffed cow in his arms. Laughing with Jaewoo as we sat in a booth at a pizza parlor, Nathaniel and Jaewoo on one side, the stuffed cow and me on the other. And maybe it's this last memory, but suddenly I'm off the bed and changing into sweats, stuffing my phone and wallet into my jacket.

A half hour later, a taxi drops me off outside Joe's Pizzeria in Flushing, Queens.

I stare at the neon sign buzzing on the quiet street. Through the frosted glass windows, a middle-aged man frowns over a crossword puzzle. Joe, perhaps?

I enter the parlor, setting off the chime above the door. As I approach the counter, my heart starts to race, knowing I'll have to order in English. While I'm fluent in Japanese and can speak a bit of French and Mandarin, English has always been difficult for me. I take out a crisp twenty-dollar bill, one of many Secretary Park had exchanged at the bank in Seoul for me before I'd left.

"One slice, please," I say slowly, making sure to pronounce each sound correctly. *Ls* are particularly difficult.

Joe nods, taking the bill and giving me back the appropriate change. "You're not from here?"

I wince. Was my accent that noticeable?

"Sorry." He scratches his head. "That didn't come out right. I know most of the kids in the area, especially the ones who turn up this late at night, and I haven't seen you before."

"I'm . . ." I struggle to find the words. "A visitor."

"Oh yeah, family in town? There's a big Korean population in this area." He places a tall paper cup on the counter with a Pepsi logo printed onto the side. "It's on the house."

I take the cup and retreat to the soda machine. After filling it with diet Pepsi, I linger by the machine until Joe finishes warming the pizza up in the oven.

The grease is already soaking through the paper plate when I take it back to the booth. I dab the top with several napkins and then carefully pick it up.

A memory overlays the moment, Nathaniel and Jaewoo sitting across from me. *Try it*, Nathaniel says excitedly. *I swear if Joe's pizza won't convince you that New York pizza is the best, then nothing will.*

I take a bite now, as I did then. It tastes . . .

Fine, but not like the pizza in Korea, which is much fluffier, and the way I prefer pizza. There's not even corn on it. Still, I finish the whole slice.

Outside, a car passes by on the street, throwing slush onto the sidewalk. A dog barks somewhere in the neighborhood. I should head back to the hotel. If my mother or Secretary Park, or Secretary Lee, for that matter, decide to check my location, I'll have a lot of explaining to do. It's just . . .

The summer I spent in New York was one of the happiest few weeks of my life, even if the reason why I was there wasn't exactly positive. Coming here, I'd wanted to feel a sliver of those feelings again. Though, sitting alone in a cold pizza parlor on a winter night isn't exactly exuding feelings of warmth.

The chime jingles as another customer enters the parlor.

"A slice of cheese for me, Joe," a young woman says. Her voice is low, melodic. "Just one of these on the counter will do."

I turn to sneak a peek at the new customer, but her back is to me. She's dressed in a leather jacket, her hair cut in a stylish bob.

"Here you go, Naddy." Joe slides an entire pizza box across the counter. "Take the whole pie home. Share it with your family."

As the young woman takes out her wallet, I stand up to throw my trash away.

"Sori?"

I look up to find her staring at me, and I realize . . . I *recognize* her. She's Nathaniel's older sister. Nadine. "It *is* you," she says, her smile widening. "What are you doing here?"

"I . . ." I'm so shocked, I blurt out the first thought that comes to mind. "I wanted pizza."

She looks incredulous. "In Queens?" She shakes her head. "I meant, what are you doing in the States?"

What are the chances I'd run into someone I know—one of Nathaniel's sisters, of all people? Then again, we *are* close to his parents' house.

"I'm here for New York Fashion Week," I hear myself answering her. "Not for the runway," I clarify, blushing. "*Dazed Korea* invited me. It's a magazine."

"Sori, that's incredible." She reaches out a hand and pats me on the shoulder. "I'm proud of you." I feel warmth spread across my cheeks.

"Where are you staying?" She switches to Korean.

I tell her the name of the hotel, which was booked by the magazine.

She frowns. "That's in Midtown, isn't it? Did you take a cab here?"

I nod, though I have a suspicion where her line of questioning is headed.

"You can't go back by yourself this late," she says. "You'll sleep over and I'll drive you to your hotel tomorrow morning."

"You don't have to do that," I protest.

"Nope, there's no arguing with me. I'm pulling the eonni card. I might not be the oldest of my sisters, but I *am* older than you. Come on." She waves to Joe as she walks out the door, not waiting to see if I'll follow.

When I step outside the pizza parlor, she grins at me before setting off at a brisk pace down the sidewalk. I hurry to catch up, zipping my coat up to my throat.

"Are you returning from somewhere?" I ask, my breaths coming out in gusts in the icy air.

"I was at a bar," Nadine says over the crunch of her combat boots in the snow. "Good thing my mom's not home or she'd *freak* out."

At twenty-one, Nadine's three years older than Nathaniel and me. Even when I was younger, I thought she was so grown-up. She wore all black and fought passionately with her mother and sisters, only to laugh with them minutes later, and she had a girl-friend who she brought over to play *Mario Kart* with us in the basement. I'd only spent a brief time with his family, but she—and the rest of his sisters—left a lasting impression on me.

As we come upon the house, I wonder how many of Nathaniel's sisters are home. Their house is three stories, including the basement, and painted a smoky-green color. The unfinished drive-way is packed with cars parked front to back all the way to the curb.

Nadine walks up the short steps to the porch, first opening the storm door, then jiggling a key into the front door lock. Shoving it open, she motions for me to go inside. I tiptoe around a front entrance covered with dozens of shoes tossed haphazardly onto the floor. The urge to line them all up in neat rows is overwhelming. My own boots I place side by side, against the wall.

A lamp glows in the next room, illuminating a cozy space with a television and sectional sofa. A grandfather clock with Roman numerals sits in the foyer, and I'm shocked to see it's almost two o'clock in the morning.

"Not there," Nadine whispers when I move toward the living area, hopping on one foot as she unzips her second boot. "You can sleep in Nathaniel's room."

I gape. "No, I—"

"It's okay." She waves off my concern. "He's not here. He's been sleeping in the suite the company booked for the tour."

30

I *know* that, but it's still awkward to sleep in my ex-boyfriend's childhood bed. But like before, Nadine refuses to brook any argument, practically shoving me up the stairs and into the first room on the left.

"The sheets should be clean," she says, flipping on a light switch. "There are spare toothbrushes in the bathroom, and towels are in the closet in the hall."

I must look lost, standing in the middle of the room, because her expression softens. "It's good to see you again, Sori. Nathaniel told us about the breakup. We were disappointed, of course, but we understand you both came to that decision together." Stepping back from the door, she yawns. "Anyway, I'll drive you back to the hotel first thing in the morning. Does eight sound okay?"

"Yes," I say. That should give me enough time to pack the rest of my belongings in time to meet the driver for the limousine service. "Thanks . . ." I hesitate. "Eonni."

She smiles. "Night, Sori."

I hear her walk farther down the hall, then the click of a door as it closes.

I'm alone. In Nathaniel's room.

On a bookshelf lined with baseball trophies and albums, a Pikachu alarm clock ticks the seconds. His books are all in English. I pick up a framed photograph of Nathaniel, Jaewoo, Sun, and Youngmin, Jaewoo's arms thrown across Nathaniel's shoulder on one side, Sun's and Youngmin's on the other. This must have been taken a few years back, before they debuted.

Putting the photograph down, I make my way across the hall to

31

the small bathroom. After brushing my teeth for the second time tonight, I go to the bed, lift back the sheets, and climb inside.

But just like in the hotel, I can't seem to fall asleep. Rising again, a little worried now that I won't be able to sleep tonight *at all*, I open Nathaniel's closet. I'm full-on snooping, but I need—

On a shelf, eye-level with me, is a stuffed bear. With black buttons for eyes and a bowtie. I grab the bear from the shelf and crawl into bed. Immediately the calmness that I'd been seeking all night settles over me. The bear's soft head fits perfectly beneath my chin. It smells clean, like detergent.

I'm drifting into sleep, a wonderful fog filling my mind. As if in a dream, I hear a distant squeal as the front door opens, then the creak of the stairs followed by footsteps in the hall. The light switches on, glaring across the room. I squint my eyes against the sudden brightness.

"Sori?" Nathaniel gapes from where he stands in the doorway. "What are you doing in my bed?"

Four

"Is that Bearemy Baggins?" Nathaniel points to the stuffed bear clasped to my chest.

"I found him in the closet," I say defensively.

I feel a bit light-headed, and I'm not sure if it's from being startled awake or Nathaniel's presence. I can't remember the last time we'd been alone together, probably not since we were dating. I try to transpose the sixteen-year-old boy he was then with the eighteen-year-old boy who stands before me now, but it's impossible. So much about him has changed, at least physically. He was always athletic, but he's grown into his body, his boyish softness gone. He's wearing layers, but that doesn't hide the fact that beneath his shirt and sweater, his shoulders are broad, his chest lean and strong. I cling even tighter to Bearemy.

"What are you doing here?" he asks, finally, and I take a deep breath.

"I couldn't sleep, and so I decided to get some pizza, and I remembered the name of Joe's Pizzeria from when I visited you that summer, but while I was there, I ran into Nadine, who wouldn't let me take a taxi back to Manhattan this late at night, and so I ended up at your house."

I stare at him. He stares at me.

"You don't even like New York pizza," he says. That *would* be his takeaway from my long-winded explanation.

"It's not proper pizza," I explain. "There's no corn or sweet potatoes in the crust."

"Sori, that's a *good* thing."

Nathaniel turns slightly, alerted by a sound down the hall. Stepping through the door, he closes it behind him.

And now we're alone together *behind a closed door*. He must realize this too because he looks away from me, only for his eyes to widen slightly.

I follow his gaze to where my black T-shirt bra dangles from the back of his desk chair where I'd carelessly tossed it before climbing into bed. My body goes hot all at once. His eyes dart sharply to mine, and then we both look away. The Pikachu clock on the bookcase ticks loudly, counting each second. I have a moment's hope that maybe this is all an awful dream, but even my subconscious wouldn't be so cruel.

My phone chirps on the nightstand and I practically dive for it.

It's a text from my father's secretary, a very lengthy and detailed text.

"Is everything all right?" Nathaniel asks once I've finished reading the whole message, and his voice is calm, even.

"I have a lunch scheduled with my grandmother at her home."

"Ah," Nathaniel says, then adds politely, "That sounds . . . fun?" He must be remembering that my father's mother isn't exactly the kindest, most loving grandmother.

"My father's secretary sent specifications on what sort of outfit I should wear, something elegant to quote 'befit the only child of

34

a future presidential candidate.' A photographer will be present at the estate to take photographs for an article that'll run alongside my father's new ad campaign."

Nathaniel lets out a low whistle. "You and Sun are like those rich people in dramas," he says, attempting to lighten the mood.

I shake my head. "Sun is on a whole different level. He's chaebol."

Nathaniel raises a brow. "And you're not?"

"My father is an assemblyman, and my mother is the CEO of Joah Entertainment. Neither owns conglomerates."

"Is that all?" Nathaniel says dryly. There's a smirk on his face, but as he looks away, his smile fades.

Here I've been arguing the difference between rich people in Korea and complaining about my wealthy family when his parents own a dry-cleaning service. Not that that's not completely respectable, but it's a far cry from being multimillionaires. Still, they've managed to help put all four of his sisters through college, *without* Nathaniel's earnings from XOXO, as I know they refused to take money from him.

He clears his throat. "I should go. You need to sleep. You're flying back to Korea tomorrow, right?"

"I swear I didn't know you were coming home tonight." Guilt makes my voice crack. "If I had, I would never have come back when Nadine asked me."

"Sori, it's fine." Nathaniel's tone is immediately gentle, kind.

I'm reminded of earlier tonight, when he'd put me in the taxi. There's so much he does for me, and I feel like I'm always intruding into his life. Even that summer, he'd invited me to his house when I needed to escape from my life in Korea for a few weeks. He's always giving me so much, and I give nothing in return. I'm supposed to be the wealthy one, but he's the one who's generous.

"Of course Nadine made you stay," Nathaniel says. "There's no way any of *my* sisters would let you go back to your hotel so late at night." He sounds so proud that I can't help smiling. "And you couldn't have known I was coming over tonight. Even I didn't know until half an hour ago, when I thought it would be funny to surprise my sisters. Joke's on me. I was the one in for a surprise."

"Then let me sleep on the couch, at least." I push back the sheets.

But he's already taking a step back toward the door, his hand on the knob. "My sisters would kill me if I let you sleep on the couch. In any case, you've already claimed my things." I frown, not understanding. He lifts his chin in the direction of Bearemy Baggins, who I still grasp in a stranglehold.

"Night, Sori." He switches off the light before closing the door behind him. I lie awake, listening to the tread of his footsteps as he walks down the hall, the creak of the steps as he descends the stairs. It doesn't seem possible, but eventually I fall asleep.

The rumbling of voices from the kitchen below wakes me the next morning. I pick up my phone to see that it's completely dead. After freshening up in the hallway bathroom, I head toward the stairs, pausing halfway when I hear Nathaniel's sleep-roughened voice. "Where're Mom and Dad?" I peek around the stairwell to see he's sitting on the sectional, his blue hair mussed and sticking up in several directions.

"They're visiting Halmeoni and Harabeoji in Toronto," Noemi, his second eldest sister, answers him. She's wearing colorful scrubs and sits on one of the two sofa chairs across from the sectional. "Mom is going to be so mad she missed you." They're speaking in English, and I have to concentrate to catch every word they're saying. Cooking sounds travel from the kitchen, as well as the strong aroma of sizzling bacon.

"You told us you wouldn't be able to visit this trip," Noemi says chidingly.

"I'm so flattered that all of you showed up for your one and only little brother's concert," Nathaniel complains loudly.

"Aw, you're welcome." This is from Natalie, his third eldest sister, who sits with her legs pulled up on the other sofa chair, reading a book.

"If you wanted us to go, you should have sent us tickets," Nadine says, from just behind me. "Good morning, Sori." I follow her sheepishly down the stairs and into the living room.

"Did we wake you?" Noemi asks, perking up at the sight of me. "We can be a bit much in the morning. How did you sleep?" She's switched from English to Korean for my benefit.

"I slept well," I reassure her, which is the truth. I slept better last night than my whole trip, even if it was only for a few hours.

"How'd Bearemy Baggins sleep?" Nathaniel drawls. "Not perished from asphyxiation, I hope?"

"You let Sori sleep with Bearemy?" Natalie looks up from

37

her book. "You wouldn't let me touch him when we were grow-ing up."

"You're *still* growing," Nathaniel says, throwing one of the couch pillows at her. She easily deflects it with the book.

"What's for breakfast?" I ask, poking my head into the kitchen. "It smells delicious." Spotting a universal charging station by the wall, I plug my phone in and place it among the many devices.

"Pancakes!" Nadine says, following me into the kitchen. "Also eggs, bacon, sausage, and breakfast potatoes."

"Sori's used to Korean food for breakfast," Nathaniel says. "Rice. Soup. Vegetables."

Nadine opens the fridge. "We have kimchi. Might be weird with pancakes."

"No, please." I laugh. "I love pancakes."

"Good morning, Sori." Nicole, Nathaniel's eldest sister, smiles at me from where she's cooking by the stove, and I quickly bow to her.

"I'll take some kimchi," Natalie says, pulling out a chair at the table.

His other sisters follow suit, with Nathaniel and I taking their parents' usual seats on opposite sides of a rectangular table. I worry that it'll be awkward, with their brother's ex-girlfriend in their midst, but it's like I'm not even there, which is exactly what puts me at ease. The conversation is lively, switching between English and Korean. They talk over each other, laugh, interrupt, tease. It's difficult to get a word in, but I don't mind, grateful to be included.

"Eonni," I say, "can you pass the eggs?" All four of Nathaniel's sisters turn to look at me. I'd meant Noemi, as she's sitting nearest the eggs, but all his sisters start reaching for dishes to offer me.

"Do you want another pancake, Sori?" This in English from Nadine.

"Have more bacon, Sori-yah." This in Korean from Nicole.

Noemi stands up from her seat to spoon an egg onto my plate, and Natalie offers me kimchi.

"So glad I've turned invisible," Nathaniel complains in English, before switching to Korean. "Sori, you want grape juice?" His chair skids against the tiles as he stands and moves to the fridge. "What happened to the grape juice?"

"It's in the outdoor fridge," Nadine answers without turning around.

He leaves the kitchen and heads toward the garage. Everyone is silent until the back door bangs. Then all four sisters start talking at once.

"Sori, I'm so glad you're here."

"We didn't think we'd see you again after . . ."

"That summer you stayed with us was the best."

"Nadine is studying abroad in Seoul this spring. I'd feel a lot better if she knew someone in the city besides Nathaniel."

I turn to Nicole, who'd spoken, then to Nadine. "You didn't say anything last night! Yes, please contact me when you get there. I'll take you shopping." It's the least I can do after all the kindness their family has shown me.

She grins. "I'd love that. What's your number?" She's plugging in my number just as Nathaniel returns with the grape juice.

After breakfast, I'm shooed from the kitchen so that Nathaniel and Natalie can clean. After quick goodbyes, Nicole and Noemi run out the door, with Nicole dropping off Noemi at the clinic before going to her job at the elementary school. Nadine sprawls on the couch beside me, flipping channels on the television. I sit cross-legged beneath a blanket, which Noemi had curled around my shoulders before she'd left, my hands circled around the glass of grape juice.

My chest feels warm. I have to leave soon to make it back to the hotel in time, but I *want* to stay a little longer. I had felt this way the last time I'd visited. As if, even if it was only for a short while, I was part of a family, a home.

"Ooh, the Korean channel," Nadine says, settling on a channel. "Our grandparents watch this one every morning when they visit." On the screen, a television presenter sits at a news desk, a foggy backdrop of the capital city, Seoul, laid out behind her.

"Last night, around 18:00, Assemblyman Min was spotted leaving a hotel suite . . ."

I sit up on the couch, the blanket falling off my shoulders. The screen changes to a late-night video of a man in dark sunglasses leaving the lobby of a hotel. "That's—that's my father."

"Wait, are you serious?" Nadine raises the volume.

"He was accompanied by an unidentified woman who was not his wife, Seo Min Hee, CEO and founder of Joah Entertainment."

"Sori . . ."

In a daze, I place the glass on a side table, standing to retrieve my phone from the charging station. As it powers on, it floods with messages and missed calls from both my parents' secretaries. My hands are shaking so much that I drop my phone and it clatters on the kitchen floor. I reach for it, but Nathaniel gets there first, picking it up.

"Are you all right?" he asks softly, handing me the phone.

I don't know how to answer that. I'm upset. I'm shocked. *I'm embarrassed.*

"I-I have to go to the hotel. I need to pack."

"I'll drive you," Nadine says. "Natalie, get the rest of Sori's things."

"I'm sorry," Nathaniel says, once they're gone, and I know he's remembering the reason why I came to his home that summer.

Because of my father's extramarital affairs, I was being bullied at school, treated like an outcast. My mother couldn't divorce my father—he owned too many shares in her company. And he wouldn't divorce her, not if he wanted to one day be president. It didn't matter that they hated each other, that they no longer slept in the same room. By then, my father had already moved out, living in a penthouse suite of a hotel. But somehow information about our private life had leaked to the public, and everyone in school found out about it.

I broke down in this very living room the morning we had to fly back. I didn't want to go back to Korea. I wanted to stay here, with his family, with *him.*

Looking at Nathaniel now, it's almost laughable how different our lives are. Seeing my father on the news is like having a bucket of ice-cold reality dumped over my head. I was a fool to have come here. I need to leave. Because the longer you stay in a dream, the harder it is to wake up.

A calmness settles over me. My hands stop shaking. This is my life, the life that was dealt to me, but also the life that I choose. A car honks from outside—Nadine.

"Goodbye, Nathaniel," I say, turning from him. Natalie hands me my coat in the foyer, then holds open the door. This time I know, when I walk out of this house, I'm not coming back.

Five

Spring in Seoul is one of my favorite times of the year as new buds appear on trees and the city's many parks grow lush with greenery and flowers. A street vendor offers me a strawberry as I wait for the bus, and I purchase a basket of them, placing them snug at the bottom of my reusable shopping bag. When the bus arrives, it's only half full, and I take a seat by the window, sliding it open to feel the breeze.

It's been a little over two months since the scandal, with my father's PR team working around the clock to clear his name. Immediately following the news report, his team had released a statement that the woman in the photograph was his assistant, working after hours with him on his campaign. All of which *are* true facts, even if key details were left out. He'd held a press conference the next day, answering reporters' questions, with my mother beside him, *her presence* doing more for his image than any statement. If Seo Min Hee, style icon, entrepreneur, and "Woman of the Year," supports her husband, then clearly the news report was blown out of proportion.

Luckily, *I* didn't have to participate, as I was somewhere over the Pacific at the time. Though, since then, I've had to appear in a few public family outings, including today's luncheon.

When I get off at my stop in Cheongdam, the road is lined with pink-hued cherry blossom trees, and I pause on my way to the restaurant to take a photo of myself beneath one, posting it to my SNS with a cherry blossom emoji as a caption.

My parents are already seated when I arrive at the sprawling Parisian-style restaurant located on the ground floor of the Sowon Hotel. I can already tell from their tense postures that they haven't spoken a word to each other beyond an initial greeting. After bowing to them, one of the waitstaff pulls a chair back from the table for me.

"Ah, Sori-yah," my father begins, as I take my seat. In his late fifties, my father is a handsome man, fit, with black hair streaked with respectable silver. Leaning across the table, he places his hand on top of mine. Behind us, I hear the rapid clicks of a camera shutter. He lifts his hand and the clicking sounds stop. "You look well. It's so rare that I get to see you."

"You saw her just the other day at the golf course," my mother says, picking up her champagne glass, "or did you not notice with all those politicians' wives fawning over you?"

Ah, that didn't take very long. I wish I had my own champagne glass, but I settle for water.

My mother is in her late forties, beautiful and refined, wearing a Celine suit, her lips a slash of red. Where many women of her wealth and status get plastic surgery, my mother has never made that choice. She has lines on her face, and she wears them with elegance.

"Sori-eomma," my father chides. "I only meant that I miss her. Sori is always so busy."

The waiter returns and my father orders from the set menu without asking our opinions.

44

"Sori shouldn't spend her time on your political campaign anyway," my mother says. "She must continue to train if she wants to debut this year. I have something planned for her in particular."

My heart drops into my stomach. I haven't told her yet that I don't want to debut. Coming off my father's scandal, it would feel like another betrayal, except worse, because I at least don't make a habit of disappointing her.

"Train?" my father scoffs. "She should be spending her time in a more productive manner. Idols have no respect."

"I was an idol." My mother sips her champagne.

Seo Min Hee was a first-generation idol, along with Lee Hyori from Fin.K.L. and Eugene from S.E.S. She was at the height of her career when she met my father and they started dating. After she became pregnant with me, they married and she retired from that side of the industry. She's never said it aloud, but sometimes I wonder if the reason she wants *me* to become an idol is because *her* dream was cut short.

"Sori-yah," my father says, as if my mother had never spoken, "I forgot to tell you, but I have someone I'd like you to meet."

The guilt in my stomach turns to dread. Since graduation, my father has been setting me up on blind dates with the sons of his influential friends, with the hope that I would date and eventually marry one of them. The frequency at which these dates occurred had slowed after the scandal. I was hoping they'd ended altogether. I look to my mother for help, but she's sifting through her salad for a crouton.

"His name is Baek Haneul. His mother owns restaurants in Seoul, as well as Daegu and Ulsan. I'll have Secretary Lee schedule a time for you to meet him."

"Sori will meet him," my mother interjects, "but only if she has time between her dance lessons."

Sometimes I feel like I'm the battlefield upon which my parents are fighting.

"Yes, Abeoji."

The food arrives, but I've lost my appetite. Having already discussed all the important matters, we spend the meal mostly in silence, with an occasional comment on the quality of the food.

As the meal winds down, my father clears his throat. "There's talk that Joah is having financial difficulties. I warned you not to get too ambitious. You might lose the company."

I look up at my mother from where I'd been poking my parfait. "Is that true?"

This is the first time I've heard that the company has been facing any problems. Last I heard, Joah was on the upward path, having acquired Dream Music, another entertainment company, as well as finalized the paperwork to renovate a new building for Joah's headquarters. Joah's success is why my mother is receiving a Trailblazer Award at this year's EBC Awards, one of the most prestigious in our industry.

"You shouldn't listen to rumors, Sori-abeoji," my mother scolds lightly. "And it's not true."

I want to ask her more questions, but I won't, not in front of my father. I might be the battlefield on which my parents fight, but I refuse to give them weapons to wield against each other.

My father pays, and together we walk out from the restaurant to the lobby of the hotel, our heels click-clacking against the marbled tiles. It's started to rain while we've been indoors, and the hotel attendants are quick to open large, dark umbrellas, holding them above our heads as the cars pull up to the curb. First Secretary Lee drives up in my father's expensive import. I bow with my mother as he slides into the back seat. Then I bow to my mother before she leaves in her own sleek vehicle.

The hotel attendant signals for one of the luxury cabs waiting in a line for guests, but I shake my head.

Grabbing a strawberry from my bag, I pop it into my mouth before lifting the entire bag over my head and running out into the rain.

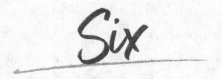

Six

It's still raining three days later when Joah sends a van to pick me up for a radio show appearance for *The Woori and Woogi Show* at EBC. Secretary Park is already seated when I climb inside, peering down at her tablet while speaking low into her Bluetooth. I nod at the driver through the rearview mirror, clipping on my seat belt as he slowly maneuvers the van down the narrow street from my house, located at the top of the hill.

After a few turns, the car passes the small corner convenience store where my mother used to take me to get ice cream after school, before the success of her company claimed more of her attention. A worker presses the door open with her back, emerging with a basket of ₩7000 umbrellas. I move my face closer to the window. Overhead, gray clouds gather above the city.

The van travels south over the bridge into Gangnam, and we hit standstill traffic near the broadcasting center. I lean back in the seat, scrolling through SNS, as rain patters against the window.

Jenny posted a carousel to her feed an hour ago. The pictures are from last week, taken at a museum in New York City where she must have performed with some of her classmates. A few of the photos are of the art exhibits, but the last is a candid of Jenny. The person who took it captured her mid-laugh. She looks ebullient, happy. A thick, uncomfortable feeling lodges in my chest, and I turn my phone face down on my lap.

Secretary Park glances up from her tablet. "Is something the matter?"

I shake my head, peering back out the window at the blurry street signs.

I haven't talked to Jenny in over a week. I know she's busy. She has classes and Jaewoo and her New York friends, along with that audition. Gi Taek and Angela, our friends from high school, would say to just *tell* Jenny I miss her, but I don't want to burden her when she's already stressed. It's better if I just deal with my feelings on my own.

The driver manages to escape traffic, pulling into the garage at EBC fifteen minutes early. The broadcasting center is a tall, multi-purpose building with studios on the upper levels and a soundstage on the bottom floor where their weekly music shows are recorded.

"Welcome!" Woori, our host, greets us as Secretary Park and I enter the spacious waiting area off the fifth-floor elevator. She's a head shorter than me with round cheeks and rosy pink hair.

The two other guests for the show have already arrived, seated on a plush leather sofa. They quickly stand as I introduce myself. "My name is Min Sori," I say, after a short bow, "a model and trainee with Joah."

A tall, slender girl with fashionably thin bangs returns my bow. "My name is Tsukumori Rina," she says. "I'm a trainee with Neptune, though I debuted in Japan . . ." She trails off with a rueful smile, implying *it's complicated*.

I smile back, wondering if she knows Angela and Gi Taek. They're also trainees at Neptune. Before I can ask her, the second girl introduces herself.

"And I'm Lee Byeol, an actress with KS Entertainment. I already debuted. You might know my drama, *Springtime Blossom*."

"Is that an adaptation from the web novel?" I ask. I haven't heard of her drama, but I've read the web novel. Though admittedly it's not one of my favorites. I'm not a big fan of the "love at first sight" trope. I prefer a second-chance romance.

I *am* curious to know more about web-novel-to-screen adaptations, however, as Sun will be starring in one fairly soon, an adaptation of a popular romantic fantasy web novel.

"It is," Byeol says, wrinkling her nose. "Please tell your friends to watch it."

We move into the recording studio where the brother half of *The Woori and Woogi Show* speaks with the producer. He's the same height as his twin, wearing hexagonal wire-framed glasses, his hair dyed a light blue-grey. After introductions are repeated, he goes over the run of show. The setup is standard for celebrity-run radio shows—Woori and Woogi themselves are indie musicians. In between playing music, we'll have short segments in which they will ask our opinions on questions that listeners will call in with, and then, at the end of the hour, we'll play a short game.

Each of the guests takes one of the three seats across from the hosts. I let the other two decide where to sit before pulling out the last seat beside Rina. The hosts and the producer show us how to use the headsets and microphones and explain how once we're on air, everything we say will be broadcasted live on the radio.

I take a deep breath to calm my nerves. This is my first time as a guest on a live radio show, but I've listened to hundreds of shows just like this one, and I know what to expect.

The producer starts counting down aloud. "Five . . . four . . . three . . ." Then with just his fingers. *Two . . . one . . .*

"Welcome to *The Woori and Woogi Show!*" the siblings say together.

"The theme of today's episode is Rising Stars," Woori says, "and here in the studio we have three incredible new talents: rookie actress, Lee Byeol, idol trainee, Rina, and model, Min Sori!"

"Let's welcome our guests!" Woogi claps.

Each of us introduces ourselves before moving on to the first caller, an older woman who asks how she can get her daughter to concentrate on her schoolwork and stop chasing idols.

Lee Byeol says that her daughter should watch dramas instead, like *Springtime Blossom*. From behind the window of the control room, Lee Byeol's manager gives her two thumbs up.

Then it's Rina's turn, and she timidly suggests that the woman take the girl to see her favorite idols at fansigning events. "As an incentive for d-doing her schoolwork."

"You want me to bribe my daughter?" the woman responds, which causes Rina to flush like a peach.

"What about you, Sori-ssi?" Woogi asks. "What advice would you give this caller's daughter?"

"Can I address the daughter directly?" I ask.

Woogi's eyes widen behind his glasses, but he nods. "Yes, of course."

"Student," I say, since I don't know her name. "I understand that you want to be close to your favorite idols because they make you happy, but there are ways to support them without following them around. Ways like Rina-ssi suggested," I add, and Rina smiles

51

at me appreciatively. "But—and this is only my opinion—the best way to show love to others is to show love to yourself." It's something Jenny had said to me, back when we were students at SAA. *You need to be strong for yourself first . . . before you can be strong and give happiness to others.* "I think your favorite idols would be happiest knowing that it was through watching them go after their dreams that you went after your own."

Woori nods with approval. "That was lovely, Sori-ssi."

I feel a little silly giving advice to someone who isn't that much younger than me, but also I'm not going to tell them to do their schoolwork. That would feel disingenuous.

After that, there's a short music break, during which an assistant brings us each a glass of water.

"Am I doing all right?" I turn to Rina who asked the question. "I've never been on a radio program before," she says, fidgeting with her bangs.

I consider her question, or at least the reason why she might have asked it. It would be easy to say yes and leave it at that, and yet . . .

"It's natural to be nervous," I say gently, "but you don't have to rush to answer the questions. You can take your time and answer them with confidence."

She blinks at me a few times, then a wobbly smile spreads across her face. "Yes, I'll do that. Thank you!"

As my eyes leave her, I notice Secretary Park watching me through the window. I raise a brow, but she shakes her head—*it's nothing.*

52

An hour isn't very long, and soon we're moving on to the last segment of the show.

"Today we'll be playing . . ." Woori pauses for dramatic effect. "Drumroll, please."

Woogi patters his fingers against his mic. "The Call the Most Famous Person in your Phone Game!"

"No!" Rina and Byeol squeal in mock-protest. I sigh inwardly. I'm not surprised the hosts—or the producer, for that matter—chose this game. It's a way for the show to feature more celebrities than those invited and therefore gain more listeners. For the guests, it's a chance to show off their celebrity friends. The more famous the friend, the more clout they'll have, and if they have a close relationship, that's even more impressive.

"We'll have Rina-ssi go first," Woogi says. "Rina-ssi, who's the most famous person in your phone?"

"Maybe, Nini-san?" she says, referring to one of the Japanese members of a rookie idol group.

Nini answers on the second ring. "Rina-chan!" she shouts, earning laughter from the hosts.

Lee Byeol then calls the costar from her drama, who also happens to be an idol. Their conversation is polite and brief—clearly, they're not close. But as he's currently a trending actor, the number of online listeners increases, with the live chat—visible on a wall-mounted monitor—picking up with comments. I watch as Woori and Woogi exchange glances with their producer.

"Now it's your turn, Sori-ssi," Woogi says.

"As you know," I begin, speaking slowly for dramatic effect,

"I'm from Joah Entertainment . . ." I might not aspire to be an actress, but that doesn't mean I can't appreciate drama.

"The home of XOXO!" Woori exclaims. "Do you happen to have Bae Jaewoo's number?"

Woori's playing right into my hands.

"I do," I say, then clarify so as not to spread any false rumors. "He's a reliable seonbae to everyone in the company."

At this information, everyone in the studio sighs, and I smile, pleased with my choice. I'd known from the start that I would call Jaewoo. Not just because he's popular, but because he'll know all the right things to say. He's my safest option.

"Should I call him?" I tease. I hand over my phone with Jaewoo's contact pulled up. His number is plugged in, and it starts to ring.

It rings.

And rings and rings. Then cuts off with, "This person is unable to accept the call . . ."

There's a short beat of silence in which Rina offers me a pitying glance. I'm the only guest whose celebrity friend didn't pick up their call.

"Oh, well, it *is* later in the day," Woori says, consolingly, "and didn't they just return from Paris?"

The world tour that had begun so many months ago finally ended in Paris late last night, local time. The members must have flown back to Seoul immediately following the last concert.

"We still have a couple of minutes, so let's try someone else," Woogi says. He reaches for my phone, which is still on the table, and starts scrolling through my contacts. I wince at the breach of privacy; he must be desperate to retain listeners. The numbers had quickly risen at the prospect of Jaewoo, but just as quickly dropped when it became clear he wouldn't make an appearance.

Woogi continues to scroll, the number of listeners decreasing with every second that passes. I have an idea to call my dance instructor, who isn't exactly a celebrity but has worked as a choreographer and backup dancer to some of the biggest stars. "What about—?"

"'Boyfriend'?" Woogi reads. A hush falls over the studio. Woogi's eyes widen, realizing he spoke aloud. An ice-cold feeling sweeps through me as I realize what's happened.

"That's an old number," I say quickly.

There's a moment when our eyes meet, before Woogi cuts his gaze to the producer. On the screen, the live chat explodes with comments. He puts the call through. It rings.

And rings and rings. I sigh with relief.

The ringing cuts off with a click.

"Someone picked up," Rina whispers into the short silence. Then . . .

"Sori?" Nathaniel's voice comes through the speaker, thickened with sleep.

Both Woori and Woogi perk up.

"Hello," Woogi says, "may we ask whom we're speaking to?"

I dart my gaze to Secretary Park, willing her to stop this. If Nathaniel gives his name, it'll be a disaster. It'll be a scandal that XOXO will never recover from.

"Who's this?" Nathaniel asks instead of answering the question.

"He's smart," Woori mutters beneath her breath.

"Do you recognize that voice?" Byeol says to Rina. "Why does it sound so familiar?"

"This is Woogi from *The Woori and Woogi Show*. We're here with Min Sori. But please, tell us who we're speaking to."

"Why don't you guess?" Nathaniel drawls. He sounds more awake now. There's a creaking sound, as if he's sat up in bed.

"You were saved under 'Boyfriend' in Min Sori's contacts," Woori says.

My eyes dart to her. If I wasn't so anxious, I'd be mortified.

There's a long pause. "I see."

"Why do you think that is?" Woogi asks, clearly fishing for information.

"Why don't you ask her?" Nathaniel responds. Even in my current state, I can admit that the way Nathaniel dodges each question is impressive.

"You sound tired," Woori muses. "Were you sleeping? It's not even dinnertime."

"I'm about to eat dinner," Nathaniel lies. It's clear he was asleep before the call woke him up. Because, as a member of XOXO, he was *also* just in Paris.

"We have to go to commercial," the producer whispers off-mic.

"Well, it looks like our time is up," Woori says, and the regret in her voice is palpable. "You'll have to remain a mystery, 'Boy-friend.'"

Nathaniel responds with a light laugh, then the line clicks.

As an ad for a delivery app begins to play, the producer lowers the volume, approaching me with his head bowed. He glances at Secretary Park through the window who's shooting daggers out of her eyes. "I hope you'll forgive our . . . enthusiasm. We had double the number of listeners at the end compared to the beginning, and that was just online listeners. We'll have to wait to get our full numbers, but thanks to you, they should be *very* satisfactory."

"Of course," I say, pasting on a smile. It's already done—no harm came of it, besides my wounded pride.

Lee Byeol and Rina join me as I walk out of the studio. "Who was that, Sori-ssi?" Byeol asks. "The boy on the radio."

"He was my first boyfriend," I say, keeping my voice casual. "Back when I was in school. He's not a celebrity." It's best to include some truths when telling a lie.

"Oh," Rina says dreamily. "It must have surprised him to get a call from you. Maybe he'll reach out to you after this."

"We've both moved on. It's best to leave first loves where they belong." I wave my hand in the air. "In the past."

Rina nods eagerly. "You're so wise, Sori-ssi."

Lee Byeol studies me, wearing a thoughtful expression. "Not a celebrity, huh? Strange, but his voice seemed very familiar."

Seven

For the rest of the week, I relive the moment Woori told Nathaniel he was saved as "Boyfriend" in my contacts. It catches me unawares—on the treadmill, in the shower. And his response, *I see.*

What did he see? It's mortifying to think that *he thinks* I might still be pining after him. I grab the nearest stuffed animal on my bed and bury my face in its stomach.

"Sori-yah?" Ajumma's voice travels from downstairs. "Min Sori, are you awake?"

Releasing the stuffed animal, I trip out of bed and open the door. "Ajumma?" I call back.

"Come down! Breakfast is ready!"

I hurry to the bathroom to brush my teeth and wash my face. Last night, I picked out my outfit for the day, and I quickly change into the white ruffled blouse and light blue jeans. As I close my bedroom door behind me, my eyes flit to the master suite at the end of the hall. It's my mother's bedroom, but she hasn't slept there in over a month, either because she's traveling on business trips or staying overnight at the company.

I wonder if I should pack up clothes to bring to her. Is she skipping meals? At least when she comes home, she can have proper meals, as Ajumma is one of the few people my mother will listen to when she tells her she needs to eat. Since before raising me, she raised *her.*

I toe on my house slippers at the bottom of the stairs and head across the front entrance to the dining room. Though it's early in the morning, the chandelier sparkles over an array of dishes that my housekeeper has laid out on the long table.

I pull the chair back from the table and sit down, admiring the spread. Surrounding a small grilled fish on a bed of lettuce are a half dozen vegetables, both pickled and freshly prepared. Directly in front of me is a bowl of beef-and-radish soup, several scoops of thick, fluffy rice, and a small plate that holds a single perfectly cooked sunny-side up egg.

"Thank you for the meal," I say, before picking up the cool metal chopsticks, cutting off a piece of egg, and placing it between my lips.

"Mm," Ajumma says approvingly, as she takes the seat opposite me. "Eat lots."

Ajumma is in her late sixties, and I've known her my whole life. My family used to also employ a driver, but my father took Mr. Kim when he left.

My mother got Ajumma and the house. My father got Ajeossi and the car. And they split me.

As usual, there's only one place setting at the long table. I've asked Ajumma to join me for meals, but she refuses. It's a quiet affair as I reach my chopsticks across the table, my spoon lightly clinking against the rim of the bowl. Not for the first time, I'm reminded of that morning at Nathaniel's house when he and his sisters had to scramble over each other to grab dishes, filling the air with lively chatter.

"Sori?" I glance up to find Ajumma watching me with a crease between her brows. "You look tired. Are you sleeping well?"

When it's not dreams of the embarrassing moment on the radio show, it's dreams of New York, not just that morning at Nathaniel's house, but the night before, when I saw him at the restaurant for the first time in several months. How at first it was awkward, because we didn't know how to act around each other, but then, as we worked together to protect Jenny, and later as he teased me at his house, it was like having a glimmer of what we were like before, when we were friends.

"I'm fine," I say. "I'll go to bed earlier tonight."

She clicks her tongue, clearly not satisfied.

"I'm seeing Gi Taek and Angela today," I say to distract her.

It works because her expression immediately brightens. She met Angela and Gi Taek when I brought them to the house, where she proceeded to thank them for being my friends. Gi Taek likes to remind me of this moment as often as possible. She's also met Jenny, who stayed with me last summer when she wasn't at her grandmother's. I'd caught Ajumma looking in on us with actual tears of joy in her eyes. It's embarrassing, but I can't blame her. Before Jenny, who came as a package deal with Gi Taek and Angela, I hadn't *had* any friends. Well, besides Nathaniel and Jaewoo.

"Actually, I need to leave soon if I'm to meet them on time." I place my chopsticks on the chopstick rest.

"Yes, of course!" she says. "You mustn't keep them waiting."

Feeling a sudden rush of affection and gratitude, I move around the table and press a kiss to her cheek. "Thank you for the meal," I say.

"Sweet girl," she says, patting my back. "Always."

"Sori!" Angela spots me across the coffee shop, pressing her hand to her head to keep her beret from flying off as she winds around the tables.

After a hug, she plops onto the cushioned seat opposite me.

"Where's Hong Gi Taek?" I ask. They were supposed to come together. This coffee shop is one subway stop away from Neptune Entertainment, where both of them are trainees, Gi Taek having joined soon after graduation.

Her eyes widen and she turns in her seat. "He's not behind me?"

I laugh. "He probably popped into a store while you weren't looking."

She turns back with a grin. "There was an Olive Young outside the subway station."

"I was on a radio show with someone from your company," I tell her once we've placed our orders at the counter and returned to the table with our drinks. "Tsukumori Rina."

"Rina!" Angela exclaims. "She's a sweetheart."

"Aw, don't tell me you're talking about me again?" Gi Taek pulls out a chair next to Angela, grabbing the drink she bought for him and bringing it to his cherry-tinted mouth.

"Yah, Hong Gi Taek," I say. "We were wondering when you'd make an appearance."

"I got distracted," he says, holding up his shoulder bag. "I got a gift . . ."—he brings the bag to his chest—"for me!"

I roll my eyes. "You should come over to my house soon. My housekeeper wants to see you both."

"Remember when she thanked us for being your friends?" Gi Taek laughs, a fact that I don't think he'll ever let go.

"No." I feign ignorance. "Did she say that?"

The morning and afternoon fly by as we catch up on what we've been up to since we last saw each other, eventually moving to another café, and then a third. We end up at Subway for dinner.

"I miss Jenny!" Angela says before proceeding to take a large bite of her tuna sub.

"Maybe she's forgotten us," Gi Taek says, twirling his straw. "Now that she has her fancy New York friends."

I know he's joking, but it's close to what I've been thinking lately. My phone buzzes and I quickly reach for it.

"Jenny?" Gi Taek asks.

I shake my head. "It's from my mother." I skim the message. "She wants me to come to Joah early tomorrow morning."

Gi Taek and Angela exchange a glance. I filled them in on my decision not to become an idol when I got back from New York. They were sad, as it was a dream the three of us shared, but they supported me. Though Angela shed a few tears.

"You haven't *told* her yet?" Gi Taek says.

"I wish I knew how she would take it. I feel like it's been *her dream* for me longer than it was something I had ever wanted."

"You need a game plan," Gi Taek says. "You have to give your mom a better career path for you than being an idol."

I nod slowly. "That's a good idea, but I don't know what that is."

"You could be a stylist!" Angela says. "You're always so stylish, Sori."

"Or a dance instructor. Remember when you taught Jenny when she took that dance class?"

I don't know if either of those are right for me, but I *would* feel better having a plan. My mother might have personal reasons why she wanted me to debut as an idol, but she's also a businesswoman. If I can give her an alternative path for me that's a better use of my time—at least in her eyes—then maybe she won't be so disappointed.

"We should do something to celebrate you deciding to talk to your mother," Gi Taek says, and Angela nods eagerly.

There's a familiar glint in his eye, and I know what his answer will be even before I ask, "What did you have in mind?"

"Noraebang!" Angela and Gi Taek shout together.

Eight

We take the subway to the next station over to find a karaoke room, choosing one at random near Exit 4. It's on the third floor of a building that contains multiple businesses, including a seafood restaurant on the second floor and a billiard hall on the fifth. Gi Taek pays for two hours' use of the room, while Angela and I inspect the small selection of snacks and sodas. We connect eyes briefly over the counter before grabbing as many items as we can, then fighting over who gets to pay.

We pile into the small room. Gi Taek immediately goes for the remote control, his fingers flying over the keys as he queues up the first few songs. Angela heads straight for the tambourine, twirling it expertly in her hand. The loud opening chord of Big Bang's "Fantastic Baby" plays, and I realize it's going to be *that* kind of night.

What is it about singing at the top of your lungs in a small room with the people you love best that makes all your worries disappear? Sometimes we sing together, other times as duos—Gi Taek and I perform a ballad that has Angela in literal tears—or as solos, because everyone enjoys a good spotlight moment when singing their favorite songs.

While Gi Taek and Angela channel Chanyeol and Punch, a glow of light catches my attention, and I turn to see Gi Taek's phone is lit up. I reach for it.

"Hong Gi Taek!" I shout, and hold the phone up so that the

screen's facing him. He steps around the table and takes it. Glancing at the screen, he brings it to his ear.

"Yah, saekki," he says, playfully. "Took you long enough to call me back."

Angela begins to rap Chanyeol's part of the song and I lose my mind, screaming like I'm being murdered.

Gi Taek presses his hand to his ear to better hear his friend. "I can't play right now, I'm out with friends. We're at a noraebang near Exit 4. Come join us."

I scowl at Gi Taek. Is he really inviting one of his gamer friends to crash our night?

But Gi Taek's already rolling his eyes. Apparently, his friend rejected the offer. "Heol," Gi Taek drawls. "I see how it is." He finally notices me watching him. "Your loss."

At that moment, Angela's song ends and the opening notes to Girl's Day's "Something" begins. I squeal and rush to my feet as Angela hands over the mic. Immediately, I get on my hands and knees, as the choreography for the song begins with a sexy floor dance.

Angela screams, pretending to faint onto the vinyl seats, and Gi Taek hollers, even though he's still on the phone.

Normally, I would never attempt to be this type of sexy, stretching my arms above my head across the floor and gyrating my hips, but I feel confident and safe with Angela and Gi Taek, also it's fun.

"Min Sori! Min Sori!" Angela starts chanting my name.

"I'm hanging up," I hear Gi Taek say, throwing his phone onto the seat. It immediately lights up again—his friend calling him back—but Gi Taek ignores it, taking up the tambourine to cheer me on.

Time passes quickly and soon our two hours in the room are almost over. The countdown clock on the screen warns that we only have another fifteen minutes until we either have to vacate the room or pay for more time.

"Should we add another hour?" Gi Taek asks.

"Yes!" Angela and I shout together.

"How about we play a game?" Gi Taek suggests. "Whoever has the lower score at the end has to pay."

Jenny had played a similar game with Jaewoo the first time they'd met, before she knew who he was. I was surprised when she'd told me, only because it seemed out of character for him. He wasn't the adventurous type, not like Nathaniel, who always managed to surprise me, catching me off guard in moments when I'd least expect it.

"Do you have any idea how many noraebang there are near Exit 4?" a low, breathless voice says from behind me.

"Nathaniel!" Angela shouts.

I twist around in my seat. He stands in the doorway, wearing a padded jacket over black jeans. His hair—still dyed that distinct midnight blue—curls slightly around ears that glint with piercings. Sauntering into the room, he flops onto the worn seat beside me, and his wood-scented cologne sets my head to spinning.

"I thought you were at your apartment playing video games," Gi Taek drawls.

I gape at Gi Taek. *Nathaniel* was the friend he was speaking to?

Nathaniel shrugs, his hands still in the pockets of his jacket.

"My sister wanted me to bring her something at her dorm. It's around here."

Nadine. I'm struck with a pang of guilt. She'd texted me when she arrived in Seoul for her study abroad program, but I never responded, too embarrassed at how I left her house after my father's scandal.

"So I thought, why not stop over and grace you all with my presence?"

"I feel graced!" Angela says.

"Really, you shouldn't have," Gi Taek deadpans.

I study Nathaniel out of the corner of my eye. The last time we saw each other was two months ago, in the living room of his house. Did he discuss the scandal with his sisters after I left? It would hurt me to know, but I wouldn't blame them if they pitied me.

"Can I have one of these?" My body tenses as Nathaniel reaches across my legs to the table, grabbing a soda. After a long drink, he reaches over again, this time retrieving a bag of chips.

As it's done this whole week, my mind chooses to remind me that Nathaniel might believe that I still have feelings for him. I feel mortified, but also nervous. I don't know what he's thinking. What if he asks me about the radio show?

When he leans back, he notices the awkward way I'm sitting. "Oh, sorry," he apologizes with a sheepish smile, rubbing the back of his head. "Not a lot of room in here. You want one?"

My mouth feels dry, so I lick my lips to wet them. I need to stop acting so nervous. If he asks about the radio show, I'll simply tell him that I had forgotten to change his name back from "Boyfriend" in my contacts, which I immediately did after the recording.

"Sure." My voice comes out breathy, having held it for too long.

His eyes flit upward, a slight frown on his face. He pops open the bag and holds it out to me, offering me the first chip.

I struggle for a safe topic of conversation as I take out a piece. "So, video games?"

"I was getting my ass handed to me by this one kid," Nathaniel says darkly. "I think he was in middle school."

His words stir a memory. "I remember in middle school when you used to play video games all day. You'd be late for practices because you stayed up all night playing them." I laugh. "You'd get in so much trouble."

"I remember that *you* loved to go to that comic book shop near the company and read manhwa all day, the one that closed down. You especially liked the romance ones. I stole a book from you once and read it aloud. You were so mad, you wouldn't talk to me for days." Now it's Nathaniel who's laughing.

"I still haven't forgiven you for that," I say, which only causes him to laugh even harder.

Our eyes meet and he smiles a lopsided smile.

I feel the tension leave my shoulders. Maybe I've been worrying for nothing, and Nathaniel hadn't given a second thought to the radio show. He's just here because Gi Taek invited him and he happened to be in the area, like he said.

"Look!" Angela points to the monitor. "The owner added minutes to our room. That's so nice."

"Enough time to add another player," Gi Taek says. "Nathaniel, you in?"

Nathaniel turns from me to grin at Gi Taek. "I don't know what we're playing, but I'm always down for a game."

While Gi Taek explains the rules to Nathaniel, Angela and I scroll through Melon for song inspiration. Songs with simple melodies are easier to get a higher score with, but we didn't come here for easy.

Gi Taek goes first. He performs the entirety of Taemin's "Move," choreography and all. My heart swells with pride to watch him. A dance major in high school, he's really improved his skills at Neptune. If I were to guess, he'll soon be selected for a group and debut within the year.

"Ninety-seven!" Angela cheers when his score appears on the monitor, then quickly realizes what that means. "We're never going to beat that!"

"You can do it, Angela," I say, raising my fist. "Fighting!"

She's chosen a TWICE song, which is difficult to sing alone, arranged as it is for nine vocalists.

I clap the loudest for Angela as "94" appears on the screen.

Then it's Nathaniel turn. He stands, rolling his shoulders like he's about to step into a boxing ring.

"What song did you choose?" Angela asks him, plopping down on the seat across from me, out of breath.

He winks at her. "It's a surprise."

Taking the controller, he keys in a song. The title "Eyes, Nose, Lips" appears alongside the artist's name, Taeyang. My heart starts to beat fast even before he brings the microphone to his lips.

While Nathaniel is XOXO's main dancer, he's also the lead vocalist after Jaewoo. His low voice is tender and sweet. He sings the first half of the song, trying to match his pitch to the melody, but as the song goes on, the lyrics start to sink in.

They're about a breakup, the longing for another person, missing their eyes, their nose, their lips, missing their touch. His voice grows more passionate. He's not singing to *me*—his eyes never stray from the screen with the lyrics—but I feel every word as if he is. As he sings, I'm remembering his eyes on me, his lips, his touch. By the end of the song, I can hardly breathe.

100.

Angela springs up from her seat with a scream. Her knees knock against the table and the soda Nathaniel had been drinking tips over the side, splashing onto my shirt. I quickly stand up.

"Oh no, Sori! I'm so sorry!"

"It's fine," I reassure her. "It won't stain. I'm just going to go clean it up a bit."

Grabbing my phone, I press open the door and escape into the short corridor. I key in the code for the bathroom and step inside. For a moment, I stand in front of the sink, waiting for my heart to stop racing.

It occurs to me that in New York, a similar thing had happened, except Nathaniel was the one who left. I doubt he was overcome with unexpected feelings. More likely, he wanted to wash the smell of alcohol from his clothing. With a sigh, I run the water in the sink, wetting a few paper towels and scrubbing at the stain.

When I step outside the door, Nathaniel is waiting for me.

"Are you all right?" he asks, stepping forward from where he'd been leaning against the opposite wall.

"It was just a little spill."

He shrugs out of his jacket. "Here, take this."

I lift my hands. "It's not cold out." Now that it's spring, the weather has gotten a lot warmer.

"You're . . ." Even in the poorly lit corridor, I can see the blush in his cheeks. I look down to see the water has seeped through my white blouse, revealing the outline of my chest. Now it's *my turn* to blush. I accept his jacket, wrapping it around myself.

Sounds of muffled singing come from behind the closed doors that line the corridor. Ads for soju brands are plastered onto the walls. From far away, someone leans on the horn of their car.

"Sori . . ." I'm alerted to the roughness of his voice, but when I look up, his expression is carefully blank. "Do you still have feelings for me?"

"I . . ."

I know why he's asking. After the radio show and my reaction to his singing tonight, I would jump to the same conclusion. For a wild moment, I imagine telling him that I *do* still have feelings for him, that when his eyes are on me, as they are now, I feel beautiful, I feel perfect. But . . . I can't.

The reasons behind our breakup haven't changed, at least the ones he knows, that he's still an idol, that he has to maintain his image, to protect not only himself but his bandmates. And then there are the *other* reasons, ones he can never know about. No, it's better to cut off any rekindling feelings before they have a chance to ignite.

"I don't."

He nods to himself, as if that was the answer he expected me to give.

"I *have* missed you though," I say, because that at least I can be truthful about. His eyes rock back to mine. "How close we used to be, when we were friends."

There's a short pause, and then he says, "You never stopped being my friend."

My heart feels almost too big for my chest, and I realize how much I needed to hear him say those words.

"I think I should probably head back home," I say, with a sigh. "Will you tell Gi Taek and Angela?"

"I will, though you should text them when you get home, so they know you got back safely. And . . ."—his eyes meet mine once more—"text me too. You have my number." His dimple deepens.

Cheeky. His teasing reference to the radio show releases the last of the tension I'd felt all week.

How does he do it? I think he's maybe the only person in the world that both annoys and amuses me in equal measure.

"I should pay for the extra hour before I go," I say. Since I'm leaving early, technically I lost the game.

He waves his hand in the air. "Don't worry about it. I already paid for the room."

I take a step, then turn to look at him over my shoulder. "Thanks, by the way. For picking up my call." And for playing along for as long as he did. He didn't have to—it was a risk for him.

"I'll always pick up your calls."

As I walk down the corridor, I hear a soft click as one of the doors down the hall closes shut.

Nine

The next morning, Secretary Park picks me up in front of my house to take me to my meeting with my mother. All night I've stewed over what I'll say to her, with Gi Taek and Angela's strategy in mind about having an alternative plan to offer her. The problem is, I don't have a career path that I'm passionate about. I like dancing and fashion, but that doesn't mean I want to be a choreographer or a stylist.

"Do you know what my mother wants to talk about?" I ask Secretary Park, buckling my seat belt. As my mother's right-hand woman, she's the closest person to my mother. She'd have the best insight into what she's planning.

"She told me a little," Secretary Park hedges, having as much trouble maneuvering down the hill as the driver a few days ago.

"Is it something I'll be pleased about?" Though, perhaps that's not the right question to ask. I've also kept Secretary Park in the dark about what it is I want, or at least *don't* want.

Secretary Park glances at me in the rearview mirror before returning her gaze to the road. "It's something you're good at."

Joah Entertainment is in the same neighborhood as my old high school. As we pass by the Seoul Arts Academy entrance, I watch as students rush through the gates, a teacher checking to make sure everyone's uniforms meet regulation. One student bounces on one foot as she pulls up her knee sock, while another adjusts his tie in one hand, gripping his backpack with the other. They bow to the teacher who waves them through.

Secretary Park pulls into the garage beneath the building, and we take the elevator to the first floor, where we go through security before entering the main part of the building. From there, we take another elevator to the fifth floor where the smaller meeting rooms are located.

My palms are sweaty and I wipe them on the skirt of my dress—I'm wearing a white knitwear one-piece with golden buttons. Chic, classic. Something my mother would approve of.

She's already waiting in the room when we arrive, dressed in a light pink silk double jacket and matching slim-leg pants. I'm surprised to find that she's not alone but with a girl I've never seen before. She's tall and pretty, in jeans and a loose top with butterfly sleeves. Her long light brown hair is pinned back with large pearl clips.

"Sori-yah," my mother says, catching my eye, "this is Woo Hyemi, the daughter of a new business partner."

I pick up on her warning. Hyemi is the daughter of someone important, someone my mother needs to impress.

I'm reminded of Jeon Sojin, the daughter of the CEO of Hankook Electric, from the restaurant in New York, but push that thought to the back of my mind, pasting on a smile instead. "It's nice to meet you."

My mother visibly relaxes. "Hyemi was born in Canada, though she's spent a few summers with her father's family here in Korea."

I look closer at Hyemi, noting her mixed heritage. She has a resemblance to Kim You Jung, the actress, with round eyes and soft lips.

"My mother is French Canadian," Hyemi says. Her voice is bright, cheerful, breaking endearingly on her words.

"You know about Joah's recent acquisition of Dream Music . . ." my mother begins.

Dream Music, a smaller entertainment company, was acquired by Joah at the end of last year, the deal finalized earlier this month. It would retain its own CEO and staff but would continue forward as a label under Joah.

"They were preparing to debut ASAP, a new girl group, at the beginning of this year. The acquisition delayed their debut by a few months, which actually worked to our benefit, as we're adding a few of our own girls as members to the group. Sun Ye . . ." She mentions another Joah trainee, one who's been at the company for as long as I have. "And Hyemi." She places a hand on Hyemi's shoulder. "And you."

This is the moment I've been dreading, and yet all the speeches I'd brainstormed the night before fly from my head. I hadn't expected any plan for my debut to be so finalized, or so . . . soon.

"You, of course, would be the leader," my mother continues blithely, "as you have the most experience. And Hyemi will make the perfect maknae to balance the group. However, because of unforeseen circumstances, we need to push up the date of the debut showcase, which is newly scheduled for two weeks from now. Which brings me to the most important part of this whole endeavor, and why I had you two meet before introducing you both to the rest of the members."

My mother's gaze focuses entirely on me. "Hyemi hasn't had any formal training, and I need you to guide her so that she's ready in time for the showcase. She'll need help learning the choreography for the title track, as well as adjusting to the team. There are four girls coming from Dream, and of course you and Sun Ye are already familiar with each other. But I think our Hyemi here will need a little more help, not just because she hasn't trained as long as the others, but there's also the matter of language and culture . . ."

"Can I talk to you in private for a minute?" I interrupt.

My mother blinks. "Of course." She then turns to reassure the younger girl. "Hyemi-yah, I'm going to talk to Sori and then I'll be right back."

Hyemi nods, though as we walk away, she glances at me with a questioning look.

Once we're out of earshot, my mother doesn't waste any breath, her voice returning to its normal clipped quality. "This might come as a bit of a surprise, but the acquisition of Dream Music and the renovations on the new building were more costly than was estimated by our financial advisors."

My heart drops. "You said it wasn't true that the company was in trouble."

"It's *not* true. Woo Hyemi's father has promised to make a sizable investment." There's a significant pause. "With the caveat that his daughter debuts as an idol."

The whole picture is starting to come together. Why Hyemi's involvement is so integral to ASAP's success—her father is

76

bankrolling her debut—and why, to secure his investment, the showcase needs to occur as soon as possible.

"Is she talented?" I ask. "Can she sing?"

"Her father assures me she can."

I raise a single eyebrow at that, a trait I ironically picked up from her.

"Sori, I'm already under enough stress as it is." She presses her fingers to the sides of her temples, massaging the skin there. "You're the only person I can trust with this."

Warmth floods my chest, that she would trust me with something so important.

"We acquired Dream Music knowing they already had plans to form a girl group. It just so happens that Woo Hyemi would make a wonderful addition. You, as well. You're soon to be nineteen, the perfect age to debut."

I have to tell her. I can't put it off any longer. It's now or never. "There's something I need to tell you. I should have told you sooner, but I was afraid . . ." *Of disappointing you. Of making you feel as if I was taking away your dream, for the second time.* "The truth is I don't want to debut anymore."

My mother blinks slowly. "What?"

I'm more certain now than ever. If my mind hadn't already been made up, the churning of my gut since I walked into the room tells me everything I need to know.

"But I think I can still help Hyemi," I quickly go on. "In fact, I *know* I can, and I'll be in a better position to help her if I'm not debuting myself, as I can concentrate entirely on her."

But my mother's already shaking her head. "Sori, you're being rash. Even with the truncated timeline, this is still an opportunity of a lifetime. So many young girls would give anything for the same chance."

"I know all that, and I *still* don't want it. This isn't a decision I came to overnight. How can you believe that of me, when I've been training to become an idol for practically my whole life?"

"I can't just let you make this decision on your own. How do you know if this is what you really want?"

"I know it's what I *don't* want."

I take a deep breath, gearing up for what I'm about to say next. "Sometimes I feel like I'm being pulled in two different directions, with you on one side, and Abeoji on the other, and the pressure of that can be . . . a lot sometimes. I don't know what it is I want *yet*, but I want to be able to choose for myself." It's the most honest I've been with my mother in months, maybe years. I always go along with what either she or my father wants, not wishing to pull on the already tenuous threads of our family, but I needed to say this, for myself.

"I can't speak for your father," my mother says slowly, "but if you manage to do this—and it won't be easy—like I said, Hyemi hasn't any formal training and there's also the matter of introducing her to the public—it will prove to me you're responsible enough to decide what you want for your own life. I won't stand in the way of that. In fact, I'll even support you. Financially."

Then she adds, as if it's an afterthought, "In all the ways a mother can."

That couldn't have been easy for her, as someone who's as rigid in her work life as she is in her family life. And maybe this conversation would have gone a lot differently if she also didn't need me to help Hyemi. But I'm grateful that she's managed to meet me halfway.

"Then it's a deal," I say. "I'll make Hyemi debut-ready in two weeks."

"Thank you, Sori." She pats me on the shoulder. "Let's have a meal together soon."

My heart lightens at the prospect. It's been a while since we shared a meal, just the two of us. "I'd like that."

On our way back to Hyemi, my mother's phone lights up. As she moves to take the call, I approach Hyemi on my own. She pulls out her earbuds, standing up from her seat. I catch a few bars of the B side of XOXO's latest single before it cuts off.

"Hi," I say in English, nervous now that it's just the two of us. We'll be spending a lot of time together, if I'm to help her debut, and I want her to feel comfortable with me. I want her to trust me. "Do you—" I begin, intending to ask her if she likes the single.

I'm interrupted by a knock at the door. A head of highlighter blue pops through the gap.

"Sori-nuna?"

"Choi Youngmin?" I say. I haven't seen XOXO's maknae since the summer, as he'd gone back to the hotel in New York City after the concert.

"I thought I heard your voice." Youngmin swings the door wide.

"What are you doing here?" I laugh, as he reaches me, wrapping me in a hug. He was always the most affectionate of the members, maybe because he's the youngest. Though, in six months, he's grown a bit taller, and I can't help noticing that his chest is rather . . . sturdy. I feel myself blushing a little.

"I'm meeting Ji Seok-hyeong to go over my school schedule," he says, releasing me.

That's right. The reason he'd gone back to the hotel after the concert was because he had schoolwork. Which reminds me . . .

I gesture to Hyemi, who's been watching our entire interaction with wide, starstruck eyes.

"Youngmin-ah, have you met Woo Hyemi? She's debuting in Joah's new girl group." She's also likely enrolling at the same school as him, Seoul Arts Academy, if she hasn't already. "Please take care of her as a hoobae and junior."

Hyemi quickly bows, her forehead hitting the table.

Youngmin laughs. "Are you okay?"

There's a loud clattering sound. I turn to where my mother has dropped her phone onto the table. She quickly picks it up again.

"Eomma?"

"My apologies, but something's come up. Sori, will you make sure Hyemi has everything she needs? I have to—" She doesn't finish the sentence, rushing out the door.

My mouth turns dry as a feeling of premonition sweeps through me. "Youngmin-ah, can you stay with Hyemi for a minute? I'll be right back."

"Sure!" He grins, then tilts his head as he regards Hyemi. "How old are you? I think we might be the same age."

"Sixteen," she says shyly.

"Great, let's be friends!" He drops the honorifics, switching to banmal.

I hurry out into the hall. With the way my mother left in a hurry, I have a bad feeling. I've been involved in enough scandals to know when one's about to drop.

Ten

The elevator opens to the foyer on the ninth floor where my mother's office is located. The whole elevator ride, I'd gone through the different scenarios of what might have happened. Had my father been caught in an affair for the *third* time? As I enter the spacious office, I spot Jaewoo and Nathaniel seated on opposite sides of a leather couch, with Sun in a sofa chair across from them. Out of the three, Sun's the only one to notice my arrival, with a slight lifting of his brow.

"How could you let this happen?" My mother is shouting.

It takes me a second to register what's going on. Secretary Park stands by a monitor that depicts a grainy photograph from the inside of a building. I recognize the dimly lit hall with ads for soju brands on the walls. The photograph was taken at the noraebang last night. There are two people in the photograph, standing close to one another. One is clearly Nathaniel, as he's facing the camera, while the other person has her back to it. I'm wearing Nathaniel's jacket, my long hair tumbling down around my shoulders.

Though we stand close, we're not touching. I'm looking down at my feet, while Nathaniel is looking at me. His expression isn't visible in the poor quality of the photograph.

"I told you last time what would happen if you messed up again," my mother continues to shout. "You don't respect this company. You don't respect your bandmates. You don't even respect yourself.

It would be doing the company a favor if you were removed from the group."

My body tenses at her words, at the way she's speaking to him. She's the CEO of the company and my mother, but it makes me want to throw myself between them.

"Director Seo," Sun interrupts. "I think that's going too far."

My mother ignores him. "Why aren't you saying anything?" she continues to shout. "Why won't you explain yourself?"

As I was leaving the karaoke place last night, one of the doors in the hall had closed shut. Someone must have recognized Nathaniel and taken a photo.

"Who's the girl in the photo with you?"

Nathaniel doesn't answer her. He's not going to, because telling her would mean revealing that it was me, and he would rather hurt himself than hurt me.

I clear my throat. "Director Seo," I say, addressing my mother by her title.

Jaewoo turns around on the leather couch, his eyes widening when he catches sight of me. Sun covers his face with his hand as if he can sense what's coming.

"Sori?" My mother's brows furrow. "Why are you here? Where's Woo Hyemi?"

Nathaniel's gaze locks on mine.

"That girl in the photo . . ." I begin, "she's . . ."

My mother goes completely still as the room falls silent.

"His sister, Nadine. She's studying at a university in Seoul."

"Is that true?" My mother turns to Nathaniel.

Nathaniel hasn't looked away from me since I spoke. "Yes."

Jaewoo sighs, pinching his arm to ease the tension.

"Ay, Jihyuk-ah," Sun chides. "I know you want to protect your sister, but it's better to tell the truth in situations like these."

"We'll have to reveal her identity to the public," Secretary Park says. "If her classmates don't already know she's your sister, they'll know after we release our statement. I think it's best if you prepare her."

"I'll call her," Nathaniel says, finally looking away. Standing, he heads out into the foyer.

"Sori," my mother says sharply, "I want to speak with you."

I follow her into the attached bedroom next to her office, which has essentially become her home in the past few months.

The full bed in the corner is made, and on the bedside table sits a vase of peonies. Through the open door of the bathroom, I can see her skincare products lined up neatly on the counter; her makeup is arranged on the vanity beside the closet.

"Did you tell me the truth?"

Light spears across the room from the window, momentarily blinding me. "Yes."

She nods, then frowns. "How do you know the person in the picture is his sister?"

"Angela told me." I'm my father's daughter, quick with a lie. "She and Gi Taek were with him last night."

She releases a sigh, and it's like a weight has fallen off her shoulders.

"Eomma?" I say, worried.

"I'm just . . ." she falters. "I'm just glad it wasn't you." Like the light, I am speared with guilt.

Nathaniel is getting off the phone when I run into him in the foyer. We have a bit of privacy as my mother remained in the bedroom to take a nap.

"How did Nadine take it?" I ask.

"She was more concerned that our stories line up," Nathaniel says. "My sister is nothing if not game for an elaborate ruse."

I shake my head with a smile, then realize, though I've avoided a scandal between *me* and him, I've dragged his sister into the spotlight.

"Sori, whatever you're thinking," Nathaniel says, "it's not true. Nadine is fine, and so am I."

How does he always know exactly what to say to make me feel better? I remember the words he spoke to me last night. *You never stopped being my friend.* My chest warms at the memory.

"Is it true what my mother said?" I ask. "That you'll be kicked out of the group if there's another scandal?"

He shakes his head. "It's not true. She just says those things because they sound dramatic, and she watches a lot of dramas."

"Nathaniel, I'm being serious."

He waves off my concern. "Don't worry about it."

"You always tell me not to worry. But I can't help worrying."

His expression softens. "I know."

The warmth in my chest seems to radiate outward.

"That was quick thinking in there," he says. "Though my sister really looks nothing like you." I recognize the signs that he's about to tease me, his eyes taking on that mischievous glint. "Not from the front, nor from the back."

Even with advance warning, I blush.

"Will the scandal affect XOXO?" I say, changing the subject. Even if the timing isn't as bad as it could have been, since they *just* returned from a successful world tour, Sun has his drama to promote soon.

"It'll blow over," Nathaniel says. "Especially when Joah releases that it was my sister in the photo. It would be a different story if it was about a girl I was dating."

"Yeah." I don't want to examine why my heart stills at the thought of him dating "a girl" that isn't me.

His gaze trails behind me. I hear the click of my mother's office door opening—apparently, she couldn't bring herself to rest. "I think that's my cue," he says. "Thanks again, Sori." He grins. "I can always count on you to save me."

Eleven

I'm so preoccupied with the scandal and the deal with my mother, I'd completely forgotten that I'd agreed to a meeting with the son of someone important to my father's political campaign. A taxi drops me off early evening the following day at the Sowon Hotel, the same hotel—and restaurant, for that matter—where I met my parents only a couple of weeks before.

It's as lovely as I remember it being, with beautiful white oak floors and an abundance of pink and white flowers in decorative pots. The hostess leads me to a table in a different part of the restaurant with floor-to-ceiling windows and low tables surrounded by cushioned seats meant for more casual dining and conversation. A boy a few years older than me sits at one of these tables, holding a wineglass in one hand and his phone with the other. He doesn't look up when I arrive. Inwardly, I sigh—it's going to be a long evening.

I take the seat opposite him, arranging my skirt around my knees. The chairs are large and cushioned, and I sink into the downy seat.

He's ordered me a glass of wine, but I ask a hovering waiter for water instead.

"You're Assemblyman Min's daughter," the boy says, glancing up from his phone, "the *idol* trainee." He says the word like its dirt on his Ferragamo loafers.

"Yes, and you are the restaurateur's son." I purposefully don't call him by his name since he hadn't bothered to learn mine. Usually, I'm a little more patient with the dates my father sets me up with, but I'm distracted by reactions online to the statement Joah released earlier today, identifying the mysterious girl in the photograph as Nadine.

The reactions have been mostly positive, as Nathaniel is known to have four older sisters. But I'm sure employees at Joah have been deleting the more vitriolic comments, claiming it's a cover-up for the truth, that Nathaniel is secretly dating another idol, and he's hurting the other members with his actions and should leave—

"Baek Haneul, second son of Kim Jinyi. My mother owns this restaurant."

"It's lovely," I say, relieved to have a topic that might interest us both. "Where does she import the flowers? The flooring is exquisite—did your mother work closely with a designer?"

He scowls. "How am I supposed to know? When I inherit my share of the restaurant, I'll have a manager to take care of all those things."

The waiter returns with my glass of water, and I carefully sip from the top. I wonder if Nadine is having trouble at her university, if reporters are dogging her steps; I hate that I've dragged her into this.

"I thought that was you," a low voice cuts into my thoughts.

I look up to find Sun approaching our table. He's dressed all in white, his icy-blonde hair swept back from his face.

Haneul stands, showing more excitement for Sun's arrival than my own. "You're Oh Sun of TK Group, right?" While Haneul's mother might own this restaurant, Sun's grandfather, as the president of TK Group, owns this hotel. "Our fathers play golf together." Haneul holds his right hand out to Sun, his left hand holding his right wrist in respect.

"Ah." Sun shakes his hand. "And you are . . . ?"

"Baek Haneul, second son of Kim Jinyi. My mother is—"

"Baek-ssi," Sun interrupts, throwing his arm around Haneul's neck. I narrow my eyes. His whole demeanor has changed, which immediately alerts me that he's up to something. "You're exactly the person I need right now," Sun says, conspiratorially. "See that woman over there?" Both Haneul and I follow Sun's gaze across the room to where a young woman sits beside the tall windows.

"I'm supposed to meet her for a blind date. My grandfather—you know, the president of TK Group—set us up. What he doesn't know is that she and I have already met, and well . . ." he trails off. "I'm not looking for anything long-term."

"I see," Haneul says eagerly, catching on quick. "I'll go in your place."

"You're a lifesaver." Sun pauses, then adds, "Hyeong."

Haneul looks like he's died and gone to heaven, pun intended.

"Bye." I wave as Haneul leaves without a backward glance.

Sun collapses into his vacated seat, long limbs sprawling. "This chair has excellent upholstery," he comments.

"Was any of that true?" I ask.

"You know me better than to ask that." He sits up straight only to reach over the table for my untouched wineglass, bringing it to his lips. He watches me over the rim. "It was all true."

I roll my eyes. "You shouldn't pawn off your dates on other people; more importantly, you should be clear and communicative in your intentions toward women."

"This is why I like you, Sori. No one nags me quite like you do."

"Just wait until you fall in love, then you'll regret all the hurt you've caused others."

He scowls. "Don't say that or I'll feel like you've put a curse on me."

"Would you like to order anything?" We look up at the smiling waiter who appears unfazed at our bickering, and that I've apparently switched dates.

"Yes," Sun says, picking up the menu and ordering a few appetizers. "Put it on his bill," he adds, pointing at Baek Haneul.

As we wait for the food, I study Sun. Even though he's only older by a year, he always *seemed* older, as the heir to a major conglomerate, and then as the leader of XOXO. He also never roughhoused with Jaewoo, Nathaniel, and Youngmin, keeping himself apart.

"Why are you looking at me like that?" His eyes narrow. "You look like you're pitying me right now. It's disturbing."

"I thought your grandfather stopped setting you up on blind dates after you made that deal with him."

His grandfather agreed to leave Sun alone as long as Sun married the woman of his grandfather's choice, at a time *after* he'd conducted his military service. Since the compulsory military service in Korea can be postponed until age thirty, Sun thought it was a good deal.

"He's back to his old ways. He's stubborn, my harabeoji." Sun speaks of his grandfather with affection. "He's under the false impression that I have more time now that XOXO is on hiatus."

Hiatus.

My stomach drops. "Is it because of the photograph?"

"No, of course not. We were always going to take a break after the tour. It was worked into our schedule for the year. We need to, otherwise we'd collapse from exhaustion, let alone the mental stress of constantly working. Rest and relaxation are good for creativity."

"It was me in the photograph," I blurt out.

He rolls his eyes. "Anyone who knows you would know that."

"My mother didn't know."

He refrains from commenting, and I don't blame him.

The servers bring out the food that Sun ordered and we enjoy a nice meal. Snarky as he is, Sun is a marked improvement from Baek Haneul.

"I never congratulated you on your drama," I say, collecting fresh pieces of lettuce with my fork. Sun ordered me my favorite salad with strawberry vinaigrette. It's a big deal for him to be the lead in his first role. Many critics have said he only got the role because of his popularity as an idol, but I know acting has been a passion of his for a long time now. "Congratulations."

"Thank you," he acknowledges, picking up the second glass of wine the server brought. "I heard about the girl group they're putting together. ASAP, isn't it? They announced the news internally. I was surprised your name wasn't on the list of members."

"Actually . . ."

He glances up, brow raised.

"I was offered a position as leader in the group, but I turned it down. After much thought, I realized I don't, in fact, wish to be an idol."

Sun frowns slightly, lowering his glass. "But don't you have a contract with Joah? Your mother might be the CEO, but she answers to a board of shareholders. They've invested in the company. And in you, as a trainee."

I raise a brow, amused. Unlike the other members, who'd hand-wave and accept things as they are, Sun is much more pragmatic.

"I honestly don't think she would have let me back out," I say, "if she didn't need my help."

I tell him about the deal with my mother. I have an inkling of unease as I explain how Hyemi's debut is tied to her father's financial support, which is undeniably transactional in nature, but Sun doesn't bat an eyelash. Since our childhood, we've witnessed our parents make questionable deals in the name of business, and I feel a rush of gratitude for him, that I can confide in him about this, without fear that he might judge my mother. Or me, for going along with her.

"I'm excited," I say. "More so than when I thought I was going to debut. I think it'll be a fun challenge, and I *like* Woo Hyemi. I want to help her."

Yesterday after leaving my mother's office, I'd gone back to the meeting room, interrupting Youngmin who'd been in the middle of doing a handstand. I got to know a little more about Hyemi— she has an older sister who lives in Canada with her partner, her favorite movie is *Kiki's Delivery Service*, and she's wanted to be an idol for as long as she can remember. We'd planned to meet after her first rehearsal to go over the choreography.

"So . . . ," Sun says, "in exchange for helping Hyemi, your mother will tear up your contract and let you walk free?"

"Maybe not as dramatically, but that's the gist of it."

"Didn't you have a dating clause in your contract?" he asks absently.

"No, I didn't. If I did, I wouldn't be able to go out on this date with Haneul."

"Ah, of course."

I never had a dating clause in my contract, even the new one I signed shortly after my scandal with Nathaniel two years ago. The promise I made to my mother was never written in words.

"You've got your work cut out for you," Sun says, with a smile. "I look forward to seeing what you can do with Woo Hyemi in two weeks."

After we've finished our food, I peek over the divider toward the windows. "Haneul-ssi is still with your date. I think they're really hitting it off. You might have inadvertently set up a love match."

"Do you think they'll send me an invitation to the wedding?" Sun quips.

As we're walking out of the restaurant, my phone buzzes with an unknown number.

"It's international," Sun says from over my shoulder.

My stomach sinks as I realize who it is. "It must be Nadine. Why do you think she's calling?"

"Probably to scold you for dragging her into this mess."

"Really?"

"Pick it up. The call's going to drop." He's ruthless.

I open the phone and bring it hesitantly to my ear. "Nadine-eonni?"

"Sori?" I remember the way she greeted me in the pizza shop, friendly and warm. All warmth is stripped from her voice when she says, "We need to talk."

Twelve

Nadine hasn't yet arrived when I exit the subway station. I check my phone to see that I'm five minutes early. A few middle school students mill about the station area, recognizable by their uniforms—gray sweater vests over white shirts tucked into ankle-length skirts. A woman walks by hand in hand with a small boy wearing a Pororo backpack. There's a little garden area, so I walk over and sit on one of the benches to wait for Nadine.

Though Sun had teased, he'd assured me after Nadine had hung up that she wasn't angry, though how can he be sure? I would be angry if my sibling and his ex-girlfriend dragged me into their business.

"Psst, Sori!" I look at the large planter in the garden that just spoke. "Sori, over here!"

Standing, I walk around the planter to find Nadine crouched on the ground. "Nadine-eonni?"

"Hurry! Get down." She grabs my hand and pulls me so that I'm also crouched behind the planter.

"What are we doing?" I whisper.

"See those girls?"

I look around the planter toward the exit of the subway station. "The middle school students?"

"They followed me from the university's campus. Nothing's more terrifying than a pack of middle schoolers." She shudders.

Like yesterday, when I realized that I'd dragged Nadine into this mess, I'm overcome with guilt. "I'm sorry. This is my fault. I should have never involved you."

"It's fine. It's actually kind of thrilling. Then again, this isn't my daily existence, so maybe that's why. My classmates think it's cool that my brother is Nathaniel from XOXO. Honestly, it's not the fans who are the problem. Nathaniel says most of them are respectful. It's the paparazzi."

"Still," I say, "you wouldn't be hiding behind a planter if I hadn't lied and said it was you at the noraebang instead of me."

"That reminds me, I *am* upset with you."

I brace for a well-deserved dressing down. "I've been in Seoul for a while now, and you haven't texted me back."

I slowly blink at her. "What?"

"I know it's probably awkward to hang out with your ex-boyfriend's older sister, but I was looking forward to seeing you."

"I'm sorry! I should have called." When we exchanged numbers, I had every intention of meeting up with her, but when I thought about it later, I *had* felt awkward, remembering how embarrassed I'd been over the circumstances in which I'd left her house.

"You can make it up to me," she says. "I have a favor to ask you."

"Anything."

She laughs. "Wait until I ask before you agree. You know XOXO is on a break from group activities, right?"

I nod. "Sun-oppa told me about the hiatus."

"That's right. It's just that with this so-called 'scandal'"—she puts the word *scandal* in air quotes—"paparazzi have started camping outside their apartment. The other members have already left to stay with their families, but Nathaniel can't exactly go home. Or he *could*, but he refuses to."

She frowns. "I'm not sure why. I think he has something he wants to stay in Seoul for, something work-related. He's being secretive about it. It's pretty annoying."

Work-related? Something *outside* of XOXO? While Sun has his passion for acting, Nathaniel has never expressed an interest in solo activities. I'm curious and wish she'd elaborate more, but she's already moved on.

"He's cooped up in that apartment, all alone. He says he doesn't mind, but I'm worried. It would be different if it was only for a few days, but it's a couple of weeks, and I won't be able to visit him often because of school. I'd feel better if he could *leave* the apartment without getting accosted, but the paparazzi follow him everywhere."

My stomach twists in knots. What she's describing is awful and completely true. All the other members have family in Korea, except for Nathaniel. Even his extended family lives in the United States. Unlike Sun, who would probably relish the isolation, Nathaniel isn't like that. He's like a puppy; he thrives on human contact. Nadine must see that I understand her completely because she reaches out to grab my hand.

"And so, I was wondering if Nathaniel could stay with you, just until the end of their vacation. That's what—two, three weeks?"

For a moment, I just stare at her, not sure if I've heard her correctly. Have Nathaniel stay . . . with me?

"I've been thinking about it," she says hurriedly, as if afraid I'll reject the idea outright, "and it seems like the perfect solution,

97

especially since, if I'm remembering correctly, you live in a residential area, which means there's less likelihood of paparazzi snooping about. Nathaniel could come and go freely, and he wouldn't be alone."

Letting Nathaniel stay at my house seems like a terrible idea, and yet . . . I do owe Nadine, not just for majorly inconveniencing her life, but also for that summer when her family let me stay with them.

I've always wanted to do something for them, *for him*, in return, and this is the perfect opportunity. And it wouldn't just be the two of us in the house, since Ajumma stays overnight every night except for the weekends. Nadine said it would only be for two, three weeks. Nathaniel and I both agreed that we're just friends. What could possibly happen—between friends—in a few weeks?

I can't believe I'm even entertaining the idea. I would have to lie to my mother—she would *kill* me if she ever found out.

"It's a lot to ask, isn't it?" Nadine says, reading my silence as unwillingness. "Never mind." She pats my hand before removing hers. "Forget I brought it up. But we do need to schedule a time to hang out. Let me buy you Korean pizza with sweet potatoes and corn on it, at the very least."

A few minutes later, as I walk her to the station to take the subway back to school, I'm surprised by the feeling stirring within me. I should feel relieved that she dropped her request, taking the decision out of my hands, and yet, for some reason, all I feel is . . .

Disappointment.

Thirteen

I'm feeling a lot of emotions from the events of the last few days, so I decide to go shopping.

Retail therapy. I'm a big fan.

I'm at the IPARK Mall browsing stickers at the bookstore when I get a text from Secretary Park about a last-minute variety show recording.

Hyemi's already in the back seat of the van when they pick me up outside the mall.

"Good morning, Seonbae," she says in her squeaky voice. Not for the first time I wonder what her role in ASAP will be, whether a vocalist or a rapper or both.

"Good morning, Hyemi. Are you excited about today's recording?"

Hyemi nods, though I can tell she's nervous, fidgeting with the bracelet she always wears around her wrist.

"An actress was scheduled to appear on the episode," Secretary Park says, as she maneuvers the van around the taxis outside the mall, "but she had to cancel last minute." This explains why Hyemi was invited at such a short notice. Joah must have requested to send her as a replacement.

It's a great opportunity for Hyemi, since she hasn't had any exposure to the public. Even I've had more exposure than her, with my modeling and radio show appearance. If netizens search for Woo Hyemi online, they'll be able to find this episode, instead of something embarrassing in her childhood, like a prepubescent middle school photo. Though, as Hyemi's first variety show appearance, it's a bit like throwing her into the deep end and hoping she can swim.

"What program is it?" I ask Secretary Park, my mind already racing with ideas on how to coach Hyemi so that she'll know how to respond in every situation that might arise.

"Catch Me If You Can."

My pulse leaps. That's one of my favorite shows. It airs every Wednesday, and Ajumma and I always watch it together after dinner. It features weekly guests—the cast of a currently airing drama or an idol group—who, after a short, silly interview with the hosts, split up into two teams to play an elaborate game of tag.

"Who are the other guests?"

"It's a Seoul Arts Academy–themed episode this week. The filming location is the school. And the guests are all SAA alumni or current students, like Hyemi."

I remember how Hyemi had told me that she'd enrolled in the school at the beginning of this year.

"And Youngmin," Secretary Park adds.

I frown. "Youngmin? But I thought the XOXO members were on hiatus."

"They are, but this was scheduled in advance. All of them will be guests. Oh, and I forgot to mention. When the producer realized *you* were also an alumnus, they insisted you join as well."

I blink. "What?"

100

"You and Hyemi will both be guests on the show."

"Congratulations, Seonbae!" Hyemi says. "I'm so happy we'll be on the show together."

Sensing my state of confusion, Secretary Park elaborates, "The producer listened to your episode of *The Woori and Woogi Show*. She says she's a fan."

A . . . fan? After *The Woori and Woogi Show* my name was trending, with netizens speculating who my boyfriend was and whether he was an idol trainee. I even reached the top fifty in the weekly search rankings. But it never occurred to me that someone had listened to the show and liked *me*.

I shake my head, pushing these thoughts to the back of my mind. I need to focus.

"When does the recording start?" I ask.

"We have about an hour and a half."

"Okay," I say. I can feel the gears shifting in my head. "Then let's make every minute count."

We pass through the gates of Seoul Arts Academy with seconds to spare, pulling into an empty space in the parking lot. I'm panting a little, the last hour and half seeming to go by in the blink of an eye. After calling up my hairstylist for hair and makeup, I'd asked Angela if she could bring some of her clothing to the salon for Hyemi to borrow, since they're about the same size and I thought Hyemi would look great in Angela's fresh, youthful style.

"Do I look all right?" Hyemi asks, nervously pulling on her shirt. She's wearing a fitted top with a square neckline and cap sleeves.

I've paired it with a flowy mini skirt—with black safety shorts underneath, of course—and white sneakers, since we'll presumably be running during the shoot. Normally I would have asked her to choose what to wear herself, as she'd feel more confident in clothing *she* felt she looked good in, but there wasn't any time.

"You look beautiful."

Hyemi blushes. "*You* look stunning, Seonbae."

I'd switched outfits with my hairstylist, Soobin, at the salon—the T-shirt dress I'd worn to the mall was too casual—and I'm in a corseted top and skintight jeans. Luckily, I was already wearing sneakers.

We exit the van and make our way toward the first filming location, right outside the front entrance of the school. It's a Sunday, which means classes aren't in session. A few students have volunteered as extras for the episode, peering from out the windows of the school. They're wearing their school uniforms, as well as face masks to protect their privacy.

"Seonbae, I'm nervous," Hyemi says as we walk.

I take her hand, squeezing it. I wish I'd had more time to prepare her. While at the salon, she'd confessed she'd only seen a few episodes of *Catch Me If You Can*.

"You'll do fine," I reassure her. "Just be yourself." And hope for a good edit.

As we bow and greet the two hosts—a large, jolly-faced comedian and a handsome, older actor who was a heartthrob in the nineties—another large black van rolls through the gate into the parking lot.

Faint screams erupt from the school as the back doors of the van slide open at the same time. Jaewoo and Nathaniel jump out on opposite sides, followed by Youngmin, then Sun from the passenger side door.

Together, they bow to the staff members and hosts who rush over to greet them.

Jolly laughs at something Nathaniel says, while Heartthrob shakes Sun's hand.

My eyes linger on Nathaniel, who's dressed in a plaid long-sleeved shirt and ripped jeans. He's dyed his hair dark brown again, from the edgy blue of the promotion cycle. Though the blue suited him, the brown is giving him strong "boyfriend" vibes and I feel my heart skip a beat.

"Good afternoon, Hyemi-ssi." Jaewoo appears at our side. Hyemi beams at him—they must have met at the company at some point. "Are you excited for your first variety show recording?"

"Yes!" she squeaks. "Please take care of me, Seonbae." She gives him a ninety-degree bow, to which he responds with an indulgent smile before sauntering away with one hand in his pocket. I shake my head, amused. He's clearly fashioned himself a role as an older brother figure. Hyemi's gaze follows him with figurative hearts in her eyes. He needs to tone it down before Hyemi develops a full-blown crush, though I guess that wouldn't be so awful. She'd want to stick around if she had a crush—long enough to debut and for her father to follow through with his investment—and it's not like anything would come of it, as Jaewoo's head over heels in love with Jenny.

He wanders over to where Nathaniel is getting his makeup touched up. One of the artists holds a thin brush to his lips, staining them a dark burgundy. For a moment, I stare transfixed as the woman dabs color onto his lips. When Nathaniel lifts his gaze, I look away.

I need to focus if I want Hyemi to not only have a positive experience but also leave a good impression on the audience. As for myself, not looking like a fool would be ideal.

The recording starts on time with Jolly and Hearthrob making introductions to the camera. My heart drops when they ask us each to do a short intro dance, only to be surprised when Hyemi performs a cute, flirty dance. Youngmin and Nathaniel are the best dancers in XOXO, but since it's a variety program, they go for laughs instead. Youngmin dances to a popular girl group song and Nathaniel spins on his head. When his shirt starts to ride up, the hosts and members pile on top of him to preserve his "modesty." I lift my hand to cover Hyemi's eyes.

When it's my turn, I channel years of dance training to effortlessly move my body, following the rhythm of the song randomly chosen for me. Since Hyemi embodies the "cute and youthful" concept, I decide to play up "sexy" and "mature." It's always good to give the viewers variety. After I finish, I spot a woman—presumably the producer director, or PD—smiling at the monitor behind the main camera.

After filming the introductions, we take a short break to retouch makeup and hydrate—Hyemi has to use the bathroom—then commence filming the next segment in which we're to pick teams for the game part of the show.

We play gawi bawi bo to decide team captains, with Nathaniel's rock beating Jaewoo's scissors to become one captain, and Sun's paper beating Heartthrob's rock to become the other. The rest of us line up in a row.

"Jihyuk-ah, why don't you choose first?" Jolly prompts.

"Then I choose you, Hyeong!" Nathaniel points to Jolly and the host gives him a high five.

Sun holds his chin between his forefinger and thumb as he considers the rest of us. Then he points to Heartthrob.

Nathaniel opens his arms. "Youngmin-ah, come to Hyeong!"

"Hyeong!" Youngmin runs into Nathaniel's arms, but he's too heavy and they topple over.

Sun's gaze lands on me, and then slides to Hyemi. "Woo Hyemi." Hyemi claps excitedly before rushing forward to join Sun's team.

Jaewoo and I are the only ones left, which is perfect because now Nathaniel has only to choose Jaewoo and I'll be on a team with Hyemi. I can watch over her throughout the rest of the recording.

"Min Sori."

My head jerks up. Nathaniel isn't looking at me, but at Youngmin, who's somehow acquired three hand warmers to juggle.

"Sori-ssi," Hearthrob calls. "Nathaniel picked you for his team."

In a daze, I walk over to stand beside them.

The final breakdown of teams are: Sun's team, consisting of Heartthrob, Jaewoo, and Hyemi, and Nathaniel's team, which is Jolly, Youngmin, and myself.

With the opening part of the episode wrapped, Hyemi and I are sent into a large tent, separate from the XOXO members, to change our clothes. I sigh at all the trouble I went through to find suitable outfits, but I guess it was worth it just for that intro.

The PD knocks on the makeshift door before sticking her head in. "The episode concept is 'student council members versus the delinquents.' Sun's team are the student council members and Nathaniel's team are the delinquents. Please dress accordingly." With that news delivered, she absconds elsewhere.

"Somehow," I drawl, "the exact right people were picked for each team."

Hyemi giggles.

We dress quickly, emerging to find Jaewoo and Sun already waiting, both in identical pressed uniforms and eyeglasses. Hyemi joins them, looking adorable in her knee-length skirt and ribboned necktie.

I've gone for the role of "Bad Girl," which probably doesn't help my image since I already give off those vibes, with a crooked tie, my skirt rolled at the waist, and heavy eyeliner. I'm also wearing track pants for range of motion.

Youngmin joins us, his hair mussed and his tie discarded altogether.

Then Nathaniel emerges and Youngmin falls on the ground, laughing.

"What kind of delinquent are you supposed to be, Nathaniel-ssi?" Heartthrob asks.

Nathaniel has fully embraced the role of delinquent, specifically one that gets into fights, presumably in an alley behind the school.

Jaewoo and Jolly hold each other, tears running down their

cheeks. "He's put a Band-Aid above his brow," Jaewoo says, pointing.

"Is that . . . blood?" Youngmin can't breathe. Nathaniel's blotted red ink at the corner of his mouth.

Nathaniel turns to the center camera with a smirk, and I can already picture an editor later adding "Bad Boy" text over the video.

We record our second intros, then move to our next locations inside the main building of the school. My cameraperson walks with me up the wide steps after introducing himself. Out of the corner of my eye, I see Youngmin's cameraperson with his hands pressed together as if pleading with him.

"What's going on?" I ask.

My cameraperson looks over. "Ah," he says, "the younger guests can be quite . . . fast."

For this part of the game, we're separated and brought to different areas of the school.

"Fighting!" I raise my fist to encourage Hyemi as her handler leads her away. My own handler wraps a blindfold over my eyes. As I walk, I go over the rules of the game in my head. It's fairly straightforward. Somewhere in the school, three tokens are hidden. The team that finds the most tokens *or* tags out of all the members from the opposing team wins.

I try to guess where my handler is leading me, but quickly lose all sense of direction. There's a whoosh of air as a door opens, and then I walk a few more steps before my handler releases my arm. She unties my blindfold and I blink several times before taking in my surroundings.

I'm in the cafeteria.

The sound of the school bell goes off, the light, familiar tune filling me with warmth, bringing me back to when I was a student here, sitting with my friends at these tables, laughing between classes. Then the cheerful melody ends.

At this moment in the episode, viewers will see eight separate boxes on their television screens, showing all of us at the start of the game.

Ready, set, go!

Fourteen

My goal is to find Hyemi so that she can tag me out, but I have to wait or it'll be too obvious.

I scan the empty tables in the cafeteria. It's unlikely they'd *start* a player in the same room as a token, but I might as well search since I have time. I move toward the kitchen area, beside the cafeteria. The lights are turned off, which indicates there's nothing to find here, and yet . . .

I start to open cabinets, crawling on my hands and knees to look through shelves stacked with stainless steel pots and pans. My cameraperson follows me, recording my every action.

I don't know what I'm looking for. They didn't tell us what the tokens look like, only that we'll know them when we see them.

I twist open the door of the walk-in cooler and a blast of cold envelops me. I immediately spot an object that doesn't belong among the frozen meats and vegetables. Grabbing it, I rush out of the fridge and hurriedly duck behind the counter. Crouched on the floor, I reveal the token to the camera. It's a little stuffed animal of the mascot of our school, a bunny holding a tiny trumpet.

It's so *cute*. I press it to my chest in a moment of bliss, then remember I'm being recorded. Opening my backpack—they'd given one to each of us at the start of the game—I tuck the bunny inside, then swing it onto my back.

"You didn't zip your backpack all the way," my cameraperson says.

I hesitate, a blush creeping up my neck. "He can't breathe if it's zipped all the way."

Oh my God, I can't believe I said that aloud. How embarrassing. I press my hands to my face and hurry out of the kitchen area and back through the cafeteria.

How much time has passed? How will I know if someone else found a token?

From the window facing the back of the school, I look out to see Youngmin sprinting across the athletics field. A few seconds later, his cameraperson follows, huffing and puffing behind him.

I'm stepping from the stairwell onto the fifth floor when I glimpse the lights of a filming crew down the hall. It's another player, likely more than one with that many cameras. Is it Hyemi? A sense of unease settles in my gut. It could be Sun or Jaewoo. The thought of being chased seems a bit terrifying. I didn't think I'd be *afraid* playing this game. I almost scream when a hand grabs my arm, pulling me into an empty classroom. My cameraperson stumbles into the room behind me.

"Nathaniel?" I gasp. *His* cameraperson—a woman with a checkered bandana around her nose and mouth—waves from behind his left shoulder.

"What are you *doing*?" he says. "That's Sun down there. I think he's met up with the host. Do you *want* them to get you out?"

The relief I feel at seeing Nathaniel is intoxicating. I almost act on impulse and throw my arms around him, then remember we're being recorded.

"Of course not," I say. I can't *tell* Nathaniel that I'm trying

110

to find Hyemi so that she can tag *me* out. He sweeps his hand through his dark hair, the metallic rings on his fingers glinting.

To remain together in the shot, I'm standing close to him. While his attention, and the attention of the cameras, is on the window and what's happening outside of it, I have a rare opportunity to study him. His lips have retained their burgundy stain, though there's a slight indent where he must have bitten them. His hair is truly a work of art, his hairstylist having used gel to keep its shape during the episode, a few strands falling across his brow; his pulse beats rapidly at his throat.

While some girls, like Jenny, prefer a student council member, I'm admittedly much more attracted to a delinquent. And Nathaniel has always embodied that spirit, at least in the group. While Sun was the heartbreaker, Youngmin the boy next door, and Jaewoo the student council president, Nathaniel was the rebel. The one who broke all the rules and made me want to break them too. If it was to defend a friend, he *would* call a bully to an alley for a fight. Or he might meet the girl he likes up on the rooftop for a kiss.

"Let's wait until they move out of the hall," he says, and I nod, my face red from the direction of my thoughts.

We crouch down beneath the window.

"Can you turn off your light?" Nathaniel asks his cameraperson, and she switches off her camera light. My cameraperson does as well. And now all four of us are crouched together in the darkness beneath the window.

There's a sound outside. Nathaniel shifts his body to cover mine, pressing his hand against the wall. When it's clear the sound was just a production assistant making the rounds, he lowers his arm.

I'm filled with gratitude that I'm not alone, that *he's* the one by my side.

"There's advantages to splitting up," Nathaniel says slowly, "but also staying together."

"I want to stay together," I say.

He lets out a breath, turning his face away. After a short pause, he says, "You watch my back, I'll watch yours?"

I wait until he turns to me before pressing my forefinger and thumb together. "Okay."

He gives me a lopsided smile.

We wait another few minutes before Nathaniel peeks through the window. "I think they're gone. Let's go."

"Wait." I grab on to the back of his uniform shirt. "I want to show you something."

I release him and swing my backpack forward, opening it to show him the stuffed animal inside. "I found one of the tokens in the cafeteria's kitchen."

"Damn, Sori!" He laughs, his eyes twinkling. "Nice work!" He raises both of his hands, palms up, and I slap mine against them.

Our camerapeople seem pleased that we've joined up. Between the two of them, they should have a variety of angles to shoot from.

Moving down to the third floor, we enter a classroom filled with students. There's already a filming crew inside, which is a very strong indicator that the producers want us to linger here.

"Is there a token in this room, by any chance?" Nathaniel asks a girl in the front row.

She giggles behind her face mask but doesn't answer him. They must have been instructed not to help us until we've earned it.

"Can you give us a hint?" He flashes his most charming smile, dimples showing.

"Maybe if you do a dance," the girl's seatmate says cheekily.

Nathaniel doesn't hesitate, backsliding across the floor. The students in the back row stand up to get a better view. They're a tough crowd, though, because even after this display, they remain silent.

"What about for me?" I ask, then do a double pirouette into a front split.

Three boys immediately point to one of the lockers in the back of the classroom. I move down the aisle, blowing them a kiss.

Inside the locker is another stuffed animal. This time the bunny mascot is holding a little drum. "I love you," I whisper.

"What did you say?"

I turn to find Nathaniel leaning against the lockers.

"Nothing," I say quickly. "You want to hold him?"

"Him?" He takes the bunny in both of his hands, turning it around to face me. Using his fingers, he maneuvers the bunny's arms so that the paw that holds the drumstick beats the little drum. My heart feels as if it's grown three times its size, watching him interact with the stuffed animal. I must make a soft sound because he looks up to catch me staring at him. His brow lifts slightly.

"Here," he says, straightening from the lockers, "turn around."

"What are you—?" My breath catches at the cool touch of

113

his fingers against my neck. Brushing my hair aside, he unzips my backpack, tucking Drum Bunny alongside Trumpet Bunny. There's one more left. What instrument will he be playing? A flute? A violin? I have a sudden, powerful need to *know*.

"You want to find the third bunny, don't you?" Nathaniel says from behind me. He hasn't removed his hands from the backpack. I can feel the slight pressure as he maneuvers the bunnies comfortably around.

"Yes," I breathe.

"Then there's only one thing left to do. Win."

He starts to zip up my backpack, but my cameraperson stops him. "Leave it a little open."

As we exit the classroom from the front of the room, the back door slides open and Heartthrob and Sun enter. There's a short pause, then Heartthrob points. "Get them!"

Nathaniel grabs my hand, and we race out of the room. I feel as if I've never run so fast in my life, my hair flying out behind me. Nathaniel takes a left at the end of the hall, and we tumble into an elevator. I press the button for the rooftop while Nathaniel pounds the close button. When the doors shut, we sink against opposite walls, then I realize what we've done.

"Nathaniel!"

"What?"

"We forgot the cameras!"

"Oh, shit."

A laugh escapes me, a snort really, and then I totally lose it, laughing so hard I can hardly breathe. Nathaniel is no better, barely holding himself up. All this time I've been careful to keep my cameraperson with me, but in that moment, with adrenaline pumping through my veins, I'd completely forgotten.

"It's okay," Nathaniel says, wiping the tears from his eyes. He points to a camera they've rigged over the security camera at the top corner of the elevator. "They'll use footage from that."

My backpack buzzes and I pull out a walkie-talkie, switching it on.

"Sori-ssi?" my cameraperson wheezes.

"We're going to the rooftop," I tell him.

"Won't Sun see we're headed that way and follow us?" Nathaniel asks after I've switched off the walkie-talkie.

"I'm sure the PD will hold them off until we're at least reunited with the cameras."

We're both breathing heavily from the running and the laughter.

"You're good at this," he says. "I knew you would be."

"Is that why you chose me for your team?" I'd wondered why he'd chosen me when he could have picked Jaewoo, who's famous for being good at variety programs. In fact, he's already been a guest on this exact show. Maybe he'd thought it made the most logical sense for two XOXO members to be on each team, but Nathaniel isn't like that. He's not like Jaewoo, or me, who'd pick for what was best for the show, or Sun, who would pick for strategy, or Youngmin, who'd pick based on who he'd have the most fun with. Nathaniel wouldn't consider any of those things.

"Why *did* you pick me for your team?" I ask.

"I didn't want to chase you," he says, and I wince. Did he finally realize I'm not worth chasing? "I wanted to run *with* you."

I catch my breath. Before I can respond, the elevator doors

open. Our camerapeople appear at the top of the stairwell, having raced to the rooftop.

Nathaniel steps out of the elevator. "Sorry about that," he says, scratching the back of his head.

"Should we search the rooftop?" he asks me. How can he act normal after what he just said?

"Sori-ssi?" my cameraperson prompts, huffing and puffing.

"Yes. Right. Let's do . . . that."

The rooftop of the school is a large, spacious area with a storage room as well as solar panels. The sky is dark beyond the high walls, the sun having set while we were filming inside. We find the last plushie behind a potted plant. It's holding—

"A cello!" I shout.

"You have an uncanny knack for finding stuffed animals," Nathaniel says. "Are *you* good at finding stuffed animals or are stuffed animals good at finding *you*?"

"I refuse to qualify that question with an answer."

My cameraperson pulls up his walkie-talkie, relaying something to the PD. A few minutes later, an announcement peals through the speakers. "All three tokens have been found. A ten-minute countdown clock has been set. The first team to tag out all the members of the opposing team before the end of the countdown wins; otherwise, the team with the most tokens wins."

"*Oh no,*" I groan. This isn't good. I can't *win*. I'd been so distracted with finding the stuffed animals that I'd forgotten my original intention to help Hyemi. I rush back to the stairs.

"What are you doing?" Nathaniel says, coming up behind me. "We should be *hiding.*"

"I need to find Hyemi," I whisper, so that only he can hear.

"Why do you need to find Hyemi?" His voice echoes loudly in the stairwell.

"Shh!" I cover his mouth; then, grabbing his hand, I tug him after me.

"Sori, seriously, what—?"

Nathaniel doesn't have time to finish that thought because suddenly there are cameras everywhere and Hyemi is flying up the stairs like she's possessed, ripping my backpack from my back. Behind her, Nathaniel and Jaewoo grapple for each other's backpacks.

"Min Sori eliminated," the announcer says. Then a half second later, "Nathaniel Lee eliminated."

Our camerapeople lead us to the first floor where the principal's office acts as a waiting room for eliminated players. We slump across from each other on the leather sofas. Shortly after, the door opens and Jolly walks in. He takes one look at us and sighs. "I think Team Delinquents is done for."

"Woo Hyemi eliminated. Bae Jaewoo eliminated."

The door opens and Hyemi and Jaewoo walk in, followed by Heartthrob who's announced as being eliminated a short few seconds later.

I sit up in my chair. "What happened?"

They don't have time to answer because the PD's voice issues over the intercom. "Oh Sun eliminated. School's out! Victory to the Delinquents!"

Nathaniel and I exchange looks of shock.

A grin spreads across Nathaniel's face. "What . . . ?"

Sun walks in, followed by Youngmin who has my backpack slung over his shoulder.

Nathaniel stands, his eyes darting from Youngmin to Sun. "Hyeong, what happened?"

"Youngmin is a beast," Sun says, as an explanation.

Youngmin does a victory dance, cartwheeling onto his knees and throwing a finger heart at the camera.

And with that, the episode reaches its conclusion.

It's one a.m., the filming having gone well into the night. While Ji Seok waited, Secretary Park went home hours ago. A replacement driver stands by the van to take Hyemi and me home. We start to walk over.

"I'll take Youngmin to his parents' home and then drop you off at the apartment," I overhear Ji Seok saying to Nathaniel, Jaewoo's mother and younger sister having come by to pick him up and Sun having absconded in a car service sent by his grandfather.

From what I recall, Youngmin's home is in the opposite direction of the apartment shared by the XOXO members.

"You can ride with us," I offer. "Hyemi's house is on the way to your apartment." I blush at my impulsive offer, but it's also the most convenient for everyone. I'm thinking of Ji Seok, who can go home earlier after dropping off Youngmin.

Nathaniel glances in my direction. "I'll go with them," he says, and Ji Seok nods.

Hyemi and I take the two middle seats, while Nathaniel climbs into the back. It's quiet for most of the drive, all of us exhausted after the long shoot.

As the driver pulls into Hyemi's neighborhood, she releases a heavy sigh.

"Hyemi, is something the matter?" I ask.

"Do you think I made a good impression?"

"Of course," I say, though I'm pricked with guilt for having spent more time playing the game with Nathaniel than actively helping Hyemi. I do mean it, though. Hyemi *was* shy in front of the camera, but that's to be expected. "They'll love you," I say, truthfully. "How could they not?"

We pull up in front of her Hannam apartment building, located in one of the most expensive complexes in Seoul. "Thank you," she says, then adds shyly, "Eonni." She's out the door faster than I can blink. As I move to sit back in my seat, feeling a little dazed, I meet Nathaniel's gaze through the rearview mirror. He turns his face so that he's looking out the window, but not before I see the small smile playing along his mouth.

Fifteen

"You can drop me off here," Nathaniel tells the driver once we've pulled up to the corner of his street. Even after their music careers took off and they started signing endorsement deals, the members of XOXO chose to remain living together. Youngmin is still in high school, and as Sun put it, they "want to watch him grow up well." But also, they genuinely enjoy each other's company.

Except none of the other members are at the apartment right now. Instead, a dark line of cars waits for Nathaniel, idling by the curb with their lights dimmed.

I lean forward in my seat. "Are those tabloid reporters?" Cigarette smoke drifts from the open windows, visible beneath the lampposts. "They wait for you like that?"

"It's gotten worse," Nathaniel says from the back seat. There's a rustling sound as he gathers his belongings.

"Doesn't your building have security?" My unease intensifies at the thought of him walking past all those cars.

"It does, but since they park across the street and not on the property, the security guards can't do anything about it. Honestly, it's fine."

My stomach tenses as I catch sight of a long-barreled camera jutting out from a cranked open window.

Nathaniel climbs from the back, sliding onto Hyemi's vacated seat as he reaches for the door.

"Wait." I catch the back of his shirt.

He stops, one hand on the door handle. His gaze flits to my fingers holding on to the sliver of fabric. Memories of my childhood steal through me, of the same dark line of cars waiting for my mother and me, outside the company, outside my school, the sudden flash as the world seemed to erupt around us in lights and shouts. *What is your statement on Assemblyman Min's affair? Did you know the other woman? Is the rumor true, that you've filed for a divorce?*

"Sori?" Nathaniel draws me back to the present. He hasn't moved. His gaze isn't on my hand that still grips the back of his shirt, but steadied on my face. I know it's unreasonable, that the paparazzi won't actually hurt him, but I have an unshakeable feeling that by letting him go outside, I'm sending him into danger.

I make a decision, then and there. "Come home with me."

His eyes widen slightly, then his gaze flicks to the driver. I'm not worried he'll say anything. He's a Joah employee, which means he's contractually obligated to keep the privacy of its artists.

I release Nathaniel and sit back in my seat. "Can you please take us to my house?"

It's close to two a.m. when Nathaniel and I exit the van. My street is quiet. My closest neighbors are halfway down the hill and around a corner. The automatic outdoor lights flicker on as I key in the code to the front gate.

"This is your house?" Nathaniel says with a whistle, stepping into the front yard behind me. "I feel like I'm in *Parasite*."

I glare at him.

"But less murder-y," he amends.

I guess I can *sort of* see where he's coming from. My mother hired a Seoul-based architect of some renown to design the house, which has five bedrooms and an indoor pool and gym. In middle school, I would sometimes invite classmates over who would tell me how envious they were that I lived in such a spacious home in Seoul.

Nathaniel trails me up the lit path to the front door.

The foyer is spotless thanks to Ajumma's diligent cleaning. Opening the shoe cabinet off to the side, I take out a pair of house slippers and place them on the floor for Nathaniel to use.

"Are you hungry?" I ask. Even if it is the middle of the night, I feel awkward leading him straight upstairs, where the bedrooms are located.

"Well, now I'm craving Chapaguri," he says with a grin, referencing the instant noodle dish popularized by *Parasite*.

I roll my eyes. "The kitchen's over here."

I lead him from the foyer, past the dining area, and into the kitchen. Chapaguri is created by combining two instant noodle brands, Chapaghetti and Neoguri. In the pantry, I open a drawer to find several brands of instant noodle packets neatly lined up, grabbing the two that I need.

After boiling the water, I place both packets of noodles and dried vegetable flakes into the pot. While it's cooking, I glance over my shoulder to see Nathaniel on the barstool behind the island. When our gazes meet, I quickly turn around, breaking the noodles apart with my chopsticks so that they'll cook evenly.

"Can I help?" he asks.

I remember how he helped his sisters that morning at his house.

I have no doubt that he's perfectly capable in a kitchen. Getting up from the stool, he makes his way around the island toward me.

"I don't know where everything is . . ." I wince as I say the words aloud. The kitchen is Ajumma's domain; the few times I've asked to help, whether with the cooking or the cleaning up afterward, she's shooed me away. Though now I'm wondering if I should have tried harder.

"That's fine," Nathaniel says easily, already opening drawers and cabinets, "I'll figure it out."

He roots out placemats in a drawer beside the stove, plucks cups from a cabinet.

"Do you need this?" he asks, holding up a strainer that he'd found in a bottom drawer.

"Yes. I think the noodles are ready."

He places the strainer in the sink while, using two hands, I bring over the pot, tilting to pour out the noodles, but making sure to keep a little bit of the broth inside. Then, transferring the noodles back into the pot, I add the packets of powder and mix thoroughly.

"There are side dishes in the fridge," I tell Nathaniel.

He moves to retrieve them while I distribute our portions of Chapaguri into separate bowls. He's already seated by the time I'm finished.

"Thank you for the meal," he says before picking up his chopsticks.

"It's not quite like the film," I say as I watch him take an inhumanly large bite.

Nathaniel shakes his head, unable to speak, reaching for a slice of cabbage kimchi to supplement his eating experience.

"It's perfect," he says, after chewing and swallowing.

Warmth suffuses me. I feel silly for being so happy. It's *instant noodles*. But he eats so heartily, taking one large bite after another. He bends his head so that the noodles have less of a distance to travel between the bowl and his mouth.

I take my own first bite and let out a soft moan. Nathaniel raises his gaze, laughter in his eyes. It's a perfect balance of the savory richness of the black noodle sauce and the spicy seafood Neoguri, of which I only used a third of the flavor packet to mitigate the spice. I don't know if it's the late night or my general state of hunger, but it's *delicious*.

Eventually Nathaniel slows down, allowing for more human bites. "So are you going to tell me what you were doing today?"

My shoulders tense. "What do you mean?"

"At the school, when Jaewoo and Woo Hyemi cornered us in the stairwell. You *let* her win."

"You can't know that for sure. She caught me by surprise. *You* didn't really put up much of a fight with Jaewoo."

"I was too distracted by you losing *on purpose*."

"Was it that obvious?" I bite my lip. The plan won't work if people believe I was trying to help Hyemi.

"It wasn't," Nathaniel says, in a gentler voice than when he accused me not a moment before. "What are you up to, Sori?"

Yesterday I'd told Sun everything, even about Joah's financial difficulties, but telling Nathaniel feels different. For one, I don't want to burden him when he's on hiatus after working so hard for the past year. And another, for all his rebellious ways, Nathaniel has a strong sense of justice—that's one of the many things I admire about him, that he speaks out against things he feels are wrong or unfair. Which is why I can't tell him that my mother is only debuting Hyemi for her father's financial support. I don't want him to think badly of her.

And, I'll admit, there's a small part of me that wonders if he'll think badly of *me* for helping her. I knew Sun wouldn't think twice about it, as toeing the moral line is par for the course for people like us, whose parents are in the topmost echelon of Korean society.

I can, however, answer his question with some of the truth. "You know Dream Music, the company Joah recently acquired? They already had a girl group set to debut at the time of the acquisition. Hyemi's joining this group, ASAP, as their youngest member, except she hasn't had any formal training. She has less than two weeks to learn the choreography, record her part in the title track, and rehearse for the group's debut showcase.

"The other day, right before the scandal, actually, I told my mother I didn't want to debut as an idol anymore. We made a deal that if I got Hyemi ready for the showcase in time, she'd let me figure out what it is I actually do want to do. I can walk away free, no strings attached." Sun had reminded me about my contract, which I'll ask Secretary Park about nullifying, but it shouldn't be a problem. My mother and I have never broken promises to each other. "I'm the best person to help Hyemi, since I'm sort of a professional trainee at this point."

The whole time I've been speaking, Nathaniel's kept the same expression, only frowning slightly when I said I'd changed my mind about debuting as an idol. I wonder if he'll say something now to talk me out of it. Before Gi Taek and Angela, *he* was the one who supported my dream the most.

"So you're telling me Hyemi basically has to join the group ASAP."

I roll my eyes, not missing the double entendre.

"That makes sense," he says. "Why you'd help her, and not just because of the deal with your mother. You like helping people."

My face warms at his words. He sounds so genuine, as if it were that simple for him. "You don't think I'm making a mistake?"

He doesn't answer immediately, and I appreciate that, because it means he's taking my question seriously. "You're not a rash person," he says slowly, "and I mean that as a compliment." I wonder if he's remembering New York, and how he said I wasn't impulsive. "You think things through, from all different angles. You really take care of yourself. Emotionally. Mentally. It's what makes you reliable, and why you're the perfect person to look out for Hyemi."

Now it's not just my face that feels warm but all of me.

After talking with Nathaniel, I realize I've spoken to everyone important in my life about this, everyone whose opinion I care about the most.

Who I care about the most. And I do care about Nathaniel. That, at least, I can admit to myself. I care about his well-being. I worry for him. I want him to be happy and safe.

"Nathaniel," I say. "Nadine told me you're the only one at the apartment right now, and with the tabloid reporters loitering outside, it's difficult to leave . . ." I take a deep breath. "Would you like to stay here, at my house, while you're on hiatus?"

It's the favor Nadine asked of me. At the time, I'd considered it for one main reason, and that hasn't changed—to return the favor of that summer I spent with his family in New York—but now, I want to do this for his sake, because I care about him, as a friend.

Nathaniel drops his eyes, only to lift them. "Can I give you an answer tomorrow?"

"Of course," I say hurriedly. "I sprung this on you." My face heats up. He must feel uncomfortable at the thought of staying at his ex-girlfriend's house. I'm too embarrassed to look at him, so I look down at my empty bowl.

Nadine had also said he had a secret work-related project. It's possible he wants to stay near his apartment for that, as well.

"Thanks, Sori," he says. When I glance up to meet his gaze, his eyes are warm. "I appreciate the invite."

"Did you get a chance to talk to Hyemi?" I say, hoping the change of subject will cover my embarrassment. "She's sweet. You'd like her. She's not that much younger than us. And she's Canadian. Her first language is English."

"Is she?" Nathaniel says, letting out a yawn.

I look at my phone to see we've been sitting in the kitchen for almost an hour.

"You're exhausted. Come on, let me show you to your room." We clean up our dishes together and head back through the dining room and up the stairs to the second floor.

"My mother's room is that last one," I say, pointing down the hall to the closed double doors. "Don't worry. She's never here. She only comes to the house to pick up clothing and spends her nights at the office."

Nathaniel frowns. "You live alone?"

"I have a housekeeper. She comes during the weekdays and stays overnight. This is the guest bedroom." I press open the door, letting it swing wide.

"Damn." Nathaniel whistles. "This is the size of our entire apartment."

"I highly doubt that." The XOXO members live in a *very* expensive apartment building. "Do you need . . . anything? Pajamas? There are towels and a spare toothbrush in the bathroom."

"I'm good," he says, leaning against the door.

"But what are you going to sleep in?" I say with a frown.

"The bed."

"But in your *outside* clothes?" I wrinkle my nose.

"No."

It takes me a second to realize what he's saying. I should be embarrassed, but I'm more curious. Is that how he always sleeps? "But won't you be cold?"

He laughs. "Maybe. Is that your room behind you?"

"Yes," I say, then add quickly, "You can't go in."

I picture what he'd see if he walked into my room right now— stuffed animals covering every flat surface, including my bed.

"I wasn't planning to," he drawls.

I glare at him. Then, realizing we're standing close, I take a big step back.

He frowns slightly at the movement.

"Well, I guess this is good night." I press my back against my door, finding the knob.

Nathaniel studies my face, his gaze lingering on my nose, my eyes, my lips. "Night, Sori."

I open my door and slip behind it, not moving until I hear the soft click of his door.

Sixteen

I must have been exhausted because I sleep the entire night through, only waking when my phone chirps with a message. Bleary-eyed, I roll over, stuffed animals tumbling off my bed as I reach for my phone on my nightstand. The message is from Secretary Lee, my father's secretary: Your luncheon with Assemblyman Min and CEO Kim is scheduled for 13:00 today. He's also provided the location—an upscale Japanese restaurant in Apgujeong—and a reminder to dress in suitable attire.

With a groan, I toss my phone across the bed. The last time I met my father and grandmother together was shortly after I returned to Korea following my father's scandal, when my grandmother had contacted a reporter to come to her home for an exclusive interview. The experience was altogether unpleasant as I had to lie through my teeth, while enduring numerous insults against my mother from my grandmother, aunt, and cousins.

I take a deep breath and toss the memory to the back of my mind. The luncheon isn't until this afternoon, and since I'm to meet Hyemi after her practice, I have the whole morning to spend exactly how I wish.

Is Nathaniel awake? My body feels oddly light, like there's a balloon in my chest. He's so close; only two doors and a hallway separate us. I feel more awake than I have all week, possibly all month. My mind races with ideas for the morning. He'll definitely be hungry. Digging through my stuffed animals, I find my phone on the bed again. More cascade off the side as I slide from the mattress, scrolling through SNS for recipe ideas. I can picture it in my head: Japanese soufflé pancakes served on porcelain plates; a white flower plucked from the garden in a crystal vase as a centerpiece, and maybe another flower for my hair.

After a quick shower, I change into a collared pale cream one-piece, the skirt swishing above my knees. In the bathroom, I apply eyeliner and curl my lashes. I'm only excited because I've never had a guest all to myself before. Ajumma was here both times Gi Taek and Angela visited, and Jenny as well. She's not here now because it's Monday, which means she won't be at the house until later this afternoon. I'd be excited for any visitor, truly.

When I leave my room, the guest room door is slightly ajar. "Nathaniel?" I call out. When he doesn't respond, I knock lightly on the door, then push it open. A double-sided shelf in the middle of the room blocks the bed from view.

Remembering our conversation from last night about pajamas, or the lack of them, my breaths turn shallow.

I clear my throat. "Nathaniel? I'm coming inside. You better be dressed." Walking around the shelf, I raise my eyes to the king-sized bed situated on an elevated platform.

It's . . . empty.

For a moment, I just stand there, confused. Then I check the bathroom, only to find it empty too.

My heart thumps heavily in my chest as I leave the room, walking downstairs and opening the cabinet in the entranceway. Inside are the guest slippers where Nathaniel had left his shoes the night before.

The balloon in my chest pops. He's gone.

I'm still thinking of Nathaniel when I show up for the lunch with my father and grandmother. When did he leave? Why didn't he say anything? I checked my phone, but he hadn't left me any messages.

A waiter pulls back the sliding door and I slip off my shoes before entering the private room. "Good afternoon, Halmeoni, Abeoji," I say, bowing to each of them—seated on either side of a low table—before sinking onto the silk floor cushion beside my father, who greets me with a warm smile. My grandmother doesn't look up.

The soothing sounds of the bamboo water fountain drift from the back of the room as the hollow chute fills with water, then drops, pouring into a basin. I feel soothed, *almost*.

A server pours tea from a clay pot into a teacup; steam lifts from the surface as he hands it to me. I accept it with both hands, and my father's eyes crinkle in approval. Though my mother is a renowned beauty, acquaintances comment on the physical attributes my father and I share. We have the same straight nose, arched brows, and thick black hair, though his is silvering at the temples.

"It's highly irregular that your father must schedule times to have a meal with you," my grandmother says, her loud voice penetrating the tranquility of the room. "This wouldn't be an issue if you just came to live with your father and me. My house is much more comfortable than that gaudy monstrosity Min Hee had designed. A waste of your father's money. And I have a professional cook, not a charity case, like the woman your mother employs."

I count to five in my head. I learned years ago not to argue or talk back to my grandmother, not just because she's my grandmother and that would be incredibly disrespectful, but because doing so only makes things worse, and ultimately my mother is the one who's blamed for my bad behavior. *It's because of her blood that Sori is acting this way.*

"Ajumma takes very good care of me, Halmeoni," I say, in the sweetest voice I can muster, "and I couldn't leave my mother in that big house, all alone."

I also learned, a long time ago, not to feel bad about lying to my grandmother, especially if it's to protect my mother. She doesn't need to know that I basically live alone.

My grandmother sniffs loudly. "You should show the same consideration to your father as you do your mother, and to myself."

There's a soft knock, followed by the sliding door opening. Servers enter with handcrafted wooden boards, artfully arrayed with pieces of sushi, placing one in front of each of us. Over the course of lunch, my grandmother and father discuss matters of which I have no interest, and so I do what I always do in these situations: I think of something else entirely.

Nathaniel must have left because he felt uncomfortable. I'd practically dragged him to my house in the middle of the night. Maybe he thinks the risk in staying at my house is too great, or—as I'd thought the night before—maybe he'd *rather* stay alone in his apartment, where he'll have it to himself without the other members around.

Then I'm struck with a horrifying thought. What if he thinks I still have feelings for him? He'd asked me if I did at the karaoke room. And the reason he left this morning without telling was to spare my feelings.

"You're not seeing that boy again, are you?" my father asks me. "From that idol group."

I almost drop my teacup. "O-of course not," I say, glad for the steadiness of my hands. What prompted him to ask such a question?

"Good. Because there's someone I'd like for you to meet, the nephew of one of my supporters. His uncle is someone very important to my campaign."

I must make a face because my father says, "I wouldn't have asked except that this young man especially requested to meet you."

I frown. "What do you mean?"

"You made an impression on him, from your recent appearance on a show."

I'm confused until I realize he must mean *The Woori and Woogi Show* since *Catch Me If You Can* won't air until Wednesday.

"Won't you consider meeting him? It would please me."

I sigh. What's one more date?

"I'll have Secretary Lee send over his information," my father says.

I arrive at Joah just as Hyemi is finishing up her first practice with her group members. Unlike XOXO, ASAP is a six-member group, with Hyemi joining as the youngest member. They exit the practice room, from youngest to oldest, bowing to the dance instructor who gives them each words of encouragement. Hyemi appears exhausted, her shoulders slumped, but spotting me, her eyes brighten. "Seonbae!"

"Hyemi-yah," I say, taking her aside to let the other girls pass, "I'll meet you in the practice room in fifteen minutes. I need to speak with Sun Ye-eonni first."

She nods, then hurries off toward the bathroom with the others.

The last member—and leader—of ASAP waits for me, leaning against the doorframe with her arms crossed. "You called?"

I grin. "Kim Sun Ye." Although we never grew close enough to hang out outside of Joah, we've been friendly over the years. Besides me, Sun Ye is the trainee who's been at Joah the longest. She had chances to leave—most significantly an offer from KS Entertainment, Joah's biggest rival—last fall. They'd offered her the "center" position in their newest girl group, but she turned it down, though I never learned why. "Can I speak with you for a moment?"

Sun Ye nods and we move to a quiet corner of the hall.

"How is she doing?" I ask.

Sun Ye doesn't have to ask who I mean. "Better than expected," Sun Ye says in her calm, measured voice. Sun Ye was the right choice for leader, not just because of her age—at twenty, she's the oldest member—but also because she's level-headed. While my mother had offered me the position, Sun Ye was always more suited for the role. "She's a quick learner. I'm surprised she's never had any training."

"And the other girls. Are they treating her well?"

"They wouldn't dream of upsetting her," Sun Ye says with a teasing smile, "not with Min Sori watching over her."

I roll my eyes. "You can tell me the truth."

She pauses, thoughtful. "Just the normal stuff. Six girls together

135

for long stretches of time in a high-pressure environment? Lots of bickering. Some hair pulling. Just kidding." She laughs.

Hyemi must not have told the other members about how her father's involved. Though, now that I think about it, she probably doesn't know the extent of it. Which means I'll have to make sure to keep it a secret from not only the members—who might grow to resent her—but also Hyemi herself, who might feel self-conscious that she didn't earn her place in the group.

"She's an amazing rapper too," Sun Ye says. "It makes sense why Joah signed her on last minute. Our diamond in the rough."

That's a relief to hear. "Thanks. I feel reassured that you're looking out for her."

"I know. It's a lot of pressure. I practically acquired five younger sisters overnight."

Sun Ye speaks as if she's long-suffering, but there's a twinkle in her eye. "I'm happy for you," I say. This is a big moment for Sun Ye. After ten years as a trainee, she's finally debuting.

"Thanks, Sori." Her expression softens.

I change into workout clothes and join Hyemi where she's stretching on the floor of the practice room.

"Sun Ye told me practice went well," I say, extending my legs out and reaching for my toes.

"Sun Ye-eonni is kind," Hyemi says. Like before, I notice how tired she looks. Not just physically. If I remember her schedule correctly, she was up at five this morning for practice, after having returned late from the variety show recording the night before.

"I know we're supposed to go over the choreography, but we can take a break."

Hyemi shakes her head. "I don't mind working hard for the next two weeks, and then sleeping afterward."

Even if she hasn't been a trainee for very long, she definitely sounds like one.

Later I'll have to tell her that it's better to pace herself, and that things will only become *more* difficult after she's debuted, but for now, I'll let her hold on to that belief a little longer.

"Okay," I say, rising to my feet and moving toward the side of the room to turn on the music. "Walk me through the steps."

The dance *is* difficult, but luckily Hyemi's positioned mostly in the back or to the side during the majority of it, only coming to the front when she has her lines. She's had *some* formal training, having gone to a dance studio in Toronto all throughout elementary and middle school. As I go through the steps with her, I offer her tips and corrections.

Hours later, we've gone through the choreography so many times that I've memorized it myself. Her dancing still needs a lot more finessing, and she'll have to put the time into practicing so that she can perform it flawlessly on a live stage, but she's improved considerably from when we began.

"I'm nervous about how I'll appear on the episode," she says as we're packing up to leave the studio.

"The episode of *Catch Me If You Can*?" I ask.

She nods. "I feel like I wasn't completely myself. I didn't want to be embarrassed, so I tried to be on my best behavior, but I think I might have come across stiff."

I consider her words. "You don't have to show your whole self to people. In fact, you *should* keep a part of yourself just for you."

"Is that what you do, Seonbae? Your image is very glamorous, but you're also glamorous in person."

"I'm really not."

"But you are," she insists.

"I can be self-conscious and mean-spirited. And annoyed and ticked off." I think of Nathaniel leaving this morning without telling me. "And maybe one day I'll be comfortable showing those sides of me to strangers, but right now I want to keep that hidden and only show the glamorous side."

"I hope to see all the sides of you one day, Seonbae," she says with a grin, and I laugh.

It's four o'clock when I step off the bus in my neighborhood, the sun setting over the mountains to the west. For a moment I just stand there, breathing in the cool night air.

The street is quiet, the occasional car lumbering by. An elderly couple walks their dogs around the block.

Instead of going straight up the hill toward my house, I head over to the convenience store at the corner. As I approach, the door opens and a boy steps out.

Nathaniel.

Seventeen

I wait for Nathaniel at one of the plastic tables in front of the convenience store. A short few seconds later, the door jingles and Nathaniel reemerges with a drink in each hand. He places a glass bottle of grape juice in front of me before taking the seat opposite. With his long fingers he carefully uncurls the tin seal from his drink.

He's dressed in a sweatshirt and joggers, his soft hair curling around his ears. His phone lights up on the table with a message from Youngmin, but he doesn't reach for it. What is he doing back here, in my neighborhood, at my local convenience store of all places?

I thought he'd given me his answer to my offer when he left this morning without a word, and now that he's here, all the feelings from the day come rushing back. Embarrassment, from when I thought he was avoiding me, annoyance that he hadn't told me he was leaving, and disappointment that he was gone.

"Why did you leave this morning?" I ask.

His eyes flit to mine, his eyebrow raised slightly. "I had a meeting, so I went back to my apartment to change."

A meeting? I frown. "But why didn't you say anything?"

"You were still sleeping. I didn't want to wake you. Sori, what's wrong?"

I shake my head. "Nothing. Everything's fine. I just—" My hands circle the glass bottle. "I thought we'd have breakfast together."

The words sound so silly as I say them aloud. It's just *breakfast*. But I was looking forward to sharing it with him. I can at least be honest about that.

My hands tighten around the bottle.

I can't look at him. He must think I'm so starved for companionship that I'd get upset over a simple *meal*. A lonely rich girl in her enormous mansion.

Nathaniel leans forward, tugging the bottle from between my clenched hands. Then he slides his hand into mine, so that I'm clinging on to him instead. I'm struck by the feeling of his hand in mine. During the recording for *Catch Me If You Can*, there were moments when we held hands, but not like this. His hands are smoother than I remember them. I slide my pointer finger down the length of his, noticing that he's trimmed his fingernails.

"I'm sorry," he says, after a beat. "I should have told you that I was leaving. I was going to text you, but then I got distracted. Next time, I'll make sure to tell you if I have to go somewhere."

Next time. I look up.

Nathaniel draws in a breath. "The meeting I had this morning was at KS Entertainment," he says, "for a collaboration I'm doing with one of their artists. That's also why I didn't want to go back to the States during XOXO's hiatus, though my parents asked me to."

He laughs shakily, and I realize he's . . . nervous. A collaboration is a big deal, and new for him, as up until now, he hasn't pursued any solo projects outside XOXO. "There's nothing in my contract that says I can't work with non-Joah artists as a producer, which is what I'll be doing.

"Honestly . . ."—he releases my hand to rub the back of his neck—"I've been a bit worried about how to get to and from KS and my apartment without starting rumors, as we want to keep the collab a secret until the release. While I was sitting out here, no one gave me a second glance. This neighborhood is so remote, and most of the people who live here seem like private people. They wouldn't want tabloid reporters around. Even if someone recognized me, I don't think they'd post my location or anything."

He bites his lip, and I follow the movement. It's so rare that I see him lacking confidence that my chest tightens. He's trusting me with this new project that he's unsure of but that he cares about. I want to treasure his trust, prove that I'm worthy of something so precious.

I reach out my hand, this time covering his. "I'll look forward to it," I say, with all the sincerity I possess.

Nathaniel stares at my hand, lying atop his. "You asked me last night, and you might have changed your mind, but . . ."

He lifts his gaze. "Can I stay with you, Sori? Until my hiatus is over."

There's no reason for him to ask me this, as I already invited him over, but I realize why he is anyway.

He's giving me a chance to back out.

And maybe I should. I've felt so emotional since we've started talking again, it'll only get worse, especially living together. But it doesn't matter, because . . .

I *want* him to stay.

"Yes."

Nathaniel's smile turns shy, and I inexplicably blush, fidgeting in the chair.

"Should we . . . go up?" he asks.

I nod.

He lets go of my hand to grab our empty bottles, heading into the convenience store to recycle them. When he comes back outside, he takes my backpack, throwing it across his shoulder.

As we walk up the hill to my house, I sneak glances at him out of the corner of my eye.

I feel silly now that I know he left because of a meeting, and not because he thinks I still have feelings for him. He wouldn't think that because I'd told him I didn't at the karaoke room. I don't know if it's a product of having grown up with four older sisters, but he's always been an excellent listener.

Same as the evening before—or, I guess, earlier this morning—Nathaniel follows me up the lit pathway to my front door. The porchlight flickers on at our approach. "We should probably set some ground rules first," I say, stopping beneath the light.

He nods. "Okay."

"Let's try our best to be discreet. If we're ever in the same place, we should make sure not to leave together."

"Makes sense."

"My mother can't know you're staying with me. To limit the chances of it getting back to her, we should try to keep it from as many people as possible. Nadine knows already."

"What about Jaewoo and Jenny?"

I bite my lip. I don't like the idea of keeping something from

Jenny, or that I have to ask Nathaniel to keep a secret from Jaewoo, his best friend.

"You know what?" Nathaniel shakes his head. "Never mind. If we tell them, we'll have to tell Gi Taek, Sun, and the others. It's better if we keep it to ourselves."

I nod, grateful that he's taking this as seriously as I am. "If at any time either of us changes our mind, then we'll end this arrangement, no questions asked. And you'll need to wear a shirt at all times."

"What?" He frowns. "Why is that a rule?"

"What if we need to wake up in the middle of the night?" I ask, reasonably. "Like, what if there's a fire?"

"I'll put a shirt on."

"But that'll take time."

"I don't know." Nathaniel sounds skeptical. "This rule seems excessive."

"You're not allowed to come into my room either."

Nathaniel arches a brow. "Why not?"

I gasp, scandalized. "What do you mean 'why not'?"

He shrugs. "I'm just curious why I can't come into your room. You can come into mine."

"Your room is a guest bedroom, so it doesn't have any personal effects. While mine is filled with my stuff."

"I'm not going to steal one of your stuffed animals," Nathaniel drawls, "if that's what you're afraid of. Not like you stole Bearemy Baggins."

"I didn't *steal* Bearemy and that's not what I'm afraid of."

143

Nathaniel goes very still, and I realize my mistake. "Then what are you afraid of?" My heart races. "Sori, what are these rules for?"

"They're just . . . rules . . ."

My eyes dart to his and my breath catches at the look in his eyes. "You should be wary about setting rules with me," he says, his voice like silk. "You know I live to break them."

Neither of us moves, and yet somehow, he's closer.

I can count every one of his long and impossibly thick eyelashes.

Slowly he lifts his hand, his fingers lightly skimming over the arc of my cheekbones, then trailing down the side of my face to slide behind my neck.

I shiver, my lips parting.

"Min Sori?" The front door swings open and Nathaniel's hand drops. "What are you *doing*?"

Eighteen

Ajumma stands in the doorway, holding a spatula. "Why are you just standing there? Come inside!" She presses the door back, gesturing for us to enter.

"Ajumma." I take a deep breath. "This is—"

"Nathaniel Lee! I am an XOXO fan, but *you* are my favorite."

I gape at her.

"You look like my first love. Or maybe it's that you look like someone who I might have loved when I was young. What do you think, Sori-yah? Doesn't he look like someone's first love?"

My heart's already racing with what *almost* happened outside. "First loves are called that for a reason," I say, needing to distance myself from that moment. "Because there are second, third, and fourth loves after."

I peek at Nathaniel to find him watching me. "You can fall in love again," he says to Ajumma, though his gaze never leaves me. "Let me be your second, third, and fourth love." I feel my heart tumble in my chest.

"Don't be silly." Ajumma waves her hand in the air. "You'd be my seventh."

"Ajumma," I say, slipping off my shoes and gesturing her to the side.

While Nathaniel takes off his sneakers in the foyer, I explain to her that he's only staying for the weeks XOXO is on hiatus, and that it needs to be kept a secret from my mother.

"It's because she wouldn't understand." This will be the hardest part, getting Ajumma to agree to lie to my mother, as she's always been nothing but loyal to her.

"Oh yes," Ajumma says, nodding her head in a vigorous motion. "Your mother can be unreasonable in that way. I think it's best she doesn't know." She catches my eye and gives me an exaggerated wink.

For the second time tonight, I gape at her. "Ajumma, I don't— that is, Nathaniel and I . . ."

"Yes, yes, of course." She motions me into the dining room. "You don't have to explain yourself. Just know I'm cheering you on. Fighting!"

"Ajumma!" But she's already hurrying out of the foyer.

"What was that about?" Nathaniel asks from behind me, and I jump.

"N-nothing. Come on, let's eat."

At the long dining table, Ajumma sets out a second place setting for Nathaniel next to mine. Then, like a chef on a culinary show, she uncovers each dish with a flourish.

If Nathaniel hadn't already won over Ajumma with his apparent likeness to her first love, he has by the end of the meal, when he enthusiastically devours everything set in front of him, including two servings of rice.

Afterward, Ajumma shoos us from the dining room so that Nathaniel can settle in upstairs.

"It might still be too early to open the pool," I say, as we make our way to the second floor, "but there's exercise equipment in the gym you can use. The code for the gate is 450928★.

"The last four digits are your birthday," Nathaniel says slowly, "but what are the first two?"

"The year we won our independence." When he doesn't respond, I glance at him to see he wears an odd expression on his face. "What?"

"You phrased it as 'our independence.'"

"Of course, I did." I roll my eyes. "You're American, but you're also Korean." I say this adamantly.

The next time I look back at him, there's a small smile on his face.

I stop outside his door. "You're allowed to go anywhere in the house. Except for my mother's room. She hasn't been back to the house in over a month, and I don't think she'll come back anytime soon." She was already busy, and that's not going to stop in the coming weeks.

Nathaniel glances down the hall, then returns his gaze to me. I wonder if we'll talk about what happened outside the house, before Ajumma interrupted us. For a moment, I thought he was going to kiss me.

I panic a little at the thought. If that happens, it will put a stop to everything.

"I'll see you in the morning," Nathaniel says, opening his bedroom door.

Relief sweeps through me and my heart fills with warmth at his words. They're like a promise.

"Oh, and one last thing." He turns back. "I found a slight flaw with one of your rules."

I narrow my eyes, sensing that he's about to say something outrageous.

"The rule about sleeping with a shirt on." He smirks. "How will you know if I break it?"

Clearly pleased with himself, he strolls into his room.

The next morning, I wake with a start. With yesterday fresh in my mind, I leap from the bed. A Pikachu flies and hits the door as I slow down in time to quietly open it, peeking my head through. Across the hall, Nathaniel's door is open. My stomach drops only to see his hoodie from the night before hanging from the back of a chair. He's *still here*, just . . . awake. Was he always an early riser?

I quickly brush my teeth and wash my face, then change from pajamas into sweats, gathering my hair behind my head and pinning it with a claw. I rush down the stairs, stopping short when I see Nathaniel seated at the dining room table. He's wearing a zip-up hoodie over a white shirt, his hair tousled from sleep. He has one leg drawn up on the chair, his elbow balanced on his knee as he stares with concentration at the screen of his laptop. Headphones cover his ears, but he looks up briefly at my arrival, lifting his hand in a wave, before returning his attention to the screen.

I remember in New York he'd said he was taking a class. Curious, I walk around the table. He's sitting toward its center, with his back to the kitchen. My eyes find the screen only to see that it's split into dozens of screens, though the speaker is highlighted. I quickly dart to the side, almost tripping over my house slippers.

Nathaniel laughs, moving his headphones to his neck. "What are you doing?"

"I don't want to be on camera." I keep my voice to a whisper.

"It's off," he says, amused, "and I'm muted." He reaches out to tug my sleeve until I'm standing next to him. "That's my professor," he says, pointing to the spotlighted box, which shows a middle-aged Caucasian woman. "And these are my classmates." He clicks an icon and more boxes appear, though most have their cameras turned off, like Nathaniel's.

"Nathaniel Lee" is displayed at the bottommost corner of his box. "You use your real name?" I ask.

"Why not? There are probably dozens of Nathaniel Lees."

He takes off his headphones completely. Grabbing his empty mug from the table, he pushes back his chair and stands.

"Don't you need to pay attention?" I ask, following him into the kitchen.

"She's going over some points from the last lecture." He places his mug on the cup tray of the coffee machine. It's a new model that my mother purchased before she left. "How did you sleep last night?"

I don't want to tell him that I woke up a few times in the middle of the night, anxious that he'd be gone in the morning. "I slept fine."

He raises a brow at my answer but doesn't question me.

"I hope it's okay that I'm using this." He nods to the machine.

"I said you could, last night. And no one uses it." My mother did, one time, but then she'd purchased a newer model for her office.

He shifts open the drawer of colorful pods. "Want to pick a flavor for me?"

"*Yes.*"

I select a pod and hold it up.

"Pink, I should have known."

He presses a button on the machine, flipping open a cover. I slot the pod in place, then click the button to begin the brewing process.

Nathaniel leans back against the counter. "Ajumma was here earlier, but she went outside to the garden. I think that's what she said. She asked me if I wanted breakfast, but I said I'd wait for you."

"I'm glad. I . . . wanted to have breakfast together."

I don't know whether it's because I'm in my house, but I'm being more honest with him than normal, and with myself. My cheeks flush. I look up, expecting to see his amused expression, but he's looking away, his own cheeks bright with color.

"We'll both be busy during the day," he says, "but let's try to have breakfast and dinner together."

"Okay."

His coffee finishes brewing, and we return to the dining room.

"I have to get back to the lecture . . ."

"Don't worry about me," I say quickly.

As he settles back in his seat, I head upstairs to my bedroom, gathering stationery supplies from the drawers in my desk. Returning downstairs, I take the seat directly across from him, laying out my materials. Others find comfort in meditation or exercise; I find comfort in aesthetically pleasing stationery. I see him smile as I place down my *We Bare Bears* sticky notepads and multicolored gel pens, but he doesn't say anything, his focus returning to the lecture.

I select a notepad and uncap my pen, but my gaze keeps straying to Nathaniel. The way he concentrates is very . . . attractive.

He has a notebook of his own—a very plain black one—and with his plain black pen, he's taking notes in English, *in cursive*; his penmanship is surprisingly neat.

He looks up, a question in his gaze. I quickly duck my head.

I try to concentrate on *my* task. Secretary Park sent over Hyemi's schedule, which I printed out the night before. I take notes on the sticky pads and affix them to the page, jotting down ideas where I can step in to help Hyemi. She's moving into a dorm with the other ASAP members tomorrow. It'll be a big change from living alone with just her father to sharing a living space with five other girls. Besides working on her choreography, I'll want to make sure she's coping well, mentally and emotionally.

A half hour passes as Nathaniel and I work on our individual tasks, and though we're not interacting besides the occasional moments when our eyes meet, it's one of the best mornings I can remember having in a long time.

Ajumma returns from the garden, and we have breakfast, all three of us, with Nathaniel coaxing Ajumma to sit and enjoy a slice of toast with blackberry jam.

Afterward, he walks me to the bus stop, which is just past the convenience store. Sliding my duffle bag from his shoulder, he hands it to me. KS is sending a car to pick him up. He gave an address of one of my neighbors around the block. The KS people don't know where he actually lives, so they won't ask questions, nor will they care, as they're used to protecting idols' private lives.

"I won't have my phone on me," Nathaniel says. He's changed out of his sweats into a black shirt. "KS is strict with devices that can take video, and I'd rather just leave it behind instead of having it confiscated. But I'll be back at the house tonight."

"Okay," I say, as the bus pulls up to the stop. "Thanks for letting me know."

He waves goodbye as I step onto the bus. I tap my card to the electronic reader by the driver, then hurry to a window seat in time to wave to him back.

The ASAP members have already been practicing for five hours by the time I arrive, and they're not alone.

"Eomeoni," I say, surprised to see my mother standing against the wall. Though she's the CEO of Joah, she rarely visits the practice rooms. My chest tightens when I see the dark circles beneath her eyes. It's only been a few days since I saw her, but they've gotten worse. I'd told Nathaniel he could stay for the rest of his hiatus, but if my mother needs to rest, then I'd rather she came home.

"Sori-yah, is that you?" A woman in her forties with wavy hair pokes her head from behind my mother. I recognize her immediately—Ryu Jin-rang, one of the most talented creative directors in the business.

She was the mind behind XOXO, as well as other popular boy groups, like 95D. If she's taking on ASAP, then this will be her first girl group, and knowing her reputation, she'll be determined to make them as big, or even *bigger*, than her boy groups.

I bow to both Director Ryu and my mother.

"Min Hee-yah," Director Ryu says casually—she might be a formidable presence in the industry, but she's also a close friend of my mother's—"was your daughter always this pretty?"

"You saw me only a few months ago," I say, "at my father's charity event at the golf course, remember?"

"Ah, yes." She looks at my mother, then up at the ceiling. As my mother's close friend, she also has strong opinions on my father. "Your mother told me how you're the one helping Woo Hyemi," she says. "I feel more confident knowing you're lending her your support."

We return our attention to the members, who are working with the choreographer to prepare for their music video shoot over the weekend. With the six of them, their screen times will be varied, with Hyemi having the least amount of time due to her having the least lines—nine seconds total of the two minutes and forty-eight second song. But even with less lines, and placement at the back of the formation, she's clearly making more mistakes than the others. When Hyemi messes up so significantly that the entire group has to stop the choreography, two of the members shoot Hyemi frustrated looks.

"What do you think of the concept, Sori?" Director Ryu asks, distracting me.

I tear my gaze away from Hyemi to consider her question. According to the document Secretary Park sent over, the concept for ASAP's debut is young women breaking into workplaces traditionally dominated by men in Korean society. The title track, "Wake Up," is an upbeat pop melody with romantic lyrics, but that's beside the point.

"I like it a lot," I say. "It's empowering and sends a good message."

Director Ryu nods. "I wanted each member to stand out as an individual, so my team and I asked the girls about their interests so that we could build each of their stories, whether they're sporty or fun-loving or have a 4D personality. We want to be as authentic to their natures as possible. When you enjoy what you're doing, the joy is expressed in the music and the performances. Woo Hyemi hasn't yet expressed what aspects of her personality or interests she'd like to focus on, so if you could help her with discovering that, it would be helpful. Right now, she's unique in that she's the youngest; the maknae of a group is always treasured by the fandom."

"I'll speak more with Hyemi," I say and put it on my mental list that I'd drawn up that morning.

"Hyemi's talented, but she's also new to this world. The four girls from Dream Music have been working toward this dream for two years, and Sun Ye for even longer. It's not just that Hyemi needs to learn the choreography, but does she have the stamina to endure the long hours of practice? Does she have the mental fortitude? Our standards are exacting but necessary for a reason. We want to ensure these girls have not only a successful career but also a healthy one, a long one. You have a short time to determine whether she's ready to walk that difficult path."

My mother interrupts. "We have a meeting with the director of the music video. Will you excuse us, Sori?"

As they leave the room, I realize my mother and I haven't yet scheduled our lunch together. She'll only get busier and busier, so I need to schedule it now. I follow my mother and Director Ryu out of the room. They're not immediately outside the door, so I head toward the hallway.

"Min Hee-yah." I'm stopped by the sound of Director Ryu's voice. "You need to rest."

"I can't stop now." They're standing in the hall, speaking low so that their voices don't carry. "Not when everything's on the line. The overseas investors are close to signing deals with Joah. Once CEO Woo signs through his investment, I can finally breathe—"

"Why don't you ask Assemblyman Min for his shares of the company? He owes you that, for what you've endured from that *awful* family. And for raising Sori so well. You've done a wonderful job with her."

"It's impossible," my mother says, mumbling words that I don't catch.

As the lead investor in Joah when my mother first started the company, my father owns the majority of its shares. My mother would have otherwise divorced my father years ago. But in the eyes of the public, he's a family man with a loving wife and daughter—a divorce would irrevocably damage that image. Those shares are the only thing keeping it from falling apart.

"Sori? What are you doing here?"

I startle. Director Ryu stands in the doorway, alone.

"I was looking for my mother. I wanted to ask her . . ." The reason why I was searching for my mother seems so small compared to the innumerable important responsibilities taking up her time. "To lunch."

"Oh, I'm sorry. She already left for her meeting. I decided to stay back and speak with the choreographer. Maybe you can call her?" It seems a reasonable enough suggestion, except that my mother and I don't contact each other except through Secretary Park.

"Is the company really in that much trouble?" I ask, hating how small my voice sounds.

Director Ryu's expression turns thoughtful. "Did you know I've known your mother for almost twenty years now? Ever since she was an idol and I was a production assistant. When her dream of being an idol ended prematurely, Joah became her new dream. And I'm so proud of her for making it a reality. She's worked so hard.

"*Your mother* was the inspiration for ASAP's debut concept. I'll never tell her that. She'd be horrified if she knew. A young woman breaking into an industry where most, if not all, of the top CEOs are men? She inspires a lot of young women; she inspires me."

"And me," I whisper. Even if work has called her away more in the past years, and we haven't spent as much time together, I've always been proud my mother is Seo Min Hee.

"Regardless of whether Joah is facing difficulties at the moment, it's not something you need to concern yourself with. You're young. Let the adults do all the worrying."

Director Ryu doesn't know me well enough to know I *can't help* worrying.

"I'll admit, when I got the list of ASAP members, I was surprised when I saw your name wasn't on it. That is, until your mother told me about your decision. I'm proud of you, Sori. Not every person who's chosen a career path can make it to the end, but it's just as difficult to *change* your path once you've decided it's not for you anymore."

I nod at Director Ryu's words, but I'm not really listening. So much is depending on Hyemi's successful debut and her father's resulting investment. I can't fulfill my mother's dream of being an idol, the one she gave up for me, but I can protect her dream of Joah.

When we return to the room, the members have split up to continue with their one-on-one training, a few leaving to work with the vocal coach, while others stay behind to practice in front of the mirror. I make Hyemi run through the entirety of the choreography. Then I ask her to do it again. And again. I change into sweats and dance the other members' parts, so that she knows where's she's supposed to be positioned at all times.

We continue practicing long after the others have left. And it's not until the maintenance workers shut off the studio lights that I realize I've kept her longer than I should have.

"I'm sorry, Hyemi-yah. I've pushed you hard today, haven't I?"

"No, Seonbae." She shakes her head, her brow glistening with sweat. "I'm so grateful for you. I want to work hard. After all, this is my dream."

I'm feeling the heaviness and exhaustion of the day on the long bus ride home. It doesn't diminish, not until I spot Nathaniel waiting for me at the same table outside the convenience store. I join him, and together, we walk up the hill toward home.

Nineteen

I'm still thinking about my mom and Hyemi the next day as I head over to the gym for a morning workout. I'll make good on my promise to ensure Hyemi is ready in time to debut, but there must be more that I can do. I could intercede with my father about the shares. I don't know why I hadn't thought of it before. He won't relinquish them freely, but maybe, like with my mother, I could strike a deal with him.

I change into workout clothes, zipping up a hoodie over my sports bra and leggings, and head over to the gym at the back of the house. Ajumma is already there when I arrive, seated on the stationary bike while watching a weekend drama.

That reminds me. The first two episodes of Sun's drama premiered over the weekend. I still need to watch them. The drama debuted with high ratings, with netizens praising the drama's writing and Sun's acting.

Arranging my yoga mat in front of the wall-length mirror, I go through my usual routine of stretches, lifting my arms above my head and extending my legs. The door to the gym opens and Nathaniel enters, dressed in joggers and a loose, sleeveless muscle shirt. He takes up position where the free weights are located, which, when I look at the mirror, are in my direct line of sight.

I try not to stare, but it's impossible. His body is a work of art; he has broad, straight shoulders and lean muscles. While I go through my floor exercises—sit-ups, planks, and lunges—he jumps rope, lifts weights, and hauls himself up off the floor in pull-ups. I'm flushed and sweaty by the time I'm finished with my floor workout. Grabbing a towel and my water bottle, I head over to the treadmill, grateful that it faces the window and not the mirror.

Putting in my earbuds, I position my phone on the stand to watch the first episode of Sun's drama. The adaptation sticks close to the original web novel, which is praised for its zaniness and romance, and I'm so engrossed that the forty-five minutes flies by.

As I'm cooling down, I take out my earbuds and place them into their case.

"Were you watching Sun's drama?" Nathaniel's voice comes from so close that I startle and miss my footing on the belt.

He catches me, one hand circling my wrist, the other sliding beneath my back.

He reaches out to press the Stop button, and the track stills beneath me.

The room continues to spin, and I blink rapidly to regain my equilibrium.

His arm is steady beneath me, secure. "Are you okay?" he asks. He's close enough that I can see the sweat trickling down the side of his face. I vaguely recall that he'd been on the second treadmill, beside Ajumma's stationary bike, though she's no longer there.

"Yes," I say, breathless.

I'm exceedingly aware of how little clothing I'm wearing, having taken off my zipper hoodie to run on the treadmill. The rough texture of his lifting gloves raises goosebumps on my skin. I'm breathing heavily, chest moving up and down, and I don't know whether it's because of running on the treadmill or his close proximity, probably both. His eyes drop, only to slowly lift to mine once more. His hands tighten infinitesimally, his eyes somehow darker than before.

He's going to kiss me. This is bad. I mean, I *want* him to kiss me. But he shouldn't. We're friends. We *can't be* more than that. Not just because of the promise I made to my mother, but for *reasons* he wouldn't understand.

If we kiss, I can't, in good conscience, let him stay. He'll have to leave. I feel a little desperate at the thought. It's too soon. I haven't been as happy *in months* as I have with him in the past few days.

"Wow, Sori," Nathaniel says, and though he's trying for levity, his voice is a little unsteady. "I didn't know you were falling for me."

I smile, my heart bursting with . . . something. Gratitude? "You can't help yourself, can you?"

He places me on my feet. Grabbing my water bottle, he uncaps it and hands it to me.

I take a long drink, letting the cool water flush through my heated system. *This* is fine. *This* will work. As long as we both lighten the mood, as long as we don't cross the line into *more*, then there's no reason to end our arrangement anytime soon.

After breakfast, Nathaniel walks me to the bus stop. He's on his way to KS, while I have plans to meet Secretary Park at Hyemi's apartment, as she's moving into the dorm today. The other members moved in last week, but Hyemi was still waiting for the rest of her luggage to arrive from Canada.

"Our episode of *Catch Me If You Can* airs tonight," Nathaniel says. Behind him, the bus rumbles toward the stop.

Though we filmed the episode a few days ago, it feels like a lifetime has passed—so much has happened since then.

"Should we watch it together later tonight?" I ask. A warm feeling stirs in my chest. I never was eager to come home before.

Nathaniel nods. "Should I invite Nadine?"

"Yes, I'd love that." As the only person who knows he's staying at my house, she's the perfect guest to invite. "I'll pick up pizza on the way home," I tell him, as I step onto the bus.

On the ride to Hyemi's apartment complex, I scroll through restaurants on Naver, starring a few of my favorites. When I arrive, Secretary Park is already there, helping Hyemi with her luggage.

"Are you excited to move into your dorms?" I ask Hyemi once we've finished loading her three suitcases into the trunk of the van. The dorm is located near Joah's new building, about a thirty-minute drive in Seoul traffic.

When Hyemi doesn't immediately answer, I look over to see that her face is turned toward the window.

"I hope I get along with everyone," she says quietly.

My heart softens. She must be nervous. This is her first time living away from her parents.

"Even though we're moving you into the dorms," I reassure her, "you'll still stay at your apartment tonight." This was a special request from Hyemi's father, who wanted to spend time with his youngest before she was completely immersed in her hectic debut schedule.

She nods, though her gaze remains out the window.

We arrive at the apartment building, each of us rolling one of Hyemi's suitcases into the elevator, and press the button for the fifth floor. As we approach the door to the apartment, the sounds of shouting come from within. Secretary Park and I exchange glances. She keys in the code, opening the door to . . .

Chaos.

It's as if the clothing and accessories floors of a department store exploded over the room, with haphazard piles of clothing covering most pieces of furniture, plus multiple standing racks packed with jackets, dresses, skirts, and hoodies. Not to mention the massive amounts of shoes crammed into shoe organizers at the entrance. This could have been *my* living situation. I shudder at the thought.

The ASAP members all stand and bow as we enter, but once Secretary Park acknowledges them, they resume their individual activities. The shouting is from the girls playing a video game on a large television set. One member, dressed in a bathrobe with bunny ears, is playing some sort of tennis game with another member who's in oversized pajamas, both of them swinging their arms recklessly through the air. They almost step on another member who's painting her toenails at their feet. Her scream startles Secretary Park. The second youngest member—Jiyoo—is sitting cocooned on the couch between two clothing piles, crocheting what looks like a carrot with a face.

It's not dirty, just very cluttered. But maybe I shouldn't speak too soon. I haven't seen the bathroom.

Sun Ye walks out of the leftmost room, and Hyemi yelps. An LED mask covers her entire face, giving her the appearance of a pink Iron Man.

"Oh, Hyemi-yah, you're here," she says. She doesn't take off the mask. "The biggest room is a triple," she says, pointing to the room across from the kitchen. "But you're in the double with Jiyoo. Come, I'll show you." She heads to the room next to hers and across from the bathroom.

"I'm going . . . to . . ." Secretary Park edges toward the kitchen. Is that sweat on her brow? "Do . . . the dishes."

Hyemi and I manage to follow Sun Ye around the fire hazards and into the room.

"I'm sorry all of my stuff is everywhere," Jiyoo says, having followed us inside. She starts to move her clothing off Hyemi's bed, throwing them onto her unmade one. "If there's anything you need to move, feel free to toss it here."

The room is small, but rather spacious for two people. In between the beds are two desks, side-by-side, facing a window that allows in natural light. Hyemi and Jiyoo are still in school, which is probably why they've been accorded a bit more space.

"If you ever need some peace or quiet, please come into my room," Sun Ye says. She has the only single.

Once Sun Ye leaves to finish up her skincare routine, Hyemi and I start to unpack her belongings.

"Do you need help?" Jiyoo asks, hovering over us.

163

"Thank you, Jiyoo-yah," I say, handing her Hyemi's toiletry bag. "Can you put this in the bathroom?"

Jiyoo, looking like I've given her a live grenade, nods bravely, heading off to the bathroom in search of an available space. I figured Hyemi might be too shy to ask the older members to move their stuff around, but Jiyoo, who's been the maknae of the four girls from Dream for a while now, will feel more comfortable making room for Hyemi.

We manage to unpack two of her suitcases in a little over an hour, shoving her third—filled with her fall and winter clothes—beneath her bed, as well as organizing her side of the room.

"You're lucky, Hyemi-yah," Jiyoo says. "My family is in Gyeong-ju, so I had to move in by myself. You must be happy to have Sori-seonbae helping you." I study Jiyoo's face, but she doesn't appear jealous so much as wistful.

"I'm very grateful," Hyemi says softly.

In the time we've been unpacking, Secretary Park has cleaned the kitchen and cooked a meal of spicy cold noodles with kimchi. Unearthing a low wooden table, she lays out the meal with the help of the other members who've put away their video game and even folded some of the laundry and vacuumed. We gather in the living room, enjoying our meal while seated on the floor around the table. The members chatter away about the music video shoot, about their costumes, and what jobs each member was chosen to portray. I notice Hyemi doesn't interact as much with the others, picking at her bowl of noodles.

She'd been so excited to join ASAP that I wonder if something happened. Sun Ye had assured me that none of the girls were giving her a hard time, but maybe, as the oldest, she missed some of the dynamics between the younger members.

I broach the subject once we're in the van headed back to her father's apartment. "Hyemi, is something the matter? I noticed you were quiet with the other girls."

At first, I don't think she'll respond, her shoulders hunched forward, but then she says in a quiet voice, "I don't know why I feel this way. Everyone is so nice. It's just that . . . they've been together for so much longer. They have inside jokes, and they're comfortable with one another, teasing and laughing. I feel like I'm an intruder, like I don't belong, like I'm too late."

Her words strike a chord with me. That's how *I* felt, back in high school, like everyone had already formed their group of friends, and if there was ever a chance to join one, I'd missed it.

"I've felt the same way," I tell her. "For most of middle school and high school, I didn't *have* any friends. I used to blame it on my classmates. I don't think I was wrong to believe that some of them *were* only friends with me because of who my parents were. But after a while, I pushed everyone away, even people who could have been genuine friends. I gained a reputation as someone stuck up, who thought she was better than everyone else." For a long time, I thought that was fine because it protected me from disappointment and hurt, but all it did was emphasize how alone I was.

"It wasn't until I got a new roommate that my high school life changed. Eventually we became best friends, but we started off as enemies. She accidentally read one of my private letters and I mistakenly believed she'd done it on purpose."

Hyemi appropriately gasps. The letter had been a postcard that Nathaniel had sent me when we were dating. He'd ended it with, *Chin up, Songbird. You will always have my heart. XOXO.* He'd mailed it to me when he was in Los Angeles, after I'd called him in tears over an incident that happened at school—one of my classmates had filled my locker with soap bubbles.

"But then Jenny kept reaching out to me in both subtle and sometimes over-the-top ways. If it wasn't for her *trying*, again and again, we might not have become friends. Now, I couldn't imagine my life without her."

The back of my eyes heat a little with the realization that Jenny never giving up on me is the reason we're friends, and the reason I'm friends with Angela and Gi Taek too.

This conversation with Hyemi is a reminder that I need to reach out to Jenny, just as she reached out to me countless times before.

"Try not to put up your walls too high." I give the advice I would give myself from two years ago. "Thinking that others won't accept you. You have to give them chances, multiples ones, and keep trying yourself. Otherwise you might miss out on forming true friendships."

Hyemi nods. "I will, Seonbae. And . . . thank you. For sharing with me. It's comforting to know that even if I'm not as close to the other members *now*, there's a chance that I will be in the future."

As we draw near to Hyemi's neighborhood, her cell phone pings. She glances down to read her message, her mouth forming a frown. "My father can't make it tonight," she says. Disappointment colors her voice.

"Should we turn back to the dorm?" I ask. "Or . . ." A sudden thought pops into my mind.

"Do you want to come to my house? I was planning to watch the episode of *Catch Me If You Can* with some friends."

Hyemi's whole face lights up. "Seonbae, I would love that!"

Twenty

As Secretary Park turns the car around, I pull out my phone and text Nathaniel. I'm bringing Hyemi back to the house to watch the episode with us.

His response is immediate. Nice. I'm assuming Hyemi's staying the night. Should I clean out the guest bedroom?

I hadn't thought of that, and I immediately feel guilty. I'd invited him to stay, only to kick him out.

Don't worry about it, Nathaniel texts, reading my mind. Jaewoo's in Seoul, staying at the apartment, so I'll go hang out with him. Seriously, it's not a big deal.

I make a split-second decision. Invite him over. If he asks, tell him I wanted to have a viewing party for everyone on the episode who's in Seoul. Sun is currently in the countryside, filming his drama, and Youngmin is on a field trip. And you don't have to clean out the guest bedroom. Hyemi will stay with me in my room.

So . . . He sends in a single message block.

Then another appears below it. Hyemi gets to see your room, and I don't?

I laugh out loud. Both Secretary Park and Hyemi glance at me.

"It's just . . ." I gesture at my phone, embarrassed. "Something . . . my friend said."

Hyemi eyes me knowingly.

"Secretary Park," I call up to the front seat. "Do you mind stopping over at a pizza restaurant on the way home?"

* * *

Nadine's stepping out of a taxi when we pull up outside my house, her short hair swept back with a studded headband.

After thanking Secretary Park for driving us, I call out to her. "Eonni!"

I gesture with the pizza boxes in my hands to Hyemi, who's holding fried chicken and cola. "This is my friend, Woo Hyemi. She's debuting next week with ASAP, Joah's first girl group."

"It's lovely to meet you, Hyemi," Nadine says warmly. She's dressed in a black cropped shirt and leggings, with her leather jacket thrown across her shoulders and silver glinting from her ears. "Congratulations on your debut."

Hyemi beams. "Thank you!"

As we enter through the front gate, Nadine turns her head to view the garden. "Your house is beautiful, Sori."

"Thank you. Nathaniel says it reminds him of the house in *Parasite*."

"Ah, my sweet brother," Nadine drawls, "always says the most charming things."

I open the front door.

As we walk through, Hyemi says, "Nathaniel . . . Lee?"

Nathaniel slides sideways into the foyer in his house slippers. Over his clothes, he wears an apron printed with a large penguin. "Welcome!"

"You look like you've made yourself at home," Nadine says.

My eyes dart to Hyemi, but she doesn't seem to take notice of the comment, too busy gaping at Nathaniel.

"Nuna!" Jaewoo yells, emerging from the dining room.

"Jaewoo!" Nadine yells back. They run toward each other, then stop to do a very long and complicated handshake.

"I'll take those," Nathaniel says, walking over to Hyemi and me. He tucks the jug of cola beneath one arm, grabbing the bag of fried chicken. When he reaches for my pizza boxes, I hold them closer to my chest.

"I'll bring them in."

His fingers briefly trace the back of my hand as his eyes lift to mine. "Welcome home."

"So it *is* true," Hyemi says, and I freeze. "That *was* your sister in the photo."

It takes me a moment to realize what she's referring to. When I do, I'm a little shocked she brought it up. Hyemi must also realize what she's said because she goes completely scarlet. "I didn't mean—I wasn't thinking—I'm sorry."

Nathaniel laughs. "Don't stress about it. I don't think we were ever really introduced. My name's Nathaniel."

"I know," she says, flushing prettily.

"Hyemi-yah." Jaewoo approaches. "I'm glad you're here. We need to represent Team Student Council Members tonight."

"Don't spoil the episode!" Nadine shouts from behind him.

We head into the dining room. I place the boxes of pizza on the table, then open them.

"Ooh," Nadine says, shifting forward in her seat. "You didn't tell me each slice has different toppings."

"Stay strong, Naddy," Nathaniel says, in a faux-pleading voice. "Don't be tempted by the beautiful pizza. Remember Joe."

"When in Korea," she says ruthlessly, in English, "do as the Koreans do." She grabs a slice with a half a cob of corn in the middle.

Nathaniel eyes me with hostile judgment as I pull out a fork and knife to eat my pizza.

Hyemi doesn't speak much throughout dinner, but she laughs often, her wide-eyed gaze flitting between Nathaniel and Jaewoo, who for some reason decide to sit on opposite ends of the long table and keep on asking each other to pass things. Ajumma declines to join us but takes a few pieces of fried chicken and a cup of pickled radish back to her room, chuckling appreciatively about the "noisy house."

When it's close to seven o'clock, Nadine checks her phone. "Wait, isn't your episode of *Catch Me If You Can* airing soon?"

We clean the table and hurry to the living room, where I turn on the television, switching to EBC.

As I turn around, I notice there's only two empty spots on the sectional sofa, between Nadine and Hyemi or beside Nathaniel, as Jaewoo has decided to sprawl his entire body over the chaise part. There's clearly more space between Nadine and Hyemi, and yet . . . I walk over and plop myself beside Nathaniel.

"I'll get the lights," Jaewoo says, jumping up to dim them. I can hear the others shift to fill the space, and Nathaniel moves as well, but only slightly.

The episode opens with an aerial pan of Seoul Arts Academy. Text overlays explain the school's history, as well as a few of its most illustrious graduates. It's also the alma mater of a certain popular boy band, the text reads. The video switches to a clip from XOXO's newest music video.

Jaewoo points to the screen and laughs when Nathaniel appears, holding a red apple. "Your hair was so long!"

"And *blue*," Nadine adds.

"I kind of liked the blue." Nathaniel sweeps his hand through his hair. "Whoops, sorry, Hyemi," he says, when his movements jostle her. He moves closer to me to give her space, and now we're touching completely, from hip to shoulder.

I liked the blue hair too, but I don't say that aloud.

Hyemi appears on screen and introduces herself.

"Hyemi, you're so cute!" Nadine exclaims. Even though it's clear she's nervous, her personality comes off bright and cheerful.

Then it's my introduction. *My name is Min Sori*. I cringe. I refused to listen to the recording of the radio show; watching myself is a new kind of torment.

After commercials, the TV splits into eight screens showing all the players. The next part is the game portion of the show, which I'm genuinely interested in if only to see what everyone else was up to while we were separated.

The camera pans to Hyemi first, who starts off the game in the gymnasium.

She's clearly someone who talks when she's nervous, speaking so quickly that the editor jokingly added subtitles. *"I don't know what to do. I'm so scared. What if I run into someone on the other team? Should I run? What if I'm caught first? Not that whoever is caught first should feel ashamed or anything. The first to lose is actually quite brave. Though still, please don't let me be the first."* The subtitles eventually become gibberish themselves as she continues to speak at a rapid rate. The text edit reads: Is she rapping?

The episode cuts to different clips of Youngmin speeding through the school, rifling through storage closets and ending up in very odd places—one time in an air vent in the boy's locker room.

"Youngmin-ah, what are you doing?" Jaewoo is laughing so hard he slides off the sofa to the floor.

The text beneath reads: Choi Youngmin finds hiding places that even the producers couldn't find.

Jaewoo, Nathaniel, and Sun are all much calmer than their youngest member, though Jaewoo shares a bit of that energy, mostly running or jogging the whole time, and clearly searching for tokens.

I don't think Sun runs even once, leisurely walking outside the school. At one point he stops to admire the flowers and explains to viewers how he had the responsibility of watering them when he was a student. Does he think he's on a gardening show? the editor adds.

As for Nathaniel, though he keeps a fast pace, he only glances into every room he passes, covering the most territory out of everyone, but not actively searching for tokens. The text reads: Is Nathaniel on the hunt? But for what . . . or whom?

"Were you going straight to tagging people out?" Jaewoo asks. "I respect your strategy."

Nathaniel doesn't answer, though I can feel his body tense at the question. Then the screen switches to me and I'm completely distracted.

The cafeteria. I remember the musical tune of the bell as the game started, the nervousness and excitement that raced through my veins. When the Sori on screen finds the first token, even I feel a sense of satisfaction.

"Damn, Sori," Jaewoo says, impressed.

I wait for the camera to cut to the next person, but it remains on me. *He can't breathe if it's zipped all the way*, I say, holding the first plushie.

My cheeks go up in flames. I thought they might edit that out. A tough girl exterior but a soft interior? the text reads. Who are you, Min Sori?

"It is a cute mascot," Jaewoo acknowledges.

Nathaniel's gaze remains riveted to the screen.

The episode *continues* to follow me. I check the time. I've officially had more screen time than everyone else in the episode. A nervous feeling flutters in my belly—will XOXO fans resent that I've had more screen time than the members?

The screen splits, showing my point of view as I go up the stairs and, at the same time, Nathaniel's POV hiding from Sun in a classroom.

The camera shows Sun turning, making it appear as if he's about to catch me down the hall.

Then a hand reaches out, grabbing my wrist. The episode cuts to commercial.

"That's where they end it?" Nadine shouts. "I'm so mad. Who-ever edited this is a genius."

After a commercial for a popular instant coffee brand and the grand opening of a new Ferris wheel by the Han River, the Seoul Eye, the episode returns. There's a short scuffle as I'm dragged into an empty classroom. The camera pans the room in a haywire movement before focusing on Nathaniel and me crouched close

174

together on the floor. Two delinquents meeting after school, the text reads.

The camera angle switches from me to Nathaniel, focusing on his face. "Can you turn off your light?" Nathaniel asks, and then the screen goes dark.

The video *finally* cuts to someone else, and it's Jaewoo who's already with Hyemi, the editor having removed their meeting.

"Jaewoo-seonbae found me hiding in the teachers' office," Hyemi says. I sneak a glance at Hyemi to see if she's upset that she hasn't had as much screen time, but she's absorbed in the episode, laughing at the students who ignore Nathaniel's dancing.

I feel embarrassed when I'm shown finding the second token. "They clearly gave me the ace edit."

"Don't question it, Sori," Nadine says. "Embrace your inner variety show goddess."

Next is the chase to the elevator, then the screen switches to footage from one of the cameras set up inside, with Nathaniel and me standing on either side of the elevator car. They don't play the audio from our mics. Instead, the text reads: We will be reunited with them soon.

By the time I'm shown finding the third token, I'm resigned to my starring role in the episode. When Youngmin appears out of nowhere like some silent tagging assassin, I'm cheering him on with everyone else.

"I have to head back to school," Nadine says once the episode is over. "Jaewoo, can you drive me?" I hadn't seen Jaewoo's car, but he must have parked it down the street.

"Sure. Nathaniel and I can drop you off on the way back to the apartment."

As Hyemi and I walk Nathaniel and the others to the door, I have the reckless thought of blurting out the truth so that he can stay, but quickly smash the impulse.

When I glance up, I find Nathaniel watching me. *Tomorrow*, he mouths, and my heart lightens in response.

Afterward, Hyemi and I go up to my room. I lend her a pair of pajamas and a spare toothbrush. Normally, I'd be on my phone, looking up reactions to the episode, but I don't want to cause her any stress, so I'm careful to leave my phone face down on the side table.

"How do you know Jaewoo and Nathaniel-seonbaenim?" she asks once we're settled in my large four-poster bed. She's chosen not to displace any stuffed animals but sleep with them piled atop her, same as me.

"I've known them since middle school . . ." I begin, then explain how because we were all trainees at Joah, and also attended SAA, we became friends.

"My friends are all in Canada," Hyemi says. "We text and talk over video but it's not the same."

"I won't say that you'll make new friends," I say gently, "but you'll make *more*. And the friends that you were meant to keep, you *will* because you'll put in the effort."

"I hope you're right, Seonbae," Hyemi says, softly. A few minutes later, she asks, "Do you think Nadine got a haircut recently?"

"I don't know. Why do you ask?"

But Hyemi's already fallen asleep.

The next morning, Hyemi heads out after breakfast. She needs to get back to the dorms in time to leave for the airport, as the ASAP members are flying to Thailand to shoot their music video. While munching on a piece of toast, I finally open SNS to see viewer reactions to the episode. They're unanimously positive. I sink into my chair with relief.

XOXO hold their titles as reality TV kings. Hyemi is praised for her fresh appearance, and excitement is already drumming up for ASAP's debut.

Then I catch sight of another article.

> WHO IS MIN SORI? DO WE HAVE A NEW VARIETY SHOW
> QUEEN?

And another and another.

> ALL YOU NEED TO KNOW ABOUT MIN SORI, DAUGHTER OF
> SEO MIN HEE
>
> MIN SORI IS THE ACE OF TONIGHT'S EPISODE OF *CATCH ME
> IF YOU CAN*

My gaze lands on the number one trending article, upvoted to the top of the site.

> ARE NATHANIEL LEE AND MIN SORI . . . DATING?

Twenty-one

Nathaniel and I are trending on all the major sites, sometimes separately, sometimes together. In a panicked flurry, I skim article after article, not exactly sure what I'm searching for but feeling as if my stomach will drop at any moment. Besides the one voted to the top of the site, they're all mostly informative articles—what happened on the episode, my background and age—rather than mean-spirited gossip. Even the top article's headline is clickbait; the actual article is a recap of the episode. The comments section is the real test. But as I scroll, these also seem harmless, and my heart starts to resume a steady rhythm.

In fact, the comments are amusing. The top comment, the one with the most likes, says they're like that high school couple that everyone admires.

I scroll to read more. They look so good in high school uniforms.

I know everyone's here envying Min Sori, but I envy Nathaniel.

I think I need to learn to play an instrument.

Then I see a comment that makes me almost drop my phone. Remember Lee Jihyuk's dating scandal when XOXO first debuted? The girl was never named, but they said she was a trainee at Joah. What if it was Min Sori?

The comment only has ten likes. Still, it's on the front page of comments, for everyone to read.

Beneath it someone's replied, Don't spread rumors without proof. That would mean they're flaunting their relationship. That would be too brazen of them both. This comment has twenty-eight likes.

And now the anxiety is back but tenfold. I have to talk to someone about this. I could text Gi Taek and Angela, but there's only one person I need right now. I open up my chat with Nathaniel, reading back our messages from last night. Jaewoo and I just got to the apartment. Try not to wake up Hyemi with your snoring.

I don't snore!

How do you know? I didn't warrant this with a response.

I type in the chat box, then press Send. Have you seen the articles? I wait for him to read my message, but when the "1" remains beside his name, indicating he hasn't read it, I text him again. Can you call me when you see this?

I hurriedly open my chat with Jaewoo. Nathaniel isn't answering his texts.

Jaewoo's response is immediate. He went to KS.

Of course. He's been going there every day to work with one of their artists. I remember he'd told me they confiscate visitors' phones, which explains why he isn't messaging me back.

I sit back in my chair. I could wait for him to come home later tonight—I glance at the clock on the wall—six hours from now. Or I could . . . go to him.

My heart starts to race at the reckless thought. And yet waiting until tonight, stewing alone while my thoughts spiral out of control, feels unbearable.

Before I can talk myself out of it, I request a taxi through the app on my phone.

Even if this plan is impulsive, at least I'm *doing* something. I quickly change out of my pajamas, checking the app to see the driver is five minutes away. I've enough time to put on sunscreen and light makeup before rushing outside the gate.

I greet the driver and settle into the back seat of the taxi, having already input the address in the app. I resist the urge to scroll through more articles, as that'll only make my anxiety worse.

The taxi drops me off outside KS Entertainment. As I stare at the company's intimidating edifice—the building is huge, twice the size of Joah, all clean, dark glass—I realize I have no way of getting inside. A few fans linger outside the building, posing cutely and taking selcas.

An unassuming man approaches the front entrance, waving his keycard over the scanner, which lights up green, granting him access.

I could throw my weight around and say that I'm the daughter of Seo Min Hee, but that information might get back to my mother, who would not be pleased that I'm at KS, practically in enemy territory.

A black car pulls up to the curb, and the back seat window shifts downward.

"Sori?" My father looks out at me from the window.

I'm so shocked to see him that I don't immediately respond. His offices aren't near this part of the city. "Abeoji?" I say finally. "What are you doing here?"

"I have a meeting with CEO Cha." He doesn't elaborate, likely because the *reasons* for meeting KS Entertainment's CEO might not be entirely ethical. "What are you . . . ?"

"I . . ." I struggle for a lie, my eyes landing on the Starbucks down the street. "I met a friend for coffee, but she left already."

"I see," he says, rubbing his clean-shaven chin. "Actually, I'm glad that I've run into you. CEO Cha's nephew is the man I wish for you to meet. It might also benefit you to know CEO Cha, as well. Why don't you get in the car, and we'll go through together?"

This seems like both the answer to my problem and a terrible idea. Still, I walk around to the other side, slipping into the back seat.

Secretary Lee maneuvers the car to the back of the building, where a security guard lets us through into an underground garage. He drops my father and I off outside the indoor entrance before parking the car on a lower level.

CEO Cha's secretary is there to greet us, bowing and opening the door to the front lobby. She leads us to the security desk where a guard offers us a tray in which to place our phones. "My apologies, but it's company policy for all visitors," she explains.

"Of course," my father says, relinquishing his phone easily.

As the guard opens a drawer to secure our phones, I catch a glimpse of Nathaniel's tucked among the rest.

"CEO Cha is finishing up another meeting at the moment," the KS secretary says politely. "Would you like a tour of the building meanwhile?"

"That's not necessary—" my father begins.

"I'd love that!" I interrupt. Once I'm ensconced with my father and CEO Cha, I probably won't have a chance to look for Nathaniel.

"You go on ahead," my father says. "Is there a place where I can wait?"

"Yes, follow me." She leads my father past security. When she returns, I walk behind her to the nearest elevator bank, watching with frustration as she presses the button for the basement floor.

Nathaniel won't be there. He'll be in one of the recording studios on an upper level.

The layout of KS is similar to Joah, with music, vocal practice, and dance practice rooms on the lower levels, and the recording studios, meeting rooms, and offices on the upper levels.

Like Joah, KS has photographs of their talent decorating the walls. Along with recording artists, they also represent actors and actresses. The last photograph at the end of a particularly long hall is the promotional poster for *Springtime Blossom*, with the lead actress, Lee Byeol, gazing up lovingly into the eyes of her costar, who plays a man who was once an alien cat from another planet. Also, he's a time traveler.

As we step off the elevator on the third floor, the secretary's ringtone goes off. She glances down at the screen with a frown. "I need to take this. Will you be all right by yourself? Feel free to look around."

"Yes." I nod, but she's already walking away, her phone to her ear.

I step back onto the elevator and press the button for the eighth floor. After peeking into a few of the empty rooms, I quickly realize this isn't the floor I'm searching for. Heading back toward the elevator, I catch sight of my father down the hall. He's walking toward me, deep in conversation with another man, presumably CEO Cha. Darting forward, I push open a door that leads into a stairwell and hurry down to the floor below.

This time it's CEO Cha's secretary approaching from down the hall, peering into rooms as if in search of me. I feel like I'm on another episode of *Catch Me If You Can*. Grabbing the nearest doorknob, I slip through into a room, closing the door quietly behind me. I let out a sigh in relief.

"Sori?"

I whip around. Nathaniel's seated behind a large mixing console, his eyes wide in shock. "What are you doing here?"

"Are you alone?" I ask, hurrying over to him. A window separates the control from the recording studio, but the lights are shut off.

He eyes my approach. "Yeah . . ."

"I needed to talk to you. I tried texting you, but then I remembered you were at KS." I take a deep breath. "I don't know if you saw this morning, but our names are trending together after last night's episode. A lot of the articles are harmless, but some of them are about us . . ." I blush. "Dating."

"Did you see anything we need to let Joah know about?" I know why he's asking. If the articles are vitriolic . . . or defamatory, then Joah would have to take legal action.

"No. They're mostly just clickbait, but . . . I'm worried. What if it escalates?"

183

Nathaniel seems to consider my question, his brow furrowed. "There's no reason to worry," he says slowly, "as long as there's no truth to the rumors."

He's right. Lots of celebrities are paired together, but nothing comes of it because it's not true.

"Even if they find out that we dated in the past," Nathaniel says, "that was a while ago. It's only a scandal if we're dating now."

His words sink into me, and I can feel the tension from this morning leave my shoulders.

Maybe I didn't have to come all the way here to see him—I could have waited until he came home—but I also feel so much better now than I had before.

"What are you doing?" I ask. Now that I can concentrate on more than just the articles, I realize I've practically barged into Nathaniel's workplace.

"I just finished arranging the music for the track," he says. "We're going to bring in the artist soon to record the vocals. Do you want to . . . listen?"

"Yes!"

Nathaniel laughs, standing. I take his seat, sinking down into the cushioned chair. Picking up the large headphones, he places them over my ears.

After a few seconds, music floods through the speakers—the track that the vocalist will sing over, carrying the melody.

"You composed this?" I say, then blush, remembering how I was shocked when I discovered he was taking a class, but I'm not shocked now. I'm just so . . . impressed. And proud.

He nods, his smile shy but confident.

"It's incredible!" I shout over the speakers. I listen to the entirety of the track, then ask him to start it over for me again.

"Producer Nathaniel," I say, once it finishes playing for the second time. "What made you want to produce?"

He leans back against the console. "Maybe it's because I come from a big family, or because I'm part of an idol group, but sometimes I want to create something that's just my own."

I'd never thought he felt this way, but it makes sense; how, though he has a family that loves him and members that support him, he'd want to have his own accomplishments, be judged on his own merits.

"I can understand why you'd see yourself as part of a group," I say. "I see myself as my mother's daughter. For what it's worth, I've always seen you for you." Although he's a part of XOXO, he's stood apart to me, the only one I see.

I look away, embarrassed at the turn of my thoughts.

"I'm envious, though. You're passionate about so many things, not just with XOXO and your family but also music producing and your university class. I seem to be lacking in not only passion but direction. Even helping Hyemi, I don't know if I'm the best person for the job."

"Don't sell yourself short," Nathaniel says. "Who's better suited to help Hyemi than you? Someone who's grown up in this industry. Maybe you can't make Hyemi into an idol like those who've trained for ten years, but you're helping make the transition for her as smooth as possible. And maybe while working with her, you'll find something you *are* interested in."

"Gi Taek and Angela think I'd make a great stylist or dance instructor," I quip.

"You would," Nathaniel says seriously, his voice intent. "But I think there's something else for you. Something better for you."

Nathaniel's eyes are dark as he looks down at me where I sit at the edge of the chair.

The way he looks at me. The way he makes me feel. His belief in me. It's like a drug, heady and intoxicating. My limbs feel weak and yet my blood runs hot, and all I want to do is reach up and bring his face closer to mine, until there's nothing left between us.

"Nathaniel?"

A woman stands in the doorway. I've been so absorbed in him and our conversation that I hadn't even noticed the arrival of another person.

I recognize her—Naseol, the lead singer of KS's third-generation girl group. She must be the artist Nathaniel's collaborating with.

I stand and bow, which Naseol returns politely.

"This is my friend . . ." Nathaniel introduces me.

"Min Sori, right? The model from last night's episode of *Catch Me If You Can*. I was rooting for Team Delinquents, by the way." She winks. "No wonder you two have such great chemistry . . ."

Neither Nathaniel nor I move. Had she seen something between us?

"You're friends in real life. Did you invite her to the studio, Jihyuk-ah?"

"I came with my father," I hurriedly explain. "He's . . . an

186

acquaintance of CEO Cha. Actually, they're both waiting for me. I should probably go."

"Ah, I see," she says, and she truly looks regretful. "It was nice meeting you."

Later, sitting with my father and CEO Cha, listening to them discuss business and the innumerable accomplishments of CEO Cha's nephew, I think of Nathaniel and Naseol in the studio, and how I wish I was with them instead.

Twenty-two

After Hyemi returns from filming ASAP's music video, we spend basically sunup to sundown at Joah perfecting the choreography. I work with not only Hyemi but the other members as well, making sure they're eating properly and getting enough rest. Their showcase is scheduled for Friday in the evening, after the release of ASAP's first single, "Wake Up." I mark the days on my calendar, crossing them off one by one; Saturday passes, then Sunday and Monday.

Besides working with the members, I also assist Director Ryu, who's subsisting solely on adrenaline and caffeine at this point. She has a whole team to help her, so I spend most of my time running to cafés within a three-hundred-meter radius of Joah to sustain the team members. I don't complain. It's an honor just to see Director Ryu and her team at work.

A huge vision board takes up the majority of the wall space in Director Ryu's office, and sometimes I stand in front of it in awe, studying all the details that went into the creation of ASAP. She's thought of everything, down to each individual member's hair color and their astrological and zodiac signs.

She's the person who signs off on their final outfit selections—brought to her by a team of stylists—including hair accessories and footwear, as well as overseeing the final edits for ASAP's debut documentary, which will go live next week after their single release. The last episode will air before their full EP drops at the end of this month.

I might not be debuting as a member of ASAP, but working with the girls and Director Ryu, I feel like I'm part of a team.

With how busy I've been at Joah, I'd have thought that other aspects of my life might suffer, but that isn't the case. Every evening at six, I leave the company. Just like I tell the ASAP members, I also need to rest, and life outside work is just, *if not more*, important.

Getting off at my bus stop Tuesday night, I round the corner to see the bright lights of my local convenience store. Nathaniel waits for me at one of the tables outside, as he has been since last week. He's sipping from a canned drink, a book in hand. My gaze moves to where he's left the bottle of my favorite grape juice on the table.

This is our routine, sitting and chatting about our days before walking up the hill to the house together. The sweet, rich drink cool in the balmy spring night. The neighborhood quiet as the sky turns to dusk. Nathaniel, the back of his hand brushing against the back of mine. I'd never thought I'd have a favorite part of the day, but this becomes it.

After dinner with Ajumma, we spend a few hours in the living room together. He plays a video game while I snuggle in the corner of the couch reading a web novel.

Nathaniel's phone lights up on the coffee table, but he doesn't reach for it. He's in the middle of an intense zombie battle. Then my own phone chirps with a message.

Are you busy? It's from Sun.

When my phone rings with an incoming call, I get up from

the couch and head to the kitchen. I balance the phone against the coffee maker, then press Accept, leaning back against the counter.

Sun's not even at his phone when the video loads. I'm staring at an empty high-backed chair. Behind it is a floor-to-ceiling bookcase with works of classic literature and a few translated works from English and Japanese.

"Oh, you picked up," I hear Sun say as he swivels the chair toward him, then sits down, rubbing his neck with a towel. He's wearing a bathrobe and pajamas pants, his hair swept back from his face. "I called Nathaniel first. He didn't bother picking up."

I keep my expression neutral. Why would he mention Nathaniel to me? None of the members know that he's been living with me.

"I have an unusual request," Sun says. "It's coming from the director of my drama. Apparently, he's a MinLee fan."

I'd been so worried that someone would discover our past relationship that I hadn't thought our interactions on *Catch Me If You Can* would have the *opposite* effect.

Apparently, we had so much chemistry on the episode that netizens started teasingly referring to us as "the MinLee couple."

MinLee couple, Nathaniel had quipped, *I guess that's better than SoNath.*

Of course, the irony is that, while people are happy for us to be in a fake relationship, if it were *real*, all the support would turn to judgment and scorn.

"The director wants to capitalize on your fake relationship," Sun says, uncapping a bottle of toner, splashing the product onto

190

his hands, then tapping it onto his face. "He asked me if I'd use you two for ratings, and I said, 'I couldn't have thought of a better idea myself.'"

The urge to roll my eyes is strong. "So what are you asking?"

"For you and Nathaniel to cameo in my drama. Your scenes will film this Thursday for the episode that will air next week. Most of the episode was filmed earlier, but the scriptwriter agreed to write in short roles for you two."

"I see . . ." Sun's drama follows the live-shoot system, so while the first few episodes were filmed beforehand, the others are being shot as the series airs. This way, the producers can make changes, like the inclusion of a cameo, or respond to viewer feedback to improve ratings.

"I'll do it," I say, "*if* you also let Hyemi appear on the episode." I would have done it anyway, to support Sun, but I might as well leverage this opportunity for Hyemi's sake.

"Woo Hyemi?" Sun raises a brow. "She's the girl you're mentoring, right? Whose debut will determine whether her father pays the big bucks." He makes it all sound so mercenary.

"Is there a problem?" I say. "If you can't do it, then—"

"No, I can." He waves me off. "And this is perfect. I was feeling unnerved at the idea of owing you a favor."

I look upward and hold that position. "What about Nathaniel?" I ask, recovering. "He might say no."

"Oh, he'll do it," Sun says with complete confidence.

When I return to the living room, Nathaniel is waiting for a new map on his game to load. He looks up when I enter, a soft smile on his face. My heart beats a little faster. On the coffee table, his phone chirps with a new message.

"That's from Sun-oppa," I say quickly.

"Were you talking with Sun-hyeong in the kitchen just now?" He picks up his phone. I watch him read through the long message. "You said you'd do the cameo?"

"Yes."

The map for the game loads. Nathaniel quickly writes out a response, then throws his phone onto the couch, picking up his controller and maneuvering his character to gathering weapons.

"What did you say?" I ask, annoyed that he's so focused on his video game.

He glances at me. "You're doing it, right? I said yes."

There's something so matter-of-fact about his response, that because I'm doing it, of course he would too. I feel my annoyance immediately melt away.

I still have a half hour before I need to get ready for bed. I pick up my phone to read my web novel. Instead of settling in the corner of the couch, I snuggle up next to Nathaniel. His body tenses and I watch as his character on screen take a few hits, but then he relaxes, adjusting his arm so that I'm more comfortable. We remain like that for the next half hour.

At Joah the following morning, I tell Director Ryu and Secretary Park about Hyemi and my cameos in Sun's drama.

"The timing works out," Secretary Park says. "The ASAP members are supposed to take the day off before the showcase anyway."

I don't bring it up to Hyemi until after she's finished dance practice with the other members.

"Are you sure it's all right that I'm in the episode?" she asks, fiddling with her bracelet. We're sitting in the same room where I'd met her for the first time. Since then, she's gotten a stylish haircut and gained some healthy weight after working with a nutritionist and personal trainer. "I don't have any acting experience."

"It'll be a small role. A cameo." In a text this morning, Sun had said the drama's writer had agreed to write in a part for Hyemi. "Nathaniel and I also don't have any acting experience."

"But you'll be a natural," she insists. I smile at her indulgently. At least one of us has confidence in me. "Seonbae, I've been wanting to ask you . . ." She twists her bracelet around her wrist. It's a braid of colorful strings woven together in a continuous loop. "How do you feel that you're trending as a couple with Nathaniel-seonbae? It must be burdensome."

My heart warms at her concern. It *would* be burdensome to be paired so publicly with a stranger, or worse, someone I felt uncomfortable being associated with, but . . .

"I'm fine," I say truthfully. Now that I know there isn't a scandal brewing, I'm feeling much calmer about the situation, though there are still the negative comments that give me anxiety.

"Seonbae, have you ever had a crush on someone in the company?"

My eyes widen, startled by her question. "Why do you ask? Is there someone you like?"

I try to go through the possible candidates. There's Youngmin, who's the same age as her and is also her classmate at SAA. And then Jaewoo, who was on Team Student Council with her and who I know she admires. There are also Joah's other trainees, who I've grown somewhat familiar with, if only because I'd seen Director Ryu's potential "teams" for future groups. One of the top trainees, a boy of Malaysian descent, is particularly cute.

She shakes her head. Quickly. Too quickly.

Hyemi has a crush.

I feel giddy at the thought. "You don't have to tell me who, just know that I support you."

She giggles. "Thanks, Eonni. Is it true that dating is forbidden? My father's lawyer looked over the contract and it didn't say anything about it."

"It's not," I tell her. "It's just tricky because of reactions from the public, especially for younger artists who don't have as many fans to support them yet. But Joah isn't as strict as other companies," I add when I see her expression fall. "There are Joah artists who date."

I think of Jenny and Jaewoo, who had a scandal early on in their relationship when a photo was leaked of the two of them. Joah stood behind Jaewoo, releasing a statement that didn't confirm or deny the relationship but stated they would take action against any defamatory articles.

"Really?" Hyemi's eyes are wide. "Who?"

"I can't tell you that," I chide.

She sighs. "You're a good friend, Eonni."

* * *

Nathaniel has a project for his class, so I go for a run later that night. It rained earlier, and the streets have that distinctive after-rain smell. I jog past an older man collecting bottles and cans with a grabbing tool, dropping them into separate bags for glass, plastic, and other waste. A woman putters by on her motorbike, a dog tucked snugly into her backpack, its eyes closed and tongue wagging. All of the businesses are closed, except for the convenience store, glowing like a beacon on the dark corner.

As I run, I mull over my conversation with Hyemi. It's true that Joah has been more lax with the idea of their idols dating in the past year, ever since they took the stance of protecting Jaewoo's relationship. The expectations around idols dating in the industry has changed too, with more and more fans supporting their favorite idols rather than turning their backs on them, like they have in the past.

If the industry had been like it is now two years ago, could Nathaniel and I have kept our relationship? Since the atmosphere *has* changed, could we enter into a relationship now?

I'm surprised at the turn of my own thoughts. I never thought I'd ask myself these questions. For one, there's the promise I made to my mother, and I've never broken a promise to her.

And yet circumstances have changed since that day, not just with Joah's stance on their idols dating but also the status of my mother's company. With the success of XOXO, Joah has become a company that others in the industry respect. Because of how my mother has led Joah, she's winning the Trailblazer Award at the EBC Awards. And now with the debut of ASAP, she'll prove to anyone who might have doubted her that she isn't going anywhere.

The matter of Nathaniel and me seems so small in comparison . . .

I slow to a walk until I stop entirely, dropping my hands to my knees to catch my breath. I've run as far as the neighborhood playground. A slide set with swings sits atop a blue cushioned ground covering. I head over to the bottom of the slide, sit down, and pull up my feet. Pillowing my back against the slide, I take out my phone. The screen emits a low glow as I press the contact for the only person who knows better than anyone what it's like to date an idol.

Jenny answers on the third ring. "Sori?" Her face appears on the screen. There's a shuffling commotion as she drops her phone. I briefly view a high ceiling before she picks it up again. "Whoops," she says, breathless.

"Where are you?" I calculate the time in my head, and it must be early morning in New York City.

"I'm at the library. Hold on a sec." She disappears from the screen. I can hear the soft tap of her footsteps as she walks from the library, then the squeal of a door opening.

Jenny angles the phone so that I have a view of her standing in a stairwell. The sound of her voice echoes around her. "What time is it there?"

"Ten o'clock."

"That's late! Where are you?"

I move the phone so that she can see the children's play area behind me. "I needed to think, so I went for a run."

"Should I be concerned?" Jenny asks.

I shake my head. "I just wanted to hear your voice."

I close my eyes as I listen to her tell me about her school life.

She's taking music theory, as well as a class on modern composers. The final selection for the quartet is this week.

"If I get it, I could be in Seoul as early as this month," she says. "I'm sorry I haven't called much."

"No!" I say vehemently. "I'm the one who's sorry."

Jenny wrinkles her nose like she wants to argue with me, but then she laughs. "Well, we're talking now. I'm also happy to hear your voice, but you called for a reason, didn't you?"

Her ability to read me across an entire ocean and continent is truly astounding.

I tell her everything, about my deal with my mother, that in exchange for helping Hyemi's debut, she'll give me more independence, but also about Nathaniel living with me for the duration of his hiatus. I feel a tad guilty that I'm telling her, when I made Nathaniel swear not to tell his bandmates, but I think he'd forgive me—I'm calling her because of him, after all.

"How do you feel?" she asks quietly.

She already knows without me having to tell her, that my feelings for Nathaniel have returned, not that they had ever gone away.

I think of the feeling that comes over me when I step off the bus to find him waiting for me.

"I feel happy." Saying it aloud, it feels like a confession. "Tell me what I should do."

"I don't think I have to," Jenny says, a smile on her face. "I won't lie, it's not easy, dating someone who spends half his life in the spotlight. It helps to remember that Jaewoo's just a person, and that, even if he wasn't a member of XOXO, I'd still want to be with him.

Of course, it *has* helped that we've kept our relationship a secret. Though some fans have theories that are eerily accurate." She shudders. "But unlike Jaewoo and me, you and Nathaniel wouldn't be long distance."

No, and I wouldn't want us to be. I'm not strong like Jenny. I want to be independent with my career but not my relationship. I want to need someone, just as much as I want to feel needed.

"I think there are obstacles in any relationship," Jenny continues. "You just have to decide whether that feeling—happiness—is worth any hardships that might come up."

I don't know if it's worth it; I just know I'm not ready to let it go.

"When are you going to tell him?"

"I can't tell him anything until after I talk to my mother. She's in Japan right now . . ." Secretary Park had informed me shortly after my mother had already left. "But she's coming back to Seoul for ASAP's debut showcase." I could talk to her as early as that night.

My chest flutters with nervousness and excitement. With hope.

"I'm rooting for you!" Jenny says. "You and Nathaniel. I think if any couple deserves a second chance, it's you two."

Twenty-three

I read the script for Sun's drama on the train ride to the filming location, which is a small town on the eastern coast of the peninsula. *The Sea Prince* is a fantasy romance about an amnesiac deity who washes up on shore during a particularly bad storm—his doing—and is rescued by a local fisherman's daughter. She's got a grudge against the god for sending all those awful storms. She, of course, doesn't know the identity of the mysterious naked man. Rom-com hijinks ensue as the heroine is a level-headed country girl and the sea prince is literally a fish out of water.

Hyemi's role in the episode is that of a schoolgirl who stumbles upon a magical conch shell holding the Sea Prince's memories. Nathaniel plays a water god who inhabits a local bathhouse. And I . . .

"I'm playing a mermaid?" I look up from the script. Secretary Park sits across from me. As Joah's representative, she's accompanying Hyemi and me to the filming site. The scriptwriter, who must have worked through the night to come up with our individual storylines, sent the revised script to Secretary Park, who in turn, reviewed the contents before printing them out and delivering them to us.

"Yes," Secretary Park says, "a mermaid who's fond of warmer temperatures, which is why you eventually end up at the bathhouse."

Hyemi stirs from where she's curled up in the window seat.

Immediately upon boarding the train, she'd fallen asleep, and neither Secretary Park nor I had the heart to wake her.

Hyemi's role in the episode, unlike Nathaniel's and mine, is actually significant to the plot. Her character's family puts the magical conch up for sale after she brings it to them, leading Sun to discover the conch and restore his memories, the catalyst for the second half of the drama.

But even with such an important role, she doesn't have many lines to memorize. It's a better use of her time to catch up on much-needed sleep.

Three hours after leaving Seoul, we arrive at the station, which consists of a single platform and three tracks. I haven't been to the sea in a while, and as we exit out front, I take a deep breath of the salty, crisp air. It's a little warmer than in Seoul, and the sun is out, so I let my cardigan fall to the crook of my elbows. Closing my eyes and tipping my head back, I stay like that for a brief moment, the sunlight warming my face and shoulders.

A production assistant waits for us in the parking lot and we drive another fifteen minutes along the coast to where the production crew has set up base camp beside the beach, with several tents and food carts.

The "set" is a functioning fishing village, whose elderly residents are being compensated for the use of their homes and businesses. They were also extended invitations to act as extras in the drama itself, with many of them taking up the offer if only to impress their grandchildren.

"Min Sori-ssi, Woo Hyemi-ssi." A man wearing black metal

frame sunglasses with orange gradient lenses and stubble on his chin—presumably the drama's director—greets us upon arrival. While giving us a brief tour of the set, he explains the day's schedule. Hyemi will film her first scene by the beach, which is where she'll discover the magical conch shell, and then I'll film mine by the tidepools. And then later tonight, Nathaniel and I will film our scene together in the bathhouse.

As we walk from the beach toward the actors' tent, I notice a dazed-looking woman walking along the coastline holding two cups of coffee and drinking from both.

The director follows my gaze. "That's the scriptwriter," he whispers. "Let's not bother her."

Over by the tents, Sun lounges beneath a large umbrella, sunglasses on the bridge of his nose. He's also drinking coffee, though he only has a single iced americano.

"Youngmin sent over a coffee truck," Sun says, raising his cup. "Help yourself." He nods to indicate a brightly colored coffee truck set up between the tents. Two baristas in matching green-striped uniforms take orders from a short line of crew members. The drinks are already prepaid by Youngmin, his face depicted on a banner that runs atop the truck with a message to Sun: CONGRATULATIONS TO THE SEA PRINCE, OH SUN! FIGHTING!

"Maybe later," I say, my stomach feeling a little queasy now that I'm about to film my scenes.

"Where's Nathaniel?" Sun asks. "I thought he'd come with you from Joah."

At the mention of Nathaniel's name, my heart starts to pound faster. I haven't seen him since my talk with Jenny. When I got back to the house, he was on a call, and so I'd hurried upstairs. It's unreasonable, but I have this sudden fear that he'll know, with one glance at my face, that I've been thinking about being with him again, and I'm not ready for that conversation, not until I talk with my mother.

"He's coming later with Ji Seok-oppa," I tell Sun.

"Hyemi-ssi," Sun says, having apparently just noticed Hyemi hovering behind me. "Hello."

She gives him a ninety-degree bow. "Thank you so much for inviting me."

He nod-bows back to her. "If I'm forced to endure Nathaniel's company," he drones, "I, at least, can have the pleasure of yours."

"Oh, but Nathaniel-seonbae is much more talented and charming than I am," Hyemi says.

"I see you're a Nathaniel fan," Sun drawls.

"I like you too! I mean . . ." Her entire face turns beet red.

I intervene, throwing a protective arm around Hyemi's shoulders, then lead her away. She's due to costume and makeup anyway. "Don't let Sun tease you," I say. "He wants you to say you like him best in XOXO, but he's too old for you. You should prefer someone closer to your age." Just like I prefer Nathaniel, who was born in the same year as me.

"Not too close," she says, so soft I almost don't catch it.

I raise a brow, letting my arm drop as she walks ahead. She's not interested in Youngmin, then. Which leaves Jaewoo. I watch her pityingly. She's in for heartbreak, as Jaewoo is very much a boy already in love.

202

I only have time to see Hyemi start her scene before I'm rushed to hair and makeup.

Stepping inside the tent, I'm surprised to discover that the hairstylist is none other than Kim Soobin, my friend who'd saved Hyemi and me before our recording of *Catch Me If You Can*.

"Eonni!" I squeal.

"Sori-yah!"

"Thank you for letting me borrow your outfit the other day," I say, after we hug. "You were a lifesaver."

"It was exciting to see my clothes on the episode!" She giggles.

Her girlfriend, RALA, is the makeup artist, and together they blow out my hair and affix me with rhinestones.

When the costume designer—a thin man with a shaven head and tortoiseshell glasses—arrives carrying a garment bag, Soobin introduces me. "This is our mermaid, Min Sori."

His blue eyes—colored lenses, presumably—widen. "Oh, you are *perfect*." He hurries forward, unzipping the garment bag. "Your secretary already sent over your measurements. This is what we were thinking." Inside is a corseted bodysuit intricately beaded with pearls and stones in aquamarine, cobalt, and sapphire blue. The costume is shoulderless, and while it'll cover my stomach and chest, it won't cover much else. He also holds up a pair of black shorts. "You'll wear these underneath, of course."

He rubs the top of his head. "I know it's a little much . . ."

"It's stunning," I say. And probably wildly uncomfortable, but I'd endure much in the name of fashion.

I smile at him. He's clearly a genius. "I'd be honored to wear it."

"It's going to fit snug against your chest, is that all right? We'll also probably have to sew you in. You ate today, right? And drank plenty of water?"

I hesitate, then say, "Yes." Which isn't quite the truth. I was too nervous to do much of either, but I'm *feeling* fine, fueled by nerves and adrenaline.

I undress behind a screen for privacy, and put on the corset, stepping out with the back untied. I breathe in as he tightens the strings of the corset, and then breathe out, feeling the pressure against my chest.

"Does it hurt?" the designer asks. "I can loosen it if it's uncomfortable."

I take several deep breaths. It's a little tight, which makes me a tad uneasy, but . . . "I'm fine," I reassure him.

He gestures me over to a floor-length mirror. "What do you think? We don't want to show too much cleavage or we'll get censored." He laughs, as if he's joking, but I have a feeling he isn't. "Your long hair will cover most of it."

I study my reflection in the mirror, turning around to admire the outfit from all sides. The structured corset is fitted perfectly to my body, clinging to my chest, narrowing at the waist, and flaring slightly at the hips. With Soobin's makeup and the costume, the effect is stunning. "I love it," I gush.

An assistant brings me a robe to wear over the costume, then escorts me from the tents to my first filming location, a tidepool that the set designers have accented with fake starfish and jewels. A fog machine billows a white vaporous trail over the pool, giving it a dreamy, mystical atmosphere.

After removing my robe, a different production assistant helps me step into the pool, and I find a spot to sit that isn't *too* uncomfortable. I hope I'm not disturbing some poor crustacean.

"In this scene we want to give off a mysterious, ethereal aura," the director says from behind the camera. "You're a beautiful mermaid, caught in a tidepool with a mission to deliver a message from the Sea King to his son, but alas, you cannot speak outside the water! What to do!" I'm caught up in the director's fervor, nodding along. "Perfect, hold that face exactly." He films me from different angles, moving the camera along a temporary track. "Now shiver, like you're cold. You long for warmer waters. If only there was a place you could go."

It's a lot like modeling, since I don't have any lines. I'm grateful to the scriptwriter who found a workaround so I wouldn't have to speak. Soon the director yells, "Cut!"

"That was perfect, Sori-ssi," he says. "You're a natural on camera."

I step out of the pool, eagerly reaching for the robe, this time for warmth.

On the way back to the tents, there's a crowd gathered outside Youngmin's cart. Sun is nowhere in sight, presumably having left to film his scenes with the lead actress.

I approach Hyemi, who's waiting by the cart, her cheeks flushed. She's still wearing her school uniform, her character's name printed on a small metal tag affixed to her blazer. "What's all the commotion?" I ask.

"Nathaniel was just here," she says, her eyes bright. "He was taking photos with some of the staff members. I took one with him too. Want to see?"

She holds up her phone. In the picture, Hyemi poses back-to-back with Nathaniel, her hand raised halfway to her face, caught mid-laughter. He must have said something to amuse her. Then my gaze travels to Nathaniel. He's laughing too, nose scrunched, dimples on full display. I'm arrested by the sight, feeling slightly out of breath, which isn't conducive to wearing a corset.

I'm just looking at him *in a photo*, and this is how I feel. How will I feel later tonight when we film our scene together? I need to make sure he doesn't suspect anything has changed; nothing *has*, at least not outwardly. I just need to hide my feelings from him a little longer. I've done it for the past two years, what's two more nights?

Twenty-four

The production crew has commandeered the only bathhouse in the village for our scene. Old tiles line the bathing area in the women's quarters where three pools sit snug among shower stalls and a tiny kiln sauna. While it's empty now, I imagine during the day it's filled with local women, gossiping about their neighbors while bathing.

My mother used to take me to our local bathhouse when I was younger, before she started to really get busy with Joah. We'd scrub each other's backs before soaking in the pools. She'd buy me sikhye, and I'd lick my lips between every sip of the sweet rice drink, a refreshing coolness after the heated rooms. Then we'd rest in the common area, our heads on block pillows, reading manhwa and giggling at the heroines' romantic adventures. A rush of warmth envelops me at the memory. Maybe once everything settles down at the company, we can go back there again, just the two of us.

I turn as the doors open, and Nathaniel enters with the rest of the crew. He's dressed in the pajama-like uniforms customary to bathhouses, a large shirt paired with drawstring shorts. Atop his head is a towel shaped to resemble a sheep's head. I'd laugh if I wasn't so nervous.

He immediately spots me, walking over. "Hey."

"You look comfortable," I say, trying to keep my voice casual.

He smiles crookedly. "I'm guessing your costume is a lot more elaborate than mine."

"Yes." I blush, feeling suddenly very naked beneath my robe.

He tilts his head to the side.

I step away from him, feigning like I need to get my makeup touched up. I scurry off toward Soobin and RALA, but not before I see the look of confusion on his face.

My stomach churns with guilt. He's done nothing wrong. *I'm* the one who can't control my feelings.

"Sori-yah, is something the matter?" Soobin says. "You look a little pale. Is the corset too tight? I can loosen it." But as she makes the suggestion, I can see her mouth thin in worry; loosening it might cause the whole costume to fall off, the thought of which makes me more panicked than I already am.

"I'm okay. I just have to make it through this one last scene."

The setup is that Nathaniel's character comes upon mine taking a dip in the steaming hot water after the bathhouse has closed for the night.

I watch as the crew positions the lights and cameras around the pool, my nerves growing stronger with every minute that passes. The scene at the tidepool hadn't felt this intimate, maybe because we were outdoors. In this enclosed setting, with all the lights centered on the pool, I'm more exposed.

The director leads me to the edge of the pool. "You're going to swim around a bit." He moves his arm in a circular motion. "And then surface near the edge." He taps his shower slipper by the pool's edge. "Nathaniel will be waiting for you. After he speaks his line, you'll relay to him the important message the Sea King has sent you to the human world to deliver."

I'm nodding along, but frown at this. "But I thought I couldn't speak."

He adjusts his sunglasses, which he continues to wear though it's now evening and we're inside. "And so, you must relay the message to him in the way of the mermaids. With a kiss."

I blink at the director, then blink again. "That's not in the script," I say.

"Yes," the director acknowledges. With a checkered hand-kerchief, he wipes sweat from his brow. "When the scriptwriter discovered the plot hole, she thought of this solution. But only if you're comfortable . . ."

My stomach flutters, and I turn to Nathaniel, who's walking toward me. I expect him to tease, but he's uncharacteristically shy, scratching at his neck beneath the collar of his shirt. "Do you . . . ? We don't have to . . ."

"I think it's okay," I say, a little breathless. "For Sun's show . . ."

"Okay," he says. "If at any time you don't want to . . ."

I nod. "Okay."

"Sori-ssi," the director nods to me, "whenever you're ready."

I realize he means for me to disrobe, *while everyone's watching.* I take a deep breath, channeling my inner mermaid, or at least actress. The costume is gorgeous, and its custom-made to my proportions—I'm *proud* to wear it. I untie the knot of my robe and let it fall from my shoulders.

There's an audible gasp from the crew that hadn't been present at the tidepool shoot. I throw back my shoulders, showing off the costume to its best advantage. Idols have worn more risqué outfits than this on stage; *I've* worn more risqué outfits on the catwalk. There's no reason to feel shy. I risk a glance at Nathaniel. His gaze, which had been lingering on my costume, raises to meet mine. My heart stutters at the heat in his eyes, and the already warm temperature in the room seems to raise a notch.

Before I go entirely up in flames, I turn from him and head to the pool, quickly submerging myself into the water. I can't even cool down because the water is over forty degrees celsius.

"Sori-ssi," the director says, positioned now behind the camera, "you remember what we discussed? Swim, swim, swim, and then emerge prettily by the edge of the pool. Like a fairy."

A fairy mermaid, got it. I can do this.

Taking a deep breath, I dip below the surface, silently thanking my mother for all those swimming lessons growing up. *Korea is a peninsula*, she'd said. *You must learn how to swim or you won't survive.* Now that I think about it, I wonder if she'd meant those words as a metaphor.

I move in what I hope is a graceful motion beneath the water, trying to keep my legs together to make it easier for the editor to add in a tail during post-production. Still submerged, I swim toward the edge, planting my feet at the bottom of the pool to orient my graceful emergence.

The water cascades off the top of my head, over my nose and cheeks. I don't gasp for air but take small breaths to give the illusion that I don't need air to breathe. I can feel the water catching on my lashes, and I have to resist the urge to raise my hand and wipe them away. Nathaniel comes into focus above me. He's kneeling by the pool, looking down at me.

He doesn't speak; instead, his gaze roves over my hair, my eyes, my lips. He has a line, though I can't recall what the exact words are, something about asking me why I'm in the pool. I can't deliver my message until he says his line. Did he forget it? We're going to miss the shot. My heart races. I have to do *something*. Gripping the edge of the pool, I lift myself out of the water and press my lips to his.

It's brief. I don't have enough upper body strength to hold myself above the water for longer than a peck. My lips part. He gasps softly. When I release him, his lips follow mine, as if seeking more, but I'm already falling back into the water.

I swallow a bit of it, making the next time I emerge a lot less graceful.

"That was perfect!" the director shouts, his voice echoing in the chamber. "Beautiful. Emotional! Such on-screen chemistry!"

I glance toward the corner to see the scriptwriter is wiping a tear from her eye.

I sigh with relief that we won't have to film it a second time, even if Nathaniel never spoke his line. It's very hot in the pool, and I'm feeling out of breath with having had to hold it for so long.

As I move toward the stairs, the room takes a sudden dive.

"Sori?" Nathaniel's voice is sharp.

"I can't—" I start, then realize I can't breathe. I start to panic. The room spins.

There's a loud splash, and then I feel arms lifting me from the water. Nathaniel. He's jumped into the pool. I feel him turn me around in the water, and then he's pulling at the back of my corset in rough, jerky motions.

The pressure on my chest releases, and I gasp in a lungful of air.

Letting go of me briefly, Nathaniel pulls his shirt over his head, throwing it over my exposed back and using his body to block mine from the room.

"Can you breathe now?" he asks, his voice gentle but strained.

"Yes."

"I'm going to carry you."

I nod, and he slides his arm beneath my legs. I hook my arms around his neck as he lifts me bodily from the water. I'm so embarrassed that I bury my face in his neck to avoid the stares of the crew, all of whom are expressing high levels of concern.

Everything is a blur from there. Nathaniel takes me to the on-site medic, a friendly woman who checks my vitals and gives me an IV for fluids. A few minutes later, Secretary Park rushes into the tent. "I texted your mother. She's on her way from Japan." There isn't enough room for the two of them and the medic, so Nathaniel moves out of the tent. I feel bereft, watching him go.

"She isn't coming back early because of this?" I ask Secretary Park, feeling anxious. I know her meeting in Japan was important. "Tell her that I'm all right. That she doesn't need to come."

I can see Secretary Park warring with herself, weighing what her boss needs to do for the company against what she needs to do for her daughter. "Are you sure?" she asks finally.

"Yes," I say, "I just need rest." I raise my arm that's attached to the IV. "This will do everything else."

"Okay. I'll tell her." She hesitates. "I'm glad you're all right." She pats my leg and then leaves.

I eventually fall asleep, waking up to find the medic gone and Nathaniel in the chair beside me. He's resting his head on the cot, his face turned away from mine and toward my outstretched arm that's hooked up to the IV. I wonder, briefly, if he's asleep, but when I move my hand, he stirs, though he doesn't turn to face me.

"Never wear something like that again," he says. His voice is slightly muffled by the blanket. I can't see his expression, but there's a catch in his voice, and I realize how scary it must have been for him to see me faint. My heart softens.

"There goes my short-lived stint as a mermaid," I tease.

He turns his head on the blanket, a crease between his brows. "I'm glad you can joke about it."

I raise my hand and brush the hair that's fallen over his eyes. "You look so serious. It's unlike you."

"I was really scared, Sori. You were so pale."

"You acted fast, for being so scared," I say, remembering how he jumped into the water without hesitation.

"Well, I didn't want to miss an opportunity to undress you."

"That's my Nathaniel," I say softly.

He doesn't say anything, and I feel my pulse race, which probably isn't good for my health.

"It was pretty while it lasted," I say, to ease the tension. "The costume, that is."

"It was beautiful," he says.

I open my hand, and he slides his over mine.

We fall asleep like that, holding hands. Sometime later, I wake to find him gone. Sun is stepping into the tent, letting the flap fall behind him. He walks over to the IV bag, checking it as if he knows what he's doing.

"Where's Nathaniel?" I ask.

"I sent him out. He needed to rest." He takes Nathaniel's chair, leaning backward slightly.

Neither of us speaks. Sun's expression is thoughtful. I wonder how much he knows. Sun is perceptive. He might not know that Nathaniel's been living with me, but he'll see that we've grown closer in the past two weeks.

"Are you going to say something to scare me away from him? I know what you said to Jenny." When Jaewoo and Jenny first started dating, Sun tried to frighten her off. Jenny thinks he was trying to "test" her and protect Jaewoo from a potential scandal, but I think he was just being a jerk.

"I *did* say something, didn't I?" He scratches his chin. "Damn, I'm as nosy as my grandfather." He chuckles to himself, as if *almost* causing Jenny and Jaewoo to break up amuses him.

"Even so," he says, watching me with his dark eyes, "I don't think anything could scare you, Min Sori."

"I'm going to talk to my mother when we get back to Seoul, about the possibility of dating him again. I want to. I want Nathaniel."

Sun lifts a single brow. "When you put it that way," he says slowly, "I don't think anyone could deny you. Even I'm blushing a little."

"Really?" I frown. "You look pale."

"I'm blushing *inside*."

He stands. "I came by because I wanted to make sure you were all right. And . . ."—reaching out a hand, he brushes a strand of hair from my face—"Jenny was a stranger to me. You're not. I'll always be on your side."

Oddly, I feel tears prick the corners of my eyes. Sun can be sarcastic and aloof, but he's always looked out for my best interests, like an older brother. The best kind. "Thanks, Oppa."

"I'm glad you're feeling better," he says. Then after a short pause, adds, "Though I should have known you and Nathaniel would bring drama to *my* drama set."

Twenty-five

I'm transferred to a small cozy clinic for the night—on recommendation by the medic—while the rest of the crew heads to Seoul. Since Secretary Park remains behind with me, Ji Seok offers to drive Hyemi back with Nathaniel and Sun. Secretary Park has to threaten me with calling my mother to get me to agree to stay.

"You're no help to Hyemi if you faint again," she insists.

She's right, of course. It's just that, tomorrow is ASAP's debut, and I want to make sure everything goes smoothly. I know there's a whole team to ensure that. But Hyemi is *my* responsibility, my mother entrusted me with her, and I want to see her journey through to the end.

Though it's really the beginning.

The beginning of her life as an idol. The beginning of *my* life, the one I chose for myself, where I can pursue whatever it is that I want. Though for now, I would like to work on ASAP's team awhile longer. There's so much still to do, from preparing for their promotion cycle to their full-length album. Director Ryu, the other day, spoke about album design and concepts.

Even if I can't spend the whole of today with Hyemi and the others, at least I'll make it to the showcase. Also, there's the surprise party afterward, which a few junior staff members and I planned. The ASAP girls aren't aware of it, and I'm looking forward to their reactions.

The next morning, the clinic's doctor, a sweet grandmother-type whose elderly patients visit more for gossip than ailments, teaches me Go—with her own board and set of distinct black and white playing stones—while we wait for my blood results to come back clear. After I'm discharged, it's another three-hour train ride to Seoul. I only have time to go home, shower, and change before I have to head to the arena.

The house is empty, with Ajumma having gone to her daughter's home, and Nathaniel having spent the night at Sun's—he couldn't exactly ask Ji Seok to drop him off at *my* house. On the car ride over to the arena, I send Nathaniel a text message. I'm having a surprise party for the ASAP members after the showcase. I give him the name and address of the restaurant. Do you think you can make it?

A few minutes later, my phone chirps with his response: I'll be there.

My heart races at the thought of seeing him.

Last night, when we fell asleep holding hands, something passed between us. I feel that if I don't say something soon, then *he* might.

If my mother comes to the party—Secretary Park let me know there's a possibility—then I can talk to her. I could tell Nathaniel my feelings as early as *tonight*.

What will he say? What will he *do*?

I take a deep breath, lowering my phone. If I keep on thinking about what might happen with Nathaniel, it's *all* I'll think about, so I push those thoughts to the back of my mind. Tonight is about Hyemi, ASAP, and the entire team at Joah.

I send the same text, inviting the rest of the XOXO members.

The venue for the showcase is at Sowon arena, which like the hotel with the same name, is owned by Sun's grandfather's company, TK Group. Sowon is normally used to host sporting events, but last night and this morning, it was transformed into a concert arena, outfitted with a stage and over two thousand five hundred seats. Tickets for the showcase were available through a random raffle system, all of which were claimed within an hour of its posting.

Hyemi's already dressed in her performance outfit when I find her, wearing a corset over a loose white dress, her long, light brown hair braided into a crown atop her head.

"Seonbae!" Hyemi shouts over the noise of the crowded dressing room. "You're here! Are you sure you're feeling okay, though? Nathaniel told me what happened."

"I'm fine. What about you? That corset isn't too tight, is it?" I pull at the top, and I see that it's made of a stretchy fabric instead of the more structured material of my mermaid costume.

She laughs at my concern, her eyes twinkling. "You're so funny, Seonbae." I'd expected her to be more nervous, but she's glowing.

"Are the members ready?" a voice calls from the doorway. "They need to be on stage in fifteen minutes."

"I have to go to the bathroom!" Jiyoo, dressed in a flouncy dress that hits her knees, shouts. "Do I have time to go to the bathroom?" She doesn't wait for an answer, racing off.

A makeup artist grabs Hyemi, pulling her toward the Broadway mirrors where one of the other members is finishing up with hair and makeup.

Another member practices choreography in the back of the room, while another stands in front of a pedestal fan, nervously chugging from her water bottle. When she sees Jiyoo sprint past, she stops drinking, her eyes going wide and dropping to her bottle in horror.

The camera crew that's filming ASAP's documentary captures every messy, excitement-inducing moment.

"Min Sori-ssi?" Director Ryu's assistant stands to the side. "We're having a bit of an issue. Director Ryu said you might be able to help. Could you come with me for a second?"

I check one last time on Hyemi—she's holding hands with one of the other members, talking to her excitedly—and follow Director Ryu's assistant to another room where a group of staff members surround a couch. Sitting on it, sobbing uncontrollably, is Sun Ye.

"What going on?" I say, alarmed.

Director Ryu gestures me over to the side. She doesn't appear worried, like the others. "I think she just needs someone to talk to. It's hard being the leader. Can I leave Sun Ye in your hands?"

I nod, though I don't know why she thinks *I'm* the one who should speak to Sun Ye.

"I think . . ." Director Ryu says, apparently able to read my mind, "you might understand her better than anyone else."

She turns toward the room. "Can everyone leave for a few minutes?"

As the room empties, I pick up a mug and fill it with hot water from the dispenser, then bring it over to Sun Ye.

"Sun Ye-yah," I say, sitting down beside her. "What's wrong? Are you feeling sick?"

"I'm sorry, Sori-yah." She sniffles. "I don't think I can do this."

I might have expected nerves from Hyemi or Jiyoo, the youngest members, but not Sun Ye. Not just because she's the oldest and has trained the longest, but because she's always so confident, at least outwardly so. But I should know better than most that people often say what they don't mean.

"Tell me," I say.

"It's too much responsibility. What if I fail the other members? I'm supposed to be their leader, but what if I'm terrible at it? And I'm so much older than everyone else. I already read an article that said I raised the average age of the group by a year."

The urge to find whoever posted that and yell at them over the internet is overwhelming.

"Have you been thinking these thoughts for a while?" I ask. "You should have told someone."

"I didn't want them to kick me off the team."

"They wouldn't have. Director Ryu and the others understand how tough it is, especially as the group's leader."

Sun Ye shakes her head, her thumb circling the rim of the mug.

I take a deep breath, thinking of what I would want to hear if I were in Sun Ye's shoes. Director Ryu asked me specifically to speak with her for a reason. *I think you might understand her better than anyone else.*

"We've been here the longest, you and I. This industry isn't easy, and it's always tougher on girls. Strangers judge us because we're too old, because we're too fat, because we're too smart, but that's why *this industry* needs you, so that people can look at you and see how beautiful and talented you are. How stubborn and insecure—"

"I thought you were complimenting me," Sun Ye sniffs.

"And realize that maybe you're not the most perfect idol in the world but that doesn't mean you're not perfect for the fan who will need you the most."

As a fan myself, that's how *I* feel. It's the feeling of when you connect to that one special person in a group and they become a comfort to you, someone you can admire from afar and cheer on. After today, Sun Ye will become that person for so many people, as will Hyemi and the other ASAP members.

"You're going to bring so much joy and comfort to thousands of people," I say. "Maybe even millions. That's what being an idol *is*."

"My makeup is all messed up," Sun Ye says, dabbing a tissue at her eyes.

"We'll get one of the makeup artists in here," I reassure her. "I saw at least five in the hall just now."

"Thanks, Sori-yah. You would have made a great idol, you know."

"Maybe. But I think I'm a little too selfish. I want to make myself happy first, and I want to give myself only to a few people, not everyone."

For a long time, I thought I was the opposite, that I wanted to bring joy to as many people as possible, because then they would love me in return. But I realized that's not me. I'm content being loved and appreciated by the few people who I love and appreciate. That's enough for me.

Sun Ye takes my hand, squeezing. "The people you give yourself to are lucky, Min Sori."

I call one of the makeup artists into the room and wait until Sun Ye is ready before following her out.

The other ASAP members have already headed to the stage, so I make my way to the back of the arena, where I'll be able to watch the stage with the rest of the audience. I *could* watch from one of the monitors backstage, but I want to experience the performance, as if I were one of the fans. Because I am.

On my way, I catch sight of Hyemi's father seated among other important-looking people in business suits, my mother among them. Like before, I notice the dark circles beneath her eyes, though she's managed to cover them well with concealer. Has Hyemi's father signed the contract? If he hasn't already, then tomorrow, for sure.

The MC walks onstage to welcome the audience. ASAP will perform two songs during the showcase, their title track and their B side, a mellow pop song called "Blue Heart."

The back part of the stage opens, revealing all six members standing together—as a group, they create a beautiful silhouette. Then the first notes of "Wake Up" begin to play and the audience erupts into cheers.

At first, I'm nervous, but it soon becomes clear that all their hard work paid off because their movements are clean, as if they've danced this choreography hundreds of times, because they have. They transform on stage, leaving behind all their insecurities and worries. Sun Ye gives no hint that she was crying only minutes before, her expression fearless. Timid, sweet Jiyoo is a monster with the choreography, attacking every move, and Hyemi . . .

Hyemi is a flirt! She *teases* the audience, her eye contact with the cameras unparalleled, her confidence mesmerizing.

Like the crowd, I'm entirely swept away with their performance.

Staring at the ASAP members, I search my heart for any lingering feelings I might have over my decision not to debut. I told Sun Ye I didn't want to be an idol, but is there a part of me that wishes I'd stuck to that path, that feels . . . regret?

The answer comes to me, clear and without doubt: I don't.

All I feel is happiness for the girls, and pride in myself, that I helped get Hyemi this far. And I know that even if I'm not *in* the group, I'll be a part of ASAP forever.

The happiness spreads outward, and it feels almost like a presence around me, echoed back to me by the energy of the crowd.

It rises within me like a wave, a feeling so powerful it makes *me* feel powerful, like I can have everything—a career that gives me purpose, friends that give me strength, and Nathaniel. I can have him, as well.

At the end of the performance, when the audience cheers, I think my voice might be the loudest.

Twenty-six

"Surprise!"

The girls burst into tears, walking into the restaurant beneath the loud sounds of poppers and party blowers, and enthusiastic clapping and cheers from the staff. Pink and gold streamers cascade around them, catching in their hair. They've changed out of their concert outfits into casual clothing, oversized sweatpants and hoodies. When they see that everyone in the room is wearing T-shirts emblazoned with "ASAP's Debut Showcase" and the date, they cry even harder.

I make eye contact with a junior staff member and together we hurry to the back of the room to light the candles on the custom cake—a beautiful, two-tiered cake with blue and pink piped flowers and "Congratulations" in white lettering along the top. As we bring it out, the crew sings "Happy Birthday."

As one, all six members blow out the candles. Youngmin's got a hold of a confetti cannon, and it explodes over the room to more cheers.

"Thank you all so much for supporting us," Sun Ye says, crying, but from happiness this time. "We couldn't have done it without you. I know it's been a tough few weeks . . . and years . . ." Her eyes travel to the girls who came from Dream Music. "The road will be difficult still, but because of this team, because of the other members who give me hope and inspire me to be a better leader, I look forward to the journey. Please continue to support us."

Together, the ASAP members bow deeply.

The party isn't scheduled for long, as ASAP has recordings booked for the weekend music shows, including EBC's Music Net, but it's important to celebrate as many moments as possible along the way.

"This was a good idea, Sori. I'm glad you suggested it." Director Ryu stands beside me, champagne flute in hand. "We would have done something at the company, but this is better. And we have entertainment."

The singing coach brought a karaoke machine with her, and Youngmin and a few of the boy trainees perform "Wake Up," having, of course, memorized the entire choreography by heart.

"Do you know when my mother is coming?" I ask Director Ryu.

"Oh, she didn't tell you? She couldn't make it. She's taking a few of the sponsors out to a restaurant."

My stomach drops. She's not . . . coming?

Director Ryu pats me on the shoulder. "I'm sure she would have liked to be here too."

She thinks I'm disappointed, and I am. But I'm also . . . frustrated. Tonight would have been the perfect opportunity to speak with her. The successful debut of ASAP is a triumph for both of us. There couldn't be a better time to approach her about Nathaniel and me. Now I'll have to wait even longer.

The door opens. My eyes fly to the door in time to see a junior staff member enter.

Jaewoo already texted after I sent the invitation to let me know he couldn't make it, since he's still in Busan with his family, but Sun and Nathaniel should be here any moment.

Ten minutes pass—Jiyoo screams, announcing to the room that ASAP is trending #1 on all the major sites—then another fifteen.

"Are you waiting for someone, Seonbae?"

Hyemi stands behind me. I thought I'd been discreet, but apparently not.

"No, I'm just . . ." Her head is tilted to the side, watching me curiously. I change the subject before she sees anything else in my expression. "I saw you earlier with Ruby," I say, naming the member I'd seen Hyemi holding hands with in the dressing room. "You seemed to be getting along."

"Ruby-eonni is from Hong Kong and speaks English. We like some of the same TV shows and video games. She's a big *We Bare Bears* fan."

"Really?" I need to speak with Ruby more. "Congratulations, Hyemi-yah. How do you feel?"

"Like I could do anything. Like this is only the beginning."

"It is! I'm so happy for you."

"Actually, Seonbae, I've been meaning to tell you—" she cuts off, her eyes straying behind me. I turn around to see Sun walking through the glass doors, his jacket casually flung over his shoulder.

"Hyemi, will you excuse me?" I say and hurry over to Sun. "You're late." I look past him for Nathaniel, but there's no sign of him.

"It's good to see you too," he drawls.

"Did you come alone?" Hyemi asks. I blink, surprised to find her beside me. She's also asked the question I was about to ask.

Sun studies her, his expression opaque. "Would that disappoint you?"

226

She goes white, then pink.

"Leave her alone," I say, my protective instincts kicking in.

Sun points to the cake. "Is that cake?"

"I'll get you some!" Hyemi scurries away. Sun moves to follow.

"Nathaniel didn't come with you?"

His eyes stray to me. "His mom called. He's out front."

I don't stay to watch Sun get his cake, rushing out the doors.

The night air is cool against my skin, and I wrap my arms around my body as I search the outer courtyard.

I picked this restaurant because of its secluded location. It's one of many buildings on a large, sprawling park with forests and creeks. Besides the restaurant, there's also a coffee shop and a museum dedicated to a renowned architect.

I peek my head through the gate where a pathway leads to the parking lot. I don't see any sign of Nathaniel. I don't think I could have missed him. To the right, another path—the one lit by stone lanterns—leads into a grove of trees.

It feels only natural to follow this path. The sky is cloudless. Moonlight pours through the thin canopy, silvering the trees. The path leads to a small stone bridge that spans over a tiny creek. I can see the museum through the trees, lit from within, shining like treasure in the darkness.

"Sori?"

I turn.

Nathaniel stands at the other end of the bridge. He pockets his phone—he must have just finished his call with his mother. He doesn't ask what I'm doing out here. Does he know that I came looking for him? Thoughts of my mother aside, something good happened tonight, and so I wanted to share this moment with the person who makes me the happiest.

I start walking toward him across the bridge, and then I'm running.

I launch myself into his arms. He takes a few steps back from the force, his arms going up to catch me. For a minute neither of us moves. I listen to his shallow breaths. His heart beats rapidly against my own.

His hand slides up my back, and I shiver in his arms. "Sorry we're late," he says. "Sun stopped to get gas. There were some fans . . ."

I shake my head. "Did you watch ASAP's performance?"

"I did, on the car ride over. They were incredible. You should be proud."

"It was all them. They were the ones that practiced relentlessly, put in the hours."

"You did too," he says, "or did you forget?" I lean back to see him smile, a glint of mischief in his moonlit eyes. "I saw you every night when you came back after practicing with Hyemi. You were not *not* sweaty."

I feign hitting him in the chest and he catches my arm. His long fingers circle around my wrist gently, his thumb brushes against my pulse.

This isn't the perfect order—I would have liked to have my mother's permission first—but I can't hold back any longer. It's like what Hyemi said, about feeling like she could do anything. I feel the same way. My happiness gives me wings, making me brave enough to go after what I want.

After everything I've done for Hyemi, for my mother, I can finally do what *I* want . . .

Like in the pool, I stand up on my toes and bring my mouth to his.

The kiss is sweet, if brief. When I release him, I look up into his eyes. They're half-lidded, gazing down at me.

"Do you mean it?" he asks softly. His fingers around my wrist tighten infinitesimally.

"I mean it," I say. "With my heart, with my body, with my soul."

His breath hitches, and then he's kissing me. He lets go of my wrist to drag his hand through my hair. I tremble at his touch, gripping his shoulders to keep from falling. His hand lowers, pressing me closer until I'm flush against him.

My lips open beneath his. When his tongue slides against my own, I feel as if I'm melting.

His kisses are long and soft; mine are just as ardent. I could kiss him forever, except that I made a promise. Tomorrow, after I talk to my mother, I won't have to hold back.

I give him one last lingering kiss, then step away.

He looks a little bereft, so I raise my hand to touch his cheek.

"I've wanted this for a long time," he says, covering my hand with his own.

"For two weeks?" I ask, breathless. I think of all the times I thought he was going to kiss me.

He shakes his head. "Longer."

My heart stutters. "Two years?"

He presses his forehead to mine. "I feel like I've wanted you for half my life."

I groan. How am I supposed to resist him when he says things like that?

He kisses me, harder than before. I give in momentarily, but then break away. "We have to go back."

"I was never there."

"*I* have to go back. And you have to greet everyone. Don't you want to congratulate Hyemi and the others?"

He sighs, dropping his head to my shoulder. "Can't we just text them?"

I laugh, grabbing his hand. "Come on." I tug him up the path, only letting go when we're in view of the restaurant.

No one notes our arrival together except for Sun, who raises his champagne flute as if to toast us.

Spotting me, Hyemi hurries over.

"Congratulations, Hyemi," Nathaniel says in English. He reaches out and ruffles the top of her head.

She flushes prettily, tugging at the hem of her hoodie.

"Hyemi-yah," I say, remembering that earlier, before Sun's arrival, she was in the middle of saying something. "What did you want to tell me?"

Her face turns an odd shade of scarlet. "Oh, I—" She glances at Nathaniel, then at me, panic on her face.

I frown. "What's wrong?"

"It—it's nothing."

"Are you sure?" I press. If she's having an issue, I want to help her.

"It's about what we talked about in the practice room," she blurts out. "Before we left for the drama shoot."

"What we . . . oh!" My eyes widen. We'd discussed Joah's policies on *dating*. My eyes dart to Nathaniel. Of course, she wouldn't want to talk about her crush on Jaewoo in front of him. I really put my foot in my mouth.

"We'll talk about it later," I whisper, and she nods.

I usher her over to where the ASAP members are singing karaoke with Youngmin and a few of the junior staff members.

They glom onto Hyemi, and she ends up singing a song with Youngmin, then Nathaniel. I sit at a table with Sun, who, having found the champagne too sweet, has moved on to black coffee. Every time Nathaniel catches my eye, I look away, aware of our surroundings.

The party winds down. As everyone leaves toward the parking lot, I linger behind the rest.

"Sun's expecting me to go back with him . . . ," Nathaniel says from behind me, his voice close to my ear. "I'll make an excuse."

I shake my head. "No, go with Sun. I need time to think."

There's a beat of silence. "Think?"

I realize how that must sound as if I'm second-guessing my actions tonight. I reach back, sliding my fingers through his. Sun Ye turns around to wave, and I wave back with my other hand. "About what I'm going to say to my mother tomorrow," I whisper.

Nathaniel draws in a breath. "You're going to talk to her? About us?" Now Hyemi's waving as she gets into the van with the other girls.

"Among other things."

Everyone's walked through the gate of the courtyard except for us. Nathaniel pulls me to the side, out of view. Pressing me back against the wall, he kisses me. I slide my hand through his silky hair and taste the champagne from his lips.

"I really *can* make an excuse," he says, when we part.

I laugh.

"Sori?" Secretary Park calls from the opposite side of the wall.

I lean forward and kiss Nathaniel on the cheek. "I'll see you tomorrow night."

An hour later, snuggled in bed with my stuffed animals, I text Nathaniel. I'm home. Dream of me.

His response is immediate. Always.

As I'm putting my phone on the bedstand, I receive another text.

It's from Hyemi. There was something I wanted to tell you earlier, but I didn't get a chance. Please keep this between us. I'm so embarrassed, but I can't hold it in any longer. I think I'm in love with Nathaniel.

Twenty-seven

The next morning, I read Hyemi's text again. I haven't responded, though it's likely she's seen that I've read it. I want to tell her the truth, about my own feelings for Nathaniel, but I want to share that with her in person, so I can explain everything in full. I feel awful knowing she'll be devastated when I tell her.

Below Hyemi's text is one from Nathaniel. I can't wait to see you tonight.

It's Saturday, which means Ajumma won't be at the house until tomorrow morning, a day earlier than usual, as her daughter is hosting her in-laws.

Nathaniel and I will be alone tonight. My heart thrums at the thought.

On my phone, I bring up my mother's number, skipping Secretary Park altogether. My thumbs hover over the keyboard before I quickly type a message. Are you busy today? Can I come by your office? I click Send before I can second-guess myself.

A stuffed whale slips from my bed as I push back the blankets. My phone chirps and I reach for it eagerly. But the message isn't from my mother.

Kim Sun Ye: Come to Joah immediately. There's an emergency.

Twenty minutes later, I burst into the practice room. Hyemi's hunched in the middle of the floor. Sun Ye sits beside her, rubbing her back in a circular motion.

I crouch on Hyemi's other side. "What's going on?" The other members aren't present, only Sun Ye. Secretary Park stands with her back against the mirror, furiously typing on her phone.

"I'm going to quit the group," Hyemi bawls. "It's not fair to the other girls."

My eyes widen. I look to Sun Ye to elaborate.

Sun Ye hands me her phone. "Someone left an anonymous post on a popular forum," she says, "about the agreement Hyemi's father had with Joah."

Dread curls in my stomach as I read the article.

> A Joah insider confirmed yesterday evening that ASAP member Woo Hyemi's last-minute addition to the girl group was contingent upon a sizable investment by her father, shipping magnate Woo Gongchul.

I wince. This is bad. The article goes on to slam the company's business ethics, throwing around words like *nepotism* and *bribery*, and ends with a call to boycott ASAP.

"Th-they said," Hyemi begins in a choked voice, barely able to speak through her tears, "I'm o-only in the group because of my f-father's money."

"That's not true," I say. Or at least, maybe that was the case in the beginning, but she's proven herself time and again; she *belongs* in ASAP. Anyone who watched the showcase would think this without a doubt.

"Once they see how hardworking and talented you are, none of this will matter," I say.

Hyemi starts to sob even louder.

234

I look to Sun Ye once more.

"The first episode of the debut documentary went up," she explains. "Hyemi's receiving a lot of negativity in the comments."

"I'm calling my father," Hyemi says. "I'll tell him I want to quit."

"You can't do that," I say sharply. Her father has yet to sign the contract.

My tone of voice startles her, and she looks up. The hurt and confusion in her eyes is like a dagger through the chest. For a brief moment, I sounded just like my father—coldhearted, manipulative.

I take a deep breath. "Was it such a quick decision to join the group?"

"Of course not. I've wanted this for as long as I can remember."

"Then give as much consideration to your decision to leave as you did to join. There's no need to rush. You've already debuted. Get some rest, and we'll talk tomorrow."

As I stand, I notice Sun Ye watching me. There's a question in the slight frown on her face. *Did you know about this?* I avoid her gaze.

On the way out of the room, I pass Secretary Park. She's moved on from aggressively texting to whispering loudly over the phone. "I don't care what you have to do, just get them to take the post *down*."

Without really thinking about where I'm going, I ride the elevator up to my mother's office.

It's empty, as is the attached bedroom, though there's evidence of my mother's return, her suitcase half unpacked on a luggage rack by her closet.

Collapsing on the high-backed chair behind her desk, I close

235

my eyes. This situation must be salvageable. It *has* to be. Though I can't see a way forward. Joah can deny the claims made in the post, but since so much of the article *is* true, it'll be difficult to refute it if more evidence arises.

And I feel uneasy about the thought of outwardly lying. I don't think anything is owed to tabloids and gossip magazines, but a company and a group should be honest with their fans. Otherwise, how can they build trust with one another? I also don't know what a lie like that would do to Hyemi's mental health. I remember Director Ryu's emphasis on the group's emotional health, along with their physical health. The company needs to protect Hyemi and ASAP as a group. I feel another rush of shame that it wasn't my first thought when Hyemi said she wanted to quit the group. I'd thought of her father's money. *Would* quitting be better for her?

My gaze catches on my mother's topmost drawer, pulled slightly open. When I move to shut it, the drawer catches on something crammed inside. Shimmying it open, I pull out a photograph.

I stare down at it, uncomprehending.

It's a photograph of me from my middle school graduation. I'm wearing my uniform, looking directly at the camera with a slight frown on my face.

The edges of the photograph are worn, an indication that my mother has picked it up quite a few times over the years. I feel an ache in my chest, as if I've caught my mother with a secret.

I gently place the photograph in the drawer. As I'm putting it back, I notice an envelope inside. I pick it up, slipping the documents onto the desk.

It takes me a few pages to understand what it is. A contract, outlining the acquisition of Joah by KS Entertainment. It's unsigned but dated for next week. *This* is my mother's solution if Hyemi's father doesn't invest. She's going to *sell* Joah.

The elevator pings. I quickly shove the contract back into the desk and close it just as my mother walks out of the elevator.

"Sori?" She steps from the foyer, stopping in the middle of the room. "What are you doing here?"

"Sun Ye told me to come. Because of Hyemi."

She rubs her eyes tiredly. "Where is Hyemi now?"

"She's with Sun Ye. They're going back to the dorm."

My mother collapses onto the couch, leaning back with a heavy sigh.

Moving from behind the desk, I grab a bottle of cold water from a small refrigerator filled with them and walk over to her. Uncapping it, I hand it to her. She takes the bottle, drinking half of it before placing it on the table. "How is it you always know what I need most?" she says softly.

I want to ask her about the contract in the desk, but instead I say, "You should come home. You'll rest better in your own bed, and Ajumma can cook for you."

"Soon, Sori-yah. I will, soon." I don't believe her, but I want to.

"How are you feeling?" she says.

I blink at her, confused.

"You collapsed on the set of that drama. I was so worried. I should have been there with you. Instead, I was in Japan, trying to secure more investors, except that wound up fruitless in the end.

I'm terrible at everything, aren't I? A terrible businesswoman, a terrible mother."

"You're not!" I say vehemently. "You're trying so hard. There's no one I look up to more than you. No one I believe in more."

Her life has been filled with challenges, from losing her parents at a young age—her wealthy, distant aunt had hired Ajumma to raise her—to becoming an idol, only to have that dream cut short when she became pregnant with me. To think she at least would have a loving family, only for her in-laws to reject her and her husband to abandon her, maybe not legally but in all the ways that matter. She then changed course and put all her time and energy into making this company what it is today, employing so many people, fulfilling the dreams of its artists. I've felt frustrated with her, resentful, even, but I've never stopped believing in her.

"My sweet girl." She brings her hand to my face, pressing her fingers to my cheek for a brief, halting moment. "You give me strength. You always have."

She drops her hand and closes her eyes. "As long as there's not another fire, I think I can handle this week."

Another fire. Another scandal.

"Can you turn the lights off when you leave? I think I'll just rest right here for a little bit."

She's asleep within minutes. I grab a blanket and pillow from the spare room. I lift her head gently and place the pillow beneath, then cover her with the blanket.

I don't go directly home but take the bus around the city. To me, Seoul is always beautiful, but there's something about the capital at dusk, with the sun banked on the horizon, turning the sky a hazy pinkish-purple, the bright lights of the signboards blurring like watercolors, that makes me think it might be the most beautiful city in the world.

Two years ago, I'd done this very thing, after I had the conversation with my mother that led to my breakup with Nathaniel. As I stare out the window toward the city, I think back to that conversation.

We were in my mother's office, just the two of us, the XOXO members having gone back to their dorm.

"I contacted the news outlet. They've agreed to blur out your photo. You'll be an 'unnamed trainee,'" my mother announced.

I'd frowned. "But then Nathaniel will take the brunt of the criticism."

"Sori, that's a good thing. A dating scandal with an unnamed trainee is better than a dating scandal with the CEO's daughter. All the hate would be piled onto you, the more vulnerable target, and I wouldn't even be able to protect Nathaniel because my name would be tarnished as well, as I allowed this to happen. It should have never happened. I wasn't careful. This is my fault."

BULLETIN, the infamous tabloid newspaper, had hinted that they were going to post a dating scandal involving "the lead singer of a popular boyband." Already, online speculation had concluded that the singer was Nathaniel, and XOXO's videos were being flooded with comments asking for Joah to expel Nathaniel from the group.

"You two will have to break up."

I shook my head, unwilling to accept what she was telling me. "But what if Nathaniel and I were to face this together?" Nathaniel had said as much when I'd come to him in tears. That we'd weather the storm, together.

My mother's eyes turned pitying. "You're young and in love, so you're not thinking clearly. I was the same, when . . ." She didn't have to finish that sentence, *when I married your father.* "Don't you remember what happened when you were in middle school?"

A shiver of fear swept through me, remembering the bullying at school, the comments shouted at my mother, for driving my father into having an affair—for being cold, for being unlovable.

"It would be the same, but ten times worse. People like Nathaniel can throw caution to the wind in grand, romantic gestures, but that's because they've never known what it's like to be alone. They can bear criticism and censure from the public because they have their families who will support them. You and I don't have that luxury. We've always had to stand on our own."

She'd been right. Nathaniel only knew a small part of the bullying I endured in middle school, the name-calling and isolation. Because I kept it from him. I wanted to protect him from the awfulness of my life—that shining boy, who always had a smile on his face, who always had a smile for me.

I thought of that time in New York with his family, how different our lives were. He would have them to go back to, without fail, that warm home filled with laughter.

"All we have is each other," my mother said. "It's always been just the two of us. I can't bear to see you hurt. I will protect you as best I can, but . . ."

She's my mother, but she's also the CEO of Joah. She has the company to think about, the hundreds of employees whose livelihoods depend upon her. I was racked with guilt. By causing a scandal, I'd jeopardized not only Nathaniel's career, but her company, everything she'd worked so hard for.

"I know you care for Nathaniel, but sometimes life is about making painful decisions in the present to avoid greater pain later. It's better to cut things off before your feelings grow any stronger."

I nodded. Her words sunk into my skin, wrapping around my heart.

"I'm sorry I'm asking this of you. Promise me you'll break it off?"

Nathaniel wanted to risk everything for love, but that wasn't reasonable for someone like me, with so much to lose. What if the worst happened and we broke up? He'd have his family, his burgeoning career. XOXO was already so popular. While I'd have hurt my mother's company, my own chances at a career, and in the end, I'd have been as I was before he came hurtling into my life— bringing with him laughter, friendship, and love—completely and devastatingly alone.

"I promise."

Twenty-eight

It's ten p.m. by the time I step off the bus in my neighborhood, having ridden it all the way to the last stop on the line, only to get back on and ride it to the other end. As I round the corner, I look up toward the convenience store.

Nathaniel's at our usual table, reading a book beneath the fluorescent lights. He's slouched in the plastic chair, a paperback propped on his chest as one of his long fingers skims the top. His brow furrows adorably as he turns a page.

How long has he been here? I usually get home around dinnertime, four hours ago. Was he waiting for me this whole time?

I walk up the stone steps, shifting my shoulder bag higher. Catching sight of me, Nathaniel sits up, putting the book face down on the table.

I have several missed calls and unanswered texts from him, but he doesn't ask me about them. Instead, he stands and heads into the convenience store, the bell jingling above the door as he enters. I sit in the seat across from him, glancing at the title of the book. It's the novelization of Sun's drama, *The Sea Prince*. When he returns a few minutes later, he's carrying a plastic bag.

"You haven't eaten yet, have you?" he asks.

I shake my head.

From his bag, he draws out samgak gimbap, unwrapping the plastic from the triangle, careful to keep the seaweed over the rice intact, then hands it to me so that I can hold it from the wrapped side. I nibble at the seaweed and rice.

Reaching once more into the bag, Nathaniel takes out a plastic water bottle, uncapping it and placing it in front of me.

I'm relieved when he takes out a triangle of his own, as that means he isn't planning on watching me eat.

I drink half the water bottle and Nathaniel readily takes out another, placing it beside the first.

"I was at Joah earlier," he says. I look up. "I was worried when you didn't text back," he explains. "Sun and I went together."

"How was it?" I ask, softly.

"Things aren't as bad as they seem. Only one of the broadcasting stations canceled an appearance, the one the ASAP members were scheduled for today. The rest have kept them in their lineups."

"But that doesn't mean they might not cancel tomorrow, if the story picks up further."

"The post was taken down."

I feel a rush of relief. Whoever Secretary Park was speaking to on the phone must have gotten through to the original poster. The damage has already been done—during ASAP's debut week, no less—but at least it won't pick up more momentum than it already has.

"All of it's true, you know," I say, trying to keep my voice neutral, without emotion. "What that anonymous poster said about the deal Hyemi's father had with Joah."

When my mother told me about the deal, I hadn't thought twice about it. All I cared was that my mother's company was in

243

trouble, that *my mother* was in trouble, and this was a way to fix the problem. I was also distracted by my own worries about the future of my career. Though, when I had the chance to tell Nathaniel, I'd kept him in the dark.

I'd felt ashamed, like he'd think badly of my mother, of *me*. Business practices and shady deals are normal in the spaces that people like my father and mother occupy. But Nathaniel has never been exposed to that part of this world, one that feels almost second nature to me.

"Did Hyemi's father hand over any money to Joah?" Nathaniel asks. I study his face, but his expression is uncharacteristically unreadable.

I shake my head. "Not yet."

"Then it's not true," he says simply.

"But it *will* be. That is, it has to be . . ."

"Why does Joah need Woo Hyemi's father's money?" he asks.

"I . . . It's not my place to say."

"If Joah needs money, then I can—"

"No," I say, my heart dropping. I don't want Nathaniel *anywhere* near this. "It's my mother's responsibility." And mine, as her daughter.

"It's normal for idols to buy shares in their company," Nathaniel says with a frown. "Sun already owns a few."

"He bought them as an investment at the time. You'd be buying them for . . ."

"For you."

"No." I shake my head vehemently. "I don't . . . I don't want any money to be involved."

It's not just that I don't want him to get involved in any of the questionable choices made by the company, but I also don't want money to enter into our relationship.

I think of my father, who solves everything with money, who bought my mother a house to placate her after his first public affair, who controls her life by owning the majority shares of her company. I want to protect Nathaniel from that. I want to protect *us* from that.

"You're right, I'm sorry. I'm just frustrated. I want to help." He sweeps a hand through his dark hair, leaning back in the plastic chair. It raises briefly on two legs before hitting the ground with a thump.

"Are you angry?" I ask.

He blinks at me, his brow furrowing. "About what?"

"That I didn't tell you about Hyemi. That I was helping her to debut so that her father would invest."

He sits up in the chair, looking at me. "But that's not true."

"It *is* true, even if he hasn't invested." Even if he probably never will after today's disaster.

Nathaniel shakes his head. "You were helping Hyemi because you were the only person who could get her ready to debut in such a short time. You trained with her, guided her through variety shows and drama sets. You didn't do all that because you wanted to get Hyemi's father to pay Joah, you did all that because you wanted to, because you enjoyed it, because you were good at it."

My pulse races at his words, my skin flushing. This conversation is getting out of hand. I can't *feel* this way.

"This scandal is bad," I whisper. "Joah can't have another one."

"I don't see why they would, unless Sun has a secret baby he hasn't told us about." He laughs.

"Nathaniel." That's all I say, just his name.

He goes still. "No."

His eyes meet mine. "Last night, you said you meant it."

"I did. But that was before today."

"Why? Because of the scandal?"

I could tell him about the contract, about KS acquiring Joah, but what would that accomplish? He's producing a song with an artist from KS. If he finds out that KS might be acquiring Joah, he might back out of this project he's been so excited about.

"Maybe we *should* announce a relationship," Nathaniel says. "It'll draw the heat off Hyemi."

"Nathaniel, be serious."

"That was a legitimate suggestion." He's joking, but there's a catch in his voice. I've hurt him. I'm *hurting* him.

But I have to. For his sake, and mine. For the sake of the company.

"Joah can't afford to have another scandal right now. Someone will find out about us. We weren't exactly careful at the party last night." We weren't cautious at all, kissing with only a wall separating us from the others. I don't know if I can hide my feelings from him, and I don't know if he can hide his feelings from me.

"The reasons why we broke up haven't changed," I say. "If anything, they've gotten more heightened. Hyemi hasn't even been an idol for one day and she's already receiving hundreds of hate comments. ASAP has had an appearance canceled, maybe more. It would be so much worse if the tabloids found out about us. Your career . . ."

"Don't make this about my career. I want you. I know what that means."

My stomach flutters.

"The situation with Hyemi is different," Nathaniel says, his voice low. "She's a rookie. She doesn't have fans who will support her, not yet. XOXO fans are different. They'll have my back."

I shake my head. "You can't know that for certain. What if you're wrong? What about Sun, Jaewoo, and Youngmin? Don't you care about how your actions affect them?"

This seems to get through to him because he lowers his head.

"I can't accept that you're pushing me away for my sake," he says.

"Then will you accept that I'm thinking of myself?"

"No."

"Nathaniel!"

"Do you honestly care what a stranger on the internet says about you?"

"Maybe not one stranger, but five hundred strangers? Yes!"

I take a deep breath. "But it's more than that. I have a responsibility to the company." Seeing my mother reminded me of the promise I made to her. "I have more to lose . . ."

"I have to lose *you*," Nathaniel says heatedly. "For me, that's enough." He gets to his feet, grabbing his book off the table. "Even if it doesn't matter to you." He's angry, speaking out of his emotions.

He gathers our trash and heads into the convenience store.

When he comes out, he doesn't wait for me, walking ahead of me up the hill toward the house.

I don't know if it's the stress from the day or the fight we just had, but tears start to fall from my eyes.

I stop by the vine-covered wall outside my front gate. "Nathaniel."

He must hear the tears in my voice because he turns. There's a brief pause, then he's walking back toward me. He gathers me in his arms.

"I'm sorry," he says, his breath warm against the top of my head. "I didn't mean to make you cry."

"I'm scared."

"We can be careful. We can keep it a secret."

I shake my head. "We can't."

Nathaniel's arms tighten around me, then he releases me, stepping back. "I should go. I feel like if I stay, I'll want to hold you, I'll want to . . ." He takes an unsteady breath. "I'm going to get my stuff."

I nod, sniffling. "I'll wait out here."

A few minutes later, the front gate opens and Nathaniel comes out again. At the sight of his duffle bag, I have to fight back a fresh wave of tears.

"What about the paparazzi?" I ask.

"They haven't been around, at least not for the past week."

Which means he could have left as early as last week but stayed. Because he'd wanted to.

"I'm having a party for the launch of my song on Wednesday. It's at the Sowon Hotel. Will you come?"

"Yes."

I want to be there for him.

He looks like he means to say more but stops himself.

He doesn't say goodbye. Neither do I.

I watch him walk all the way down the hill to the main road. Once he rounds the corner, out of sight, I collapse onto the ground and cry.

Twenty-nine

I wake up the next morning with red, puffy eyes, beneath a pile of stuffed animals. The low whir of a vacuum travels from below, the sound of which must have woken me. Unearthing my phone from beneath Medium Totoro, I text Ajumma. I'm not feeling well. I'm going to stay in my room today.

She doesn't respond, but a half hour later there's a knock on my door.

Ajumma enters carrying a tray with a covered stone bowl and a glass of water. Placing the tray on the side table, she presses the back of her hand to my forehead.

"You don't have a fever," she says, clicking her tongue.

"I just have a headache . . ." *From crying myself to sleep.*

"Mm-hmm," she says. She hands me two white pills, which I plop into my mouth, then the glass of water; I gulp, swallowing them down.

She doesn't ask about my swollen eyes or where Nathaniel is, though she must have noticed his empty bedroom. I'd gone into the room last night, crying anew when I saw his neatly made bed; the room was spotless, as if he'd never been there at all.

I only have myself to blame.

"I'll come check up on you later," Ajumma says, smoothing my hair back from my face.

When she leaves, I lie back on the bed, dizzy with thoughts, which only serves to intensify my headache. Had I acted too rashly the night before? Nathaniel and I had kept the fact that he was staying at my house a secret for two weeks, we *could* hide a secret relationship, at least until Hyemi's scandal has quieted down.

No, I'm thinking with my heart, not my head.

The risk is too high, the consequences of getting caught too great. I need to be the reasonable one, even if that means making the hard decisions and breaking both of our hearts.

Nathaniel will be fine. He has his bandmates, his family.

He doesn't need me, not like my mother needs me.

When I decided to help Hyemi, it was partly to prove to my mother that I could be trusted to make my own choices with my career, but it was also because I wanted to *help* her, to ease some of her burdens.

She would be horrified to know all the things I've done that would prove to her the opposite, starting with inviting Nathaniel to stay with me.

I couldn't do the two things she asked of me: staying away from Nathaniel and preparing Hyemi for debut. Director Ryu said that the secret to an idol's success isn't just practice and talent, but also the support of the people around them, that gives an idol their strength, that helps them to endure difficult times.

I've failed Hyemi on so many levels. Maybe I couldn't have prevented that anonymous poster from leaking that story, but I could have prepared Hyemi for the consequences, if it should happen. I could have told her that her father made a deal with Joah instead of hiding it from her. But I was afraid she might quit if she knew the truth, taking her father's money with her.

I'm flooded with guilt that I quickly suppress.

Mentally, I form a hardness around my heart. Maybe this is who I am. It's who my parents are, after all, and I'm their daughter.

I pull myself out of bed to brush my teeth, because one can wallow but also have good oral hygiene. Turning my phone on silent, I grab my laptop and climb back under the covers. Opening up Netflix, I click on the first episode of the newest Hong Sisters drama, because I'd rather watch fictional characters deal with their innumerable, and sometimes fantastical, problems than deal with my own.

I'm on episode six, the computer completely turned on its side, and me along with it, when an invitation for a video call pops up in the right-hand corner.

Your roommate, the caller's ID says, *Go Jooyoung*. Jenny.

I sit up. The laptop starts to fall off my four-poster, and I make a grab for it, my fingers inadvertently pressing the keypad.

Jenny's face appears, illuminated by a ring light.

"Sori?" She's in her dorm room. Behind her is a bookcase and her cello on its stand. "Are you sleeping?" Her gaze travels to the corner, as if checking the time. It's one o'clock.

"Oh, Sori. That bad, huh?" Does she somehow know about Nathaniel? "I heard about the trouble with Joah."

"How did you know?" I ask. Then I realize Jaewoo must have told her. I shift the computer so that she's looking at me and not my ceiling.

"Never mind that," she says. "I was worried about you."

"I'm fine," I say. "Well, I'm not fine, but hearing your voice is helping."

"I was going to call you soon anyway. I wanted to tell you my news. I'm going to Japan! That is, I got the place in the quartet."

I scream, and she laughs.

"I was going to come to Seoul first for a week," she says. "Can I stay with you?"

"Of course. Though don't you want to stay with your halmeoni?"

"I'll stay with her on the weekends, but she likes to go to the clinic on the weekdays to flirt with the grandfathers there."

I laugh. Her halmeoni is sweet and loving, the complete opposite of mine.

We chat for the next three hours. At one point I have to get off my bed to plug my computer into the charger at my desk. Drawing back the shades, sunlight spills into the room.

She seems to sense that I don't want to talk about the *reasons* for why I'm lying in bed in the middle of the afternoon, and so we talk about everything else but that.

Ajumma's porridge went cold, but I eat it while Jenny heats up water in an electric kettle for a bowl of instant noodles.

"What were you doing before I called?" she asks.

"I was catching up on the new Hong Sisters drama."

"It's so *good*. What episode are you on? Did you get to the kiss scene yet?"

"Not yet! Does it happen in episode six?" I'd had fifteen minutes left of the episode before she called.

"How am I supposed to remember that? But yes, at the one-hour-and-twenty-minute mark."

As we're saying our goodbyes, she catches my eye. "I'm Team Sori; you know that, right?"

"Yes, and I'm the president of your fan club. Go to sleep." It's three in the morning in New York.

I wave to her as she hangs up.

Feeling rejuvenated after talking to Jenny, I finish the last fifteen minutes of the episode, replaying the kiss scene twice.

I take a shower, forming a plan in my mind.

Actually, the idea stemmed from what Nathaniel said the night before, about buying shares of Joah. I don't have the money to buy shares, but maybe I don't have to . . .

I open a direct line to my father, skipping Secretary Lee entirely. I've been skipping both my parents' secretaries lately.

Do you have time to meet tomorrow? I text.

His response is immediate, and I wonder if he's surprised to see a text from me. Yes. Come to your halmeoni's house tomorrow morning for breakfast.

Ajumma prepares a simple meal for dinner because I'm still "sick."

"It's a bit quieter tonight," she hedges, clearly waiting for me to explain Nathaniel's absence.

"Things are just back to normal again," I say. "It's better this way."

If Ajumma thinks differently, she doesn't share her thoughts, leaving me alone to eat in silence.

Later, Ajumma and I sit down to watch Sun's drama, which in the excitement of the last few days, I'd forgotten was airing *tonight*. A lot of the episode was filmed in the previous weeks, with only Hyemi, Nathaniel, and my scenes filmed and edited so last minute.

Hyemi's character is adorable. She's a high school student who has a crush on a boy in her class, but he's oblivious.

I laugh when she kicks the magical conch shell in frustration only to stub her toe, jumping around on one foot.

"She's good!" Ajumma says.

She's reminiscent of a young Jung So Min. She delivers each of her lines with charisma. In fact, I'm fairly certain the scriptwriter added extra lines after realizing Hyemi had talent.

The episode continues with an aerial shot of a rocky beach. Fog rolls over the tidepools as a sonorous voice narrates the scene. *The Sea King's messenger has arrived from the glittering depths of the court to deliver a message to the Sea Prince.* A tail appears on screen, then the camera slowly pans upward.

Ajumma gasps. "Sori-yah. You're *beautiful*." She takes out her phone and starts recording the screen.

I'm impressed with what the editors managed to do in only a short few days. My tail is a stunning blend of violet and aquamarine, matched perfectly to my corseted top. My damp hair hangs over my bare shoulders, strung with jewels and pearls. The narrator's low baritone intones. *But mermaids cannot speak above the water. How will she deliver the Sea King's message?*

If I remember correctly from the script, my next—and final—scene isn't until the end of the episode, which is a relief, because I can actually enjoy the story. It continues with Sun and the heroine going on a date. This is the episode where they truly start to acknowledge their feelings for each other, but because of the conch shell, which will restore the Sea Prince's memories, they're torn apart.

I'm so caught up in the story that another forty minutes seem to fly by—the episode is an hour, since it's on EBC, not tvN—and suddenly the setting cuts to the bathhouse.

I grab a pillow off the couch and bring it to my chest. Nathaniel walks onto the set in his shower slippers and sheep's head towel.

He has lines as well, and though his delivery is a bit stilted, unlike Sun and Hyemi, his natural humor lends itself to his character. He's upset because he sees a light on in the bathhouse after hours and think it's one of the old women sneaking in.

His eyes catch on something in the water, a glittering tail. Kneeling on the ground, he moves toward the edge to peer over the lip of the pool. The camera angles to catch my slow emergence, the water cascading off my jeweled hair. I remember how uncomfortable I'd felt trying not to blink, and I'm glad that I hadn't, because the effect is quite lovely. A second camera shows a close-up of Nathaniel's expression. I know what *I* was thinking—I'd been freaking out that he hadn't delivered his line yet—but he appears arrested, his eyes roving over my face. I expect the director to have cut the scene, but he kept the long pause. Nathaniel and I stare at each other, as if struck by one another.

Then the moment comes. Lifting myself out of the water, I bring my lips to his.

Then I fall back into the water and the scene ends.

"Omona!" Ajumma shouts.

There's ten more minutes left in the episode but my phone floods with messages.

MIN SORI, Angela texts. At the same time, Gi Taek messages,

I'm scandalized. Then, in a separate text, That outfit was out of this world.

Jenny texts a hundred !!!s.

I stare at my phone, hoping for the chirp signaling another message, this one from Nathaniel. But it doesn't come. Maybe he didn't watch the episode?

"Sori-yah," Ajumma says, pointing at the TV, "you're missing the rest."

The episode ends with Hyemi's character giving the conch to Sun's character in the marketplace. He regains his memories, including the fact that it was *his* storm, brought about by a petty tantrum, which destroyed the heroine's family's business, leading to all their misfortunes.

After the episode ends, I read the comments on EBC's homepage.

I think the screenwriter is a MinLee fan.

Their chemistry is so convincing!

Isn't this too far for a cameo?

I can admit that Woo Hyemi knows how to act.

Min Sori is blessed.

They look like they're in love.

As I'm readying for bed, my phone pings with a new message, forwarded from Secretary Park.

To the management of talent, Min Sori,

As the CEO of EBC, I'm reaching out to invite Min Sori to cohost our annual EBC Awards, scheduled for next weekend.

In the past few weeks, Min Sori, with her charm and beauty, has struck a resonant chord with our audience. Her on-screen chemistry with Nathaniel Lee, of the popular idol group XOXO, inspired us to reach out to invite him as her cohost for this year's awards. I look forward to Min Sori's positive response to this invitation.

Yours with admiration,
Kim Seo-Yeon, CEO of EBC

Thirty

The next morning, I type out a message to Nathaniel and press Send, hopping into the shower before I can second-guess myself. I kept the message brief. Are you going to say yes? When I get out of the shower, I have a missed call. My heartbeat picks up, only to deflate when I see that it's from Secretary Park.

She would have texted if it was urgent, so I finish up getting ready for the day, blow-drying and styling my hair, as well as going through my skincare routine—toner, essence, ampoule, serum, sheet mask, eye cream, moisturizer, and sunscreen.

I call Secretary Park while sitting down for breakfast. She picks up after the first ring.

"Perfect timing. I was just about to call you again. The producer of *The Woori and Woogi Show* invited you back for a follow-up episode, scheduled for later today. Lee Byeol and Tsukumori Rina have already agreed to return as guests."

"I can't," I say, and immediately feel guilty because there's a possibility that if I don't participate, they'll cancel the episode, as they won't have all three original guests. "I wanted to go and support Hyemi," I explain. ASAP's schedule was canceled yesterday, but they have a performance at a different music show tonight.

Secretary Park takes such a long time to reply that I check my phone to see if the call dropped. "Hyemi and the other members agreed that she wouldn't promote with the group for now."

"What?" I say, loud enough that Ajumma looks up from where she's snapping the tails off bean sprouts across the table. She's leaving tonight to go on a spa retreat with her friends down south. She'll be gone for the whole week.

Secretary Park clears her throat. "Hyemi felt like she was burdening the girls, and also that she wasn't in the right mindset to perform. The other members supported her and said they would wait until she was ready to resume promotions, but Hyemi insisted. She said it would make her feel worse to know the others couldn't perform because of her."

Oh, Hyemi. "Where is she now?" I push back my chair. I should go to her, make sure she's all right, that she's not crying and making herself sick with heartbreak.

I pause.

Except that I've already made plans to see my father this morning, and I *need* to speak with him as soon as possible.

"She's with her father. I think you should do the radio show," Secretary Park says. "If they ask about Hyemi, or the episode from last night, you can say something in support of her."

I nod. "That's a good idea."

I hang up with Secretary Park and call Hyemi, but after a few rings it switches to an automated voice message.

I text her instead. Are you busy tonight? A new café opened near Seoul Forest. Want to check it out?

It takes me two hours to travel by bus to my grandmother's house in Suwon to the south of Seoul, which gives me time to mull over how neither Nathaniel nor Hyemi have responded to my texts.

Hyemi's lack of response worries me. She's never taken this long to reply back to one of my messages before. She's with her father, so she should be all right. Is she telling him that she wants to quit the group?

Opening my message history with Nathaniel is more painful. Before my text this morning, there are a dozen messages from him Saturday night, asking where I am, worrying about if I'm okay. And then before that . . .

I can't wait to see you tonight.

He *also* has never taken this long to respond to a text, at least when he has his phone with him. He hasn't read my message, but he might have seen it pop up as a notification and swiped it away, so that it only *appears* as if he hasn't read it.

I'm motion sick by the time I get off the bus and have to walk another twenty minutes uphill in my strappy heels to reach the front gate of my grandmother's house.

I press the intercom and smile sweatily at my grandmother's housekeeper who buzzes me through.

The house is a single story but spread out over two thousand square meters of space, with floor-to-ceiling windows that face Gwanggyosan, the mountain north of Suwon. Its lofty peaks appear misty against the skyline. As I head up the manicured walkway, I spot movement through the clear glass windows—Mrs. Shin, the housekeeper, on her way to inform my father and grandmother of my arrival.

She's left the front door open. I unstrap my heels in the foyer, wincing at the red lines indented into my ankles, and toe on the house slippers Mrs. Shin has left out for me.

My father and grandmother are waiting in the dining room,

which is the largest room of the mansion, with the highest ceilings. The whole room echoes with the soft sliding sounds of my slippers.

I bow upon entering. When I raise my head, I'm surprised to see they have another guest.

"Eomma?"

"Sori?" She's as shocked to see me. "What are you doing here?"

"She came to visit her father and grandmother. Is that not allowed?" Halmeoni's sharp voice rings across the room.

"My apologies, Eomeoni," my mother says, quietly.

I sit gingerly beside my mother, facing my father and grandmother.

Brunch is hansik served in beautiful ceramic dishware—dozens of small dishes arranged neatly on the table by Mrs. Shin and her assistant.

The food is exquisite, prepared as it is by my grandmother's cook. I would enjoy the meal more if it weren't for the awkward atmosphere making it difficult to swallow.

"Apologies for bringing this up again," my mother says, and I realize I must have interrupted her with my arrival. "I would only borrow the money for a short period of time. I would return it as early as next month."

I keep my expression neutral. She's here for money?

"Haven't you taken enough from my son?" Halmeoni says, her voice echoing off the walls. "You have no shame. It's because you didn't have parents to raise you. It doesn't matter that your aunt is a person of consequence. She never adopted you. Orphans never learn humility."

"Eomeoni," my father chides affectionately. "Let's not squabble among family."

"Family?" she scoffs.

"Yes, *my* family," my father says, and his eyes land briefly on me, before narrowing on my mother. "Sori-eomma, I understand what you're asking. I'll of course lend you the money."

"You'll have to sign a contract." Halmeoni sniffs. "And there will be interest. He can't just give it to you."

"Yes, Eomeoni," my mother says, lowering her eyes. "Sori-abeoji," she says, turning to my father. "Can I speak with you in private?"

"Why? So you can make threats?" Halmeoni accuses.

My father ignores my grandmother, pushing back his chair and rising from the table. Together, my parents head toward my father's office at the other end of the house.

A few minutes later, I excuse myself from the table, saying I need to use the restroom.

My mother's voice trails from my father's office, the door cracked open a sliver. "Sori-appa, Kyung-mo-yah . . . I don't ask you for many things."

"And yet you do ask. It's, honestly, shameful. If you were better educated, had a better upbringing, you would know this."

If my mother takes offense to these insults, her calm voice doesn't show it. "If you're selling your shares to KS, then the money I'm borrowing to save Joah won't matter."

"I haven't decided yet. The decisions I make aren't just for me. I have more people to consider than only myself. My role in our government is not a hobby. Please understand that if I do sell the shares, it's nothing personal against you."

I quietly return to the dining table. I'm sitting there when my mother passes through a few minutes later. She bows to Halmeoni. "I'm leaving, Eomeoni. Please stay healthy."

"Ungrateful child." Halmeoni clicks her tongue.

I follow my mother outside, where she's stopped on the stone pathway.

"Eomma?"

She turns back to look at me, and my heart drops at the sight of tears in her eyes. She quickly wipes them away. "The wind," she says weakly. "It's strong here."

"You could have told me you wanted to visit your grandmother," she says. "I would have sent a car. I can wait for you now . . ."

I can't tell her the real reason I came here today. "No, I'm fine."

I know she's stayed in this marriage because of the shares, but I wonder if it's worth it. How can she endure such cruelty from them?

"Family can be difficult, can't they?" she says, a soft sigh in her voice. "But it's good to have family. It's hard to be alone in this world."

After my mother leaves, I look for my father, finding him still in his office, smoking a cigarette by the open window.

"About your shares of Joah," I begin. "I want them. As my inheritance."

His expression doesn't change except for an infinitesimal lifting of his brow.

"I'll do whatever it takes." To save Joah. To save my mother.

"CEO Cha's nephew," he says, blowing out a long stream of smoke. "He's still asking about you."

264

I close my heart to Nathaniel. He can't help me now.

"I'll meet with him," I say. My father won't sell his shares to KS, not if he's giving them to me.

"I'll have Secretary Lee send over his information."

My father walks me outside the gate, where Secretary Lee waits to drive me back to Seoul. "I'd say you're like your mother, but you're much smarter, Sori," my father says. "You know how to make the right deals. No . . ." I look up to find him studying me, a calculating look in his eye. "You're much more like me."

In the back seat of the car, I text Hyemi again. Are you okay? Please answer. I'm worried.

Nathaniel still hasn't responded, but that's not surprising. My phone pings with a message from Secretary Lee, containing details about CEO Cha's nephew. I plug in Cha Donghyun's number. Donghyun-ssi, I write, this is Min Sori. My father gave me your number. I hope this isn't too forward, but I'm interested in meeting you. I feel numb, my heart like ice.

Three minutes later, I receive a response. I didn't think you'd reach out. I'm so happy, Sori-ssi. Are you free Wednesday?

Wednesday is the launch of Nathaniel's song.

I text back, I'm free.

"We're back with our guests, Tsukumori Rina, Lee Byeol, and the trendy model turned variety show queen, Min Sori, who also made an appearance on last night's episode of *The Sea Prince*!"

Byeol sniffs. Sun's drama has overtaken *Springtime Blossom* as the show with the highest number of viewers in their shared timeslot.

The recording proceeds very much like the previous episode, with the three of us answering a question from a caller. This time, it's a boy asking advice on how he should confess to his older sister's best friend, who's a grade above him. Rina and Byeol squeal at the forbidden love—an older girl, his sister's best friend!

I'd also be caught up in the romance except that the numbness from before persists. It's like I'm seeing and hearing everything from underwater.

"And now for the game portion of our episode," Woori exclaims excitedly. "Like our previous episode, each contestant will call the most famous person in their phone!"

"It's no question who you should call, Sori-ssi," Woogi says, skipping the other guests entirely.

It takes me a full minute to realize what he's saying. He means *Nathaniel*.

It never occurred to me that they might have decided to have a follow-up episode for this reason alone, to take advantage of Nathaniel's and my newfound popularity as a variety show couple.

"Won't her boyfriend be jealous?" Lee Byeol quips, referring to my "Boyfriend" from the previous episode.

They hook up my phone, which luckily blocks the actual number, otherwise they might recognize it.

Am I really about to *fake* a fake relationship with Nathaniel?

The phone rings and rings and rings.

Then there's an audible click and an automated voice message plays, the same that had played earlier when I'd called Hyemi.

I'm too weary to feel embarrassed. I'm also slightly relieved.

266

Nathaniel and I haven't spoken since our fight, and I don't know if I want the first time to be on a public radio show.

"I can call someone!" Byeol say brightly. She calls the same costar from before, but now they're clearly on more friendly terms, as they speak casually, in banmal.

The producer ducks his head into the recording studio, waving his hands to get Woori's attention. "Min Sori is receiving a call from Nathaniel Lee," he hisses.

"Oh! Get him on the line!"

Byeol's costar is summarily shoved off the call.

Why is Nathaniel calling back when he hadn't responded to my messages?

"Nathaniel-ssi?" Woogi says, "This is Woogi from *The Woori and Woogi Show*. I'm here with one of our guests, Min Sori. Do you have time to play a short game with her?"

There's a loud metallic sound, then someone's voice in the background—a girl's voice. My heart staggers. He's with someone. *A girl.*

"Sorry," he says. He's slightly out of breath. "What did you say?"

"This is Woogi from *The Woori and Woogi Show*. I'm with Min Sori. The challenge was to call someone—"

"Where are you, Nathaniel-ssi?" Woori interrupts.

"I'm at a batting cage."

"It sounds like you're with someone."

"Just some friends."

"Don't say that, Nathaniel-ssi," Woori croons. "You'll hurt Sori-ssi's feelings."

"Oh no, please," I say, waving my hands in the air. I'm relieved that Nathaniel can't see my face, which is most definitely red.

"You can come, Sori," Nathaniel says. His voice has gotten clearer, as if he's moved away from where he was before. "I'll wait for you."

Rina squeals. Byeol's eyes dart to me, a questioning look in her eyes.

My cheeks grow hot. I know he's just play-acting for the show. On the TV monitor, I can see the total of live listeners practically double in number.

"The game is simple," Woogi explains. "We're going to ask Sori whether she likes or dislikes something. She'll hold up an *X* for disliking or an *O* for liking, which those watching the video feed will be able to see." I have small paddles painted with the letters in front of me. "You have to match her two out of three times to win ₩1000000 to a charity of her choice. Do you understand?"

"I understand," Nathaniel says.

"Okay. Sori-ssi, hold up whether you like or dislike . . ."

"Grapefruit," Woori says.

I immediately hold up a red *X*.

"Dislike," Nathaniel says, after a brief pause. "Sori loves grapes, but she hates grapefruit."

"You know her so well! How long have you known Nathaniel, Sori-ssi?"

"For almost six years," I say softly.

"That's a long time. You two must be close."

"Nathaniel helped me with a lot of troubles when I was in middle school. Because of that, he will always be a good friend to me."

I wish I could see Nathaniel's expression. He's silent on the other end of the line.

"Okay, next question. Sori-ssi, hold up whether you like or dislike . . ."

"Snakes."

Byeol and Rina shiver.

"Like," Nathaniel says, at the same time I hold up the *O* sign. "Sori likes all animals."

"This is revealing a lot about your relationship, Sori-ssi," Woogi says. "Are you sure you're not more than friends?" He laughs, clearly meaning for his words to be a jest.

"Last question. You already won the donation of ₩1000000, so this bonus round is for an extra ₩500000 toward a charity of Nathaniel's choice. Sori-ssi, hold up whether you like or dislike . . ."

"Nathaniel Lee of XOXO," Woogi finishes.

"You should clarify, Oppa," Woori scolds. "She just admitted that they've been friends for six years. Of course she likes him."

Woogi clears his throat. "Let me rephrase, do you have feelings that are more than friendship for Nathaniel Lee of XOXO?"

Yes, I want to answer.

Before I can, Nathaniel says, "I'll donate ₩500000 of my own."

"You don't want her to answer?"

"I know the answer."

The guests, and the hosts, swoon.

"Thank you so much for playing with us, Nathaniel-ssi! Do you have anything you want to say to Sori-ssi before you go?"

"Nathaniel!" It's that voice again. "Who are you talking to?" the girl says in English. "It's your turn at bat!"

"I have to go," Nathaniel says. "Thanks for having me." The phone line goes dead.

"Oppa, is it just me, or do you have a feeling of déjà vu?" Woori asks.

"I feel it too, Woori. Nathaniel-ssi sounds similar to your ex-boyfriend, doesn't he, Sori-ssi? Maybe it's that they have similar personalities?"

I'm barely listening to what they're saying, a keening in my ears.

I recognized that voice. Hyemi.

Thirty-one

After the show, I jump into a taxi. Looking up the batting cages nearest to Hyemi's apartment, I give the address to the driver and sit back in the seat. I'm only going because I'm worried about Hyemi. She told me that she has feelings for Nathaniel. If she confesses to him, his rejection, however gentle, will devastate her. He must have invited her out to make her feel better, though I can't figure out *how* they ended up there together.

It's not just a simple crush she confessed to having either. I can see her text from three nights ago even when I close my eyes. *I think I'm in love with Nathaniel.*

I text Gi Taek and Angela on the way, for moral support.

So you're going there so that you can talk to Hyemi? Gi Taek writes.

He's still typing when Angela adds, It has nothing to do with the fact that Hyemi is with Nathaniel, and you want to make sure there's nothing going on between them?

Yes, I type quickly. The first.

Okay, whatever you say! ㅋㅋㅋ.

How do you even know where he is? This from Gi Taek.

I type out the long explanation of how I was on the radio show and Nathaniel said he was at the batting cages.

Won't his fans do the same thing?

I stare at Gi Taek's message. I hadn't thought of that. I think it'll be okay. I'm only going to check the one. It's not near Joah but Hyemi's apartment.

Text us when you meet up with him, Gi Taek messages. It's late.

Fighting!

No, Angela, I type out, I'm just going there to check on Hyemi.

ㅋㅋㅋ! Okay!

I pay the driver and exit the taxi onto a quiet street. It's more secluded than I imagined, tucked in a network of alleys behind one of the larger boulevards. A single streetlight illuminates a green single-story building with a flickering signboard that reads HOME RUN HITS!

I press open the door, peering inside before stepping through. The building is divided into a small entrance area in the front, with cages in the back, separated by a chain-link fence. There's a photobooth against the wall and a few old arcade games. The attendant must have stepped out for a moment because the room is empty.

I hear the loud crack of a baseball hitting a metal bat. Slowly, I approach the fence. All the cages are empty except for the last one where two people stand. I recognize Hyemi's laugh, brighter and clearer than it had been over the radio. I can't see Nathaniel's face; his back is to me. Hyemi wears a helmet that's too large for her, and she's laughing while fiddling with the straps. She's having a difficult time of it, so Nathaniel reaches up, his longer fingers adjusting the straps for her. Afterward, he raises a fist and knocks it gently against the top of her helmet. She grins, swatting at him.

I feel odd, light-headed. They'd both been ignoring my texts all day. Is this why? Because they were together? Then there's movement as another person comes into view.

272

Jaewoo. *They're not alone.* He must have been seated before, which is why I hadn't seen him. He takes the bat that Hyemi holds out to him.

Facing out from the cage, he raises the bat. A pitching machine releases a ball and he swings the bat, connecting with the ball. It soars skyward before colliding with a high net and dropping to the ground.

Hyemi shouts in English, "Home run!"

I realize, as Jaewoo continues his turn with the bat, that they're speaking *entirely* in English. I can only hear snatches of their conversation, echoing back to where I linger by the fence. Though it's only Jaewoo and Hyemi's voices. I strain my ears, but I can't pick out Nathaniel's among them.

Then it's Nathaniel's turn. As he takes the bat from Jaewoo, I catch sight of his face for the first time.

There are dark shadows beneath his eyes, as if he hasn't slept well the past few nights. He looks tired. And . . . unhappy.

He looks sad. My chest aches and I suddenly want to cry.

He swings the bat with both hands before adjusting his grip on the handle, bringing it level with his shoulders. He turns to face the machine. It shoots out a ball, so fast I almost miss it.

He swings, hard. Harder than Jaewoo had. The ball connects with the bat and goes flying.

Hyemi jumps to her feet. "Home run!"

The machine releases another ball in quick succession—he must have adjusted the speed. Jaewoo had more of a lull between pitches.

Nathaniel swings again, even harder this time; the ball ricochets to the left, hitting a pole. Foul ball. He continues, not letting up. With every swing, the ball soars, catching at the back of the net.

"Hey," I hear Jaewoo shout. "Slow down."

He doesn't. He keeps swinging harder, faster.

By the time he's finished with his turn, my heart is racing.

"Let's take a break," I hear Jaewoo say, and then Hyemi is rounding the corner. *She's coming this way.* I quickly turn toward the photobooth and duck inside, catching a glimpse of her as she walks past my hiding spot toward the bathrooms. I can't believe I just *hid* from her. What have I been reduced to? Pushing back the drapes, I step cautiously out of the booth.

Making my way back to the fence, I move farther along it, getting as close as possible to the last cage without stepping into view.

"I'm not sure this is helping," I hear Jaewoo say. He and Nathaniel are both sitting on the bench, with Nathaniel leaning his head back against the chain-link.

What's not helping? Hadn't they come to cheer up Hyemi? From the way she skipped past the photo booth, I'd consider their mission accomplished.

Nathaniel doesn't respond, and I press closer.

"Do you feel any better?" Jaewoo asks softly.

"No," Nathaniel says, and his voice doesn't sound like it did over the radio—casual, unaffected. It sounds broken. "It still hurts like hell."

It's as if my body moves of its own volition, moving toward the gate that separates us.

I finally admit to myself that I didn't come here for Hyemi; I came because I wanted to be with Nathaniel, and because I was jealous.

I close my hand around the latch of the gate.

In my pocket, my phone vibrates with a message. Gi Taek and Angela, wondering if I found Nathaniel, if I'm safe. I want to ignore their message, but I also don't want them to call the cops.

I take out my phone. It's a text from Cha Donghyun. What about lunch on Wednesday? I can pick you up.

The numbness from before freezes me in place, stealing away my will, my hope, my breath.

I've already made my decision. If I walk through these doors, if I go to Nathaniel now, I'll be making a promise I can't keep.

I release my hand from the gate. Before I can change my mind, I turn and rush out the doors . . .

And into a crowd.

For a moment, I just stand there, disoriented.

Then a girl points at me, so close that I can see the heart-shaped rhinestone on her fingernail. "Isn't that Min Sori?"

Suddenly faces are turning toward me, phones being lifted. I cover my face with my hands, the shutter and click of cameras going off all around me.

"Sori-eonni, look at me!"

"Min Sori, I'm a fan."

"Give her space!" a girl shouts. The crowd surges forward and I trip and fall; my phone skitters, disappearing into the rush of feet.

275

I see a gap in the crowd, and on instinct, I stand up and run. The students hang back, but some of the older people, men carrying large DSLR cameras, follow.

Tabloid reporters. *Paparazzi.*

They chase me down the street. I take a left, realizing too late that I'm heading *away* from the main boulevard.

The streets are darker here. I can hardly see my feet hitting the pavement.

The only advantage I have is that I'm smaller, quicker. Catching sight of a narrow alley, I dart inside, only to cry out when I realize it's a dead end. Backtracking, I spot a tiny space between garbage bins and lower myself to the ground. I listen to the pounding of feet as the paparazzi rush past my hiding place.

I pull my knees to my chest. I don't have my phone, so I can't call anyone. Gi Taek warned me that this could happen. I hadn't taken him seriously. Or at least, I hadn't wanted to. All I could think about was reaching Nathaniel. I shift on the ground, then wince, noticing a trickle of blood sweeping down my leg. I must have scraped my knee when I fell.

I should leave this alley. I'm trapped here with nowhere to run. If one of the paparazzi should circle back . . .

There's a noise outside the alley. Footsteps from the direction the men had run earlier. Someone's coming. I stand, looking for a way out, a door, a ladder, but it's all brick. I feel panic overtake me, my heart palpitating.

"Sori!"

Nathaniel.

He skids into the alley, as if he'd been sprinting. His eyes are bright, his breath ragged.

Crying out, I rush toward him. His arms circle around me, holding me close. "God, I'm so glad I found you. Are you hurt?"

I shake my head, unable to speak.

"Why are you here? Weren't you just on the radio show?"

I'm here because I was jealous, and I wanted to be with you.

But I can't tell him that.

"Everything's fine," he breathes, "as long as you're okay."

I realize I'm clinging to him. I let go and step back. He frowns slightly.

"How did you find me?" I ask.

"A few fans saw you come down this way." He pauses. "They directed the tabloid reporters in a different direction."

"I'm so irresponsible," I groan. "There's going to be a huge scandal because of me."

"Maybe," he says.

I glare at him. "What are you doing with Woo Hyemi?"

"Hyemi?" he says. My heart pangs at his casual use of her name. "I was at Joah. She was there with her father, picking up some of her stuff. She looked upset, so I invited her out with Jaewoo and me."

It's close to what I thought might have happened.

"We should head back," he says. "Come on. Jaewoo should be waiting for us over this way." He holds out his hand, and I take it. Slowly, we make our way toward the main boulevard, emerging onto a well-lit street. Jaewoo and Hyemi wait outside his car that's parked by the curb.

"Eonni!" Hyemi says, spotting me. Nathaniel lets go of my hand as she rushes over.

"I have your phone," she says. "I found it on the ground." She holds it out to me.

"Thank you, Hyemi-yah," I say. The screen has a crack, but otherwise it still works.

"That was so scary!"

"What happened?" I ask.

"We noticed something going on outside," Jaewoo says, walking over. "When we came out, a girl explained what had happened, that you were here, and that the tabloid reporters had chased you. A few of the girl's friends had followed you to make sure you were safe. Nathaniel . . ."

He trails off, his gaze focusing on Nathaniel beside me. He doesn't have to explain this next part. Nathaniel had gone after me.

"We should get out of here," Nathaniel says. "Those tabloid reporters might still be lurking around."

Jaewoo nods, heading to the driver's side of the car.

Nathaniel passes by me to open the front passenger door.

"Eonni, you should sit in the front this time," Hyemi says, having apparently ridden in the front on the way here. Before I can answer, she rounds the car to the other side.

Nathaniel hasn't moved from holding open the door. As I slip into the car, I have a brief memory of a similar moment in New York City, when Nathaniel had called over a taxi for me.

As I adjust my skirt, Nathaniel sucks in a breath. "Sori, you're bleeding."

I'd forgotten about the scrape from my fall. It hardly hurts anymore.

Nathaniel pushes back the door the widest it will go, then leans forward to open the glove compartment, removing the first-aid kit.

Crouching on the ground, he gently shifts my skirt away from my knee. A blush creeps up my neck. Self-consciously, I glance at Jaewoo, but he's looking down at his phone. As for Hyemi, I can't see her unless I turn around in my seat.

Then I'm brought back to myself, wincing as Nathaniel presses an alcohol swab to the wound. His eyes flicker up to meet mine.

For a brief moment, he holds my gaze, letting me see how unhappy he is. Then he drops his eyes, applying Bacitracin to the wound and pressing a Band-Aid securely over it.

"If you need help," he says softly, rising to his feet, "you should say something."

He closes my door before opening the back, sliding into his seat.

Jaewoo guides the car out of the street and onto the main boulevard.

As we're crossing the bridge over the Han River, Hyemi points to a glowing wheel in the distance. "Look, they finished building the Ferris wheel."

We drop off Hyemi first, and then it's Nathaniel, Jaewoo, and me.

As Jaewoo turns onto my street, Nathaniel breaks the silence. "You're still going to the launch of my song, right? It's this Wednesday."

The text message from Cha Donghyun burns a hole in my

pocket. I haven't responded to him yet. "I can't. Something came up. I'm sorry."

Nathaniel doesn't respond. Like before, I can't look at him unless I turn in my seat, so I continue facing forward.

"Do you . . ." I take a breath. "Do you not want to host the awards show?" I wouldn't blame him. I've done nothing but hurt and disappoint him.

"Didn't Secretary Park tell you? I said yes."

"You did?" This time I do turn around, but he's gazing out the window, his chin in his hand.

I sit back. "She didn't."

Jaewoo finally pulls up outside my gate. Nathaniel gets out of the back seat to sit in the front. He doesn't look at me when he passes me. "Night, Sori," Jaewoo says from within the car before Nathaniel shuts his door. They don't drive off immediately, and I realize they're waiting for me to go through the gate.

Turning, I key in the code and hurry inside. I wait until I hear the sound of Jaewoo's car moving back down the hill before slowly trudging up the steps to my dark, empty house alone.

Thirty-two

Cha Donghyun picks me up from my house late in the morning on Wednesday and drives us to a lunch restaurant in the trendy area of Yeonnam, the neighborhood beside Hongik University. The restaurant doesn't take reservations, but Donghyun knows the owner, so we pass the long line of people waiting outside and are promptly seated on an upper-floor terrace overlooking a quiet street.

I settle my purse onto my lap, so that I can feel my phone vibrate should I get any calls or texts. I expect, at any moment, to get one from Secretary Park, informing me that an article was posted about Nathaniel and me being spotted together outside the batting cages. Luckily, there shouldn't be any *actual* pictures of Nathaniel and me together, just the fact that we were at the same location. That's not a scandal, as Jaewoo and Hyemi were also there. Joah's PR team can spin it easily as four friends from the same company going out together. At least I hope so.

"Sori-ssi, I can't tell you how happy I am that you contacted me." Across from me, Cha Donghyun smiles shyly. He's dressed simply in a button-down shirt and slacks, though I know the sum total of his outfit is probably a couple million won. He looks like an actor, with his pale skin and clear complexion. His most charming features are his ears, which stick out rather adorably.

"I apologize for my uncle." He blushes, his white complexion making it difficult for him to hide his feelings. "I told him I was a fan of yours and he decided to do a bit of matchmaking. That must have been awkward for you."

I shake my head. "I think it's sweet. I'm mostly surprised that I *have* a fan." If my father hadn't made our getting together transactional, I might have felt completely at ease with Cha Donghyun.

"Really? But you're so charming and beautiful. Sorry."

"Thank you. You're also very handsome. And sweet." He's making this so easy for me. I could ask him to call up his uncle now and demand he rip up the contract between KS and Joah.

"I should probably tell you some things about myself, to see if you want, that is . . ." He clears his throat. He means that I should know his qualifications before considering him a candidate for a boyfriend. I forgot that this is how some people of my social class date, sharing pedigrees to see if we'd make a good match. "I'm a first-year student at SNU."

Only a first-year? According to the message from Secretary Lee, he's twenty-one.

"I already served my compulsory military service," he explains, referring to the service all male Korean citizens must fulfill. Nathaniel wouldn't have to, as he's American, but at some point, Sun, Jaewoo, and Youngmin will all enlist.

"I'm studying photography," he continues.

My eyes widen. I'd expected him to be studying business or something more . . . practical, at least in the eyes of men like his uncle and my father.

"I've always loved taking photos." His gaze connects with mine. "I have an eye for beauty."

I raise a single brow. That's something Nathaniel would say. He'd hold my gaze, a smirk on his lips, teasing me, flirting with me.

Donghyun must realize how his words come across because he blushes to the tips of his ears. "That is, I like bringing out the beauty in others. I mean, it helps when the subject is already beautiful. Wow, I'm not recovering from this well, am I?"

I laugh, finding him charming. With him, it would be effortless. He's clearly the right choice. My father would get what he wants. My mother would have what she needs. The company will be safe. And so will Nathaniel.

The server approaches us and takes our orders. Unlike my father or Baek Haneul, Donghyun asks me what I want to eat and orders both dishes when I can't decide between them.

I can't help wondering what Nathaniel would do. We've obviously never gone on a date to a restaurant, just the two of us. He'd probably have ordered his own separate dish and then eaten off my plate.

"I saw your cameo on the latest episode of *The Sea Prince*. You were lovely. I'll admit I was a bit shocked by the ending." He rubs the back of his neck with his hand. "You must be close to—"

"I'm not," I say quickly. If Cha Donghyun believes there's something between Nathaniel and me, he might tell his uncle. Who could tell my father. I shudder at the thought. "That is, we were close, but . . ."

We can't be anymore.

"I see," he says. I eye him. *How much does he see?* "He *is* Nathaniel Lee of XOXO. He probably can't date like normal kids his age. Not to imply that you were dating." Donghyun smiles, guileless.

I shake my head. I wonder if he's realized what he's said. *Kids his age*, as if Nathaniel was so much younger than him.

The servers set our food on the table, two large platters of pasta dishes infused with Korean spices. Donghyun portions out a sizable amount of each pasta onto a separate plate for me, reaching over the table to set it in front of me. In the corner of my eye, I see two of the female servers whispering to each other and giggling over his manners.

"I've met him," Donghyun says. "Nathaniel Lee."

He's currently in the middle of serving himself, otherwise he might have seen me choke on a caper. "You have?"

"He's collaborating with one of KS's artists, Naseol. We were introduced when he was at the company."

I don't know how I'm supposed to react to this information, so I say nothing. How would a normal girl who *was* interested in him react to his mentioning another boy she was *not* in love with say? My head hurts.

"He seems rather carefree, doesn't he? That was my impression of him."

I frown. Only someone who doesn't know Nathaniel would think this about him. His friends know better. His *fans* know better.

He cares deeply about his family and his bandmates. He's passionate about music and performance. He has dozens of interests and pursues them all fearlessly. Beyond being funny and kind, he's also hardworking, reliable, and the most genuine person I know.

He's never lied to me. He's so different than how I've been raised, to hide my emotions, to never cause discomfort for my parents. He's always honest with his feelings, even when it hurts. He believes everything I say, which is sometimes terrifying, because I know I can hurt him so easily; his trust is a gift.

I can feel myself getting worked up, which will only confuse Donghyun. I take a deep breath. Like before, I say nothing, shifting the pasta around on my plate.

"This date is going so well," Donghyun says, as he maneuvers his car from out of the Hongik University area. "I don't want it to end."

I smile at him. It *is* going well, much better than I'd imagined, but I just want to go home and sleep. I check my phone, but Secretary Park hasn't texted about any scandals. Maybe there won't *be* one. Two days have already passed since that night. It's possible that the tabloid reporters hadn't gotten a good photo; in all of them, I must appear scared and harassed. Not exactly titillating news.

"Sori-ssi, I'm sorry to ask, but . . ." I look up from my phone at Donghyun, driving with both hands on the wheel. "A friend of mine is having an event nearby here. I hadn't thought I could make it and was honestly feeling a bit guilty. Do you mind if we stop over for a few minutes? The event is almost over. I just want to offer my congratulations."

"Of course," I say. "Though I'm not dressed appropriately for a party."

"You look gorgeous. That is . . ." He coughs. "It's not a black-tie event."

We're moving a little fast if I'm already meeting his friends.

But I'll eventually meet them. If I'm to date him, I'd have to commit to the role. If you date someone while being in love with someone else, who are you betraying? Nathaniel and I never made any promises to each other. Donghyun, then . . .

As I glance at his eager face, my heart fills with self-loathing.

He pulls up in front of a sleek, modern building.

I glance uneasily at the red carpet leading from the porte cochere to the front doors. A few photographers line the walkway, though, as Donghyun pointed out, we're late, and most of the guests are already inside.

"I thought you said it wasn't a black-tie event."

"It's not. It's just that photographers tend to follow idols, you know? But I wanted to support Naseol-nuna."

Naseol. My heart drops into my stomach.

"I don't know if I should go. I—I wasn't invited." It's a lie. I was invited, by the other guest of honor. But I can't show up to Nathaniel's event with a *date.*

"It's fine," Donghyun says, driving up to the curb. As he reaches for the door handle, I grab his arm.

"Can we not tell people that we're, you know . . . ?"

He looks down at my hand, then up at my face. "That we're on a date?"

"Yes," I say, slightly out of breath.

"Of course. We'll tell people that we're friends, not that we came together. It'll be our secret." He presses his hand to mine, squeezes, then lets go. I feel nauseous.

Outside, the photographers perk up at our entrance. I try to cover my face with my purse, but a few of them recognize me. "Min Sori, look this way! Sori-yah, are you here to support Nathaniel? Sori, are the rumors of a real-life MinLee couple true?" I'm reminded of two nights ago, the reporters crowding around me, yelling for me. I stumble on the steps leading up to the building.

Donghyun catches my arm before I can fall, leading me through the doors and into the foyer. I'm breathing heavily, sweat on my brow.

"Sori-ssi?" Donghyun says, concern in his voice. "What's wrong?"

"Donghyun-ah?"

Both of us look up.

Naseol stands in the foyer, having apparently come out from the main event hall, where through the large flung-open doors a stage and screen are in view, along with banquet tables.

She's not alone.

"Sori," Nathaniel says. His eyes move slowly from me to Donghyun, who's still gripping my arm.

"Jihyuk-ah," Naseol says, "this is Cha Donghyun, my CEO's nephew."

"Sori," Nathaniel says again, his brow furrowed. "Are you okay?"

"I'm fine. There were just a lot of cameras . . ." I trail off, meeting Nathaniel's eyes. He isn't even trying to hide his feelings, radiating concern, confusion.

I flush.

When I turn to Donghyun, I find his gaze trained on Nathaniel, a deep frown on his face.

"Sori and I were on a date," Donghyun says. I gape at him. I expressly told him *not* to say this. "But I wanted to come congratulate you, Nuna." Though his words are meant for Naseol, his gaze never leaves Nathaniel.

Silence descends upon the hall. I can't *deny* what he's said. We are—*were*—on a date. And I haven't gotten my father's shares of Joah, the whole reason why I'd gone on it in the first place, which I can't, of course, *say*.

"You missed the event, Donghyun-ah," Naseol chides, oblivious to the tension. "But we were just on our way to a restaurant. You're welcome to join us. You and your girlfriend." She laughs.

I feel light-headed.

The sounds of voices come from the main event hall as more guests exit into the foyer. I recognize some of them: Sun, Jaewoo, Youngmin, Hyemi, a few KS artists. Lee Byeol from the radio show. They haven't seen us yet. The thought of them seeing me with Donghyun fills me with dread. How will I explain him? Sun will know what I'm doing. With one look at Donghyun, he'll know that I'm using him for *something*, even if he won't know quite what that is. What if he mentions him to my mother? She'd never allow me to make a deal with my father. But if I don't, she'll lose the company.

"Donghyun-ssi," I say, turning to him, almost pleading, "I'll meet you outside. I need to use the restroom."

His eyes widen, alerted to my panic. "Of course."

I rush across the foyer into a secluded hallway. Finding the door to the bathroom, I push it open. Luckily, it's empty, with only a few stalls.

Nathaniel catches the door as it closes behind me, following me inside.

"What are you doing?" I hiss. "What if someone saw you?"

"What's going on?" he says, and my chest tightens at the pain in his voice. "Why are you with him? Were you really on a date?"

"No. I mean . . . yes."

Nathaniel winces. "Is that why you couldn't come to the launch? Because of him?"

"Yes," I say, this time definitively.

Nathaniel's gaze drops away, then it rises to mine, stripped bare. "Sori, I want to understand. If you're breaking my heart, I need to understand why."

My eyes are hot, they feel as if they're burning.

I love him. I can admit that to myself now. I've always loved him. I love his voice and I love the way he looks at me. I love his laugh and I love the way he makes me laugh. I love the way I feel when I'm around him, like the days are warmer, the nights more beautiful. I love him so much that it makes me want to throw everything else away, if only to be with him, for one more day, for one more minute, for one more breath.

"It's not just your heart," I whisper.

I don't know who moves first, but I'm suddenly in his arms.

He kisses me as if he can't breathe without me; I feel the same, wanting, *needing* to be closer. His hands circle my waist and lift me onto the counter. Our kisses turn frantic; my hands delve into his hair. I feel out of control, like I can't have enough of him.

I kiss him with all the passion in my heart, showing him,

even if I refuse to say it, how much I want him, how much I adore him.

I'm so caught up in Nathaniel that I almost don't hear it—a knock. I break away from our kiss to hear Donghyun's voice through the door, "Sori-ssi, are you all right?" He must have come looking for me when I didn't come back.

Nathaniel's hands tighten around my waist before they let go. He backs away as I slide from the counter, my dress falling back down around my knees.

"I'm here," I call back. "I'll be out in a second."

"Sori," Nathaniel whispers, just my name.

I shake my head. "What would have happened if Donghyun had walked in on us? It would ruin everything. It could, if he suspects anything."

Nathaniel drags a hand through his mussed hair. "I'm sorry. I saw him, with you, and I didn't . . . I wasn't thinking."

"Neither of us think clearly when we're together. This was a mistake."

He looks at me, stricken by my words. "You don't mean that."

He thinks I'm just upset because of the threat of a scandal. He doesn't know it's more than that.

Every scandal he can walk away from, more or less unscathed, beloved by his fans, with the support of his members and family to fall back on, but not me, and not the people I love. Scandals for my family destroy us, have destroyed us.

I forget that when I'm with him.

"Sori . . ."

"Please, let me go."

As if hearing me through heavy fog, he steps back.

I bury my feelings, until the only evidence of them is the smarting of my eyes. Walking past Nathaniel, I open the door and slip through, hoping Cha Donghyun can believe whatever lie comes out of my mouth.

Thirty-three

On Friday, I head over to Joah to bring my mother her favorite pair of shoes. They're an old pair of champagne-colored pumps with worn heels, which don't even fit her properly, but they had belonged to *her* mother. She'd worn them on her wedding day, and now she wants to wear them tomorrow at the EBC Awards, when she accepts the Trailblazer Award in front of all her peers. Ajumma had wrapped the shoebox carefully in a bojagi, folding the silk wrapping end over end. I cradle the shoebox in my lap on the bus ride over, as if I'm carrying something precious, because I am.

In my mother's office, I place the package on her desk, then I raise the blinds to let in the light. Down below, a few fans linger outside the building, taking photos with the Joah Entertainment sign. The new building under construction is even more impressive, with a café that will be open to the public on the weekends and a museum and gift shop.

My phone chirps in my pocket, and I take it out to see that I have a text from Jenny. It's a photo of her unpacked suitcase in the middle of her bedroom floor. She's back home in Los Angeles.

I type out, You're arriving tomorrow, and you're not packed yet? And please don't tell me you're only bringing one suitcase.

Her response is immediate: Not everyone travels with their entire wardrobe, Sori.

I can hear the teasing lilt of her voice. I can't wait to hear it in person. I won't be able to see her tomorrow, because of the awards show, but we have plans to meet up Sunday.

There's still so much I have to do for the show . . . Luckily, I've taken care of most of the finer details already. I have my glam squad assembled for tomorrow, with Soobin and RALA, and my dress is a black Saint Laurent with a plunging neckline and thigh-high split. I'll have to wear an invisible Band-Aid to cover my scrape from Monday, but it'll be worth it.

ASAP will be performing; Hyemi won't be with them, but hopefully, if everything goes according to plan, that could change by next week.

I leave my mother's office, pressing the button for the ground floor.

My phone chirps once more. This time the message is from Donghyun, which I swipe away without opening.

Yesterday, at dinner, he'd asked me officially if I'd be his girlfriend. I'd asked for more time. But I can't keep putting him off. I have to make a decision soon. I just know that once I've made it, there's no turning back.

The elevator opens on the ground floor, and I walk out.

Late afternoon sunlight spills through the glass windows of the lobby, catching in my eyes. I should be excited about tomorrow: I'm hosting one of the biggest awards shows on television; I'm going to wear a beautiful dress and have my makeup done and hair styled—two of my *favorite* things; I'm going to see ASAP perform live; and I'm celebrating this industry that I love so much, with the people I respect and admire. So why do I feel like I'm walking through water? It's sunny outside, yet I feel cold. I'm not sick, at least I don't think I am.

I catch sight of Youngmin, headed toward the doors that lead to the parking garage. He's wearing headphones and I have to call out to him twice before he turns around.

He lowers his headphones. "Nuna?"

"Youngmin-ah," I say, walking toward him. "How was your break?"

"Good. I had school, mostly."

He smiles at me, waiting patiently. Out of all the XOXO members, he and I are the least close, though I've always felt comfortable around him.

"I'm back at the dorm," he says, referring to the apartment he shares with the other members. "Since Wednesday."

Wednesday. The day of Nathaniel's launch. He'd been there, at the event hall. If he knows that *I* was there as well, he doesn't show it, his expression more curious than anything.

I don't know why I stopped him or why I'm lingering here. He was clearly on his way somewhere. I was just feeling a bit . . . melancholy, and I wanted to see a friendly face. "Well—"

"I was just on my way there, actually," Youngmin says. "Even though no one's around. Sun's out on a date, Jaewoo's with his mom and sister, and Nathaniel went to see the Ferris wheel."

I feel my heart sink. "Did he . . . Did he go with anyone?"

"He said he was taking Woo Hyemi."

I look toward the windows once more. It'll be sunset in an hour. Had they gone to watch the sunset over the Han River?

When I return my gaze to Youngmin, I find him watching me,

294

his expression carefully blank. "I haven't been to see the Ferris wheel yet," he says. "It looks like a lot of fun."

Is he saying what I think he's saying?

"What do you think, Nuna?" Youngmin grins. "Want to go on a date with me?"

Ji Seok, who'd been waiting for Youngmin in the parking garage, drops us off near the park.

"Please don't do anything *I'll* regret," he begs.

"Ha, you're funny, Hyeong!"

The park is crowded, with hundreds of people having come out to watch the sunset. The most crowded area is around the Ferris wheel, with couples and groups of friends lining up to take their turn around the massive wheel.

"We need disguises." Youngmin drags me to a cart where an elderly woman is selling useful items for a day spent beside the Han River. He selects a pair of plastic sunglasses from a display and hands them to me before grabbing a pair for himself. "Ooh, and this." He picks up a sun umbrella beneath a pile of them, cranking it open. It's the gaudiest umbrella with lace and flowers. Luckily, it's a sunny day, so a lot of people also carry umbrellas.

"Youngmin-ah, that's not them, right?" I stare at a young couple sitting on a picnic blanket on the grass. I can't tell if it's them from this distance, but the girl is wearing the same bucket hat I've seen on Hyemi.

"Youngmin-ah?" I turn around, only to find Youngmin missing. I groan. Don't tell me I've already lost him.

"Nuna!" Youngmin runs up.

I'm about to scold him, but I'm immediately distracted by the churros he's holding; they're Oreo-flavored and filled with cream cheese.

As we walk toward the area around the Ferris wheel, enjoying our churros, a group of teenage girls pass us.

"Wasn't that Nathaniel Lee just now?" I overhear one of them say.

"Who was that girl with him?" her friend asks.

"Whoever it was, it wasn't Min Sori."

"Don't tell me you're a 'MinLee' fan?"

"I don't know, but I *am* a fan of both of them."

"Even Min Sori?"

"Yes! She's so pretty, and I like how she looks like she's mean but you can tell she isn't, you know?"

"Yeah, I like that about her too."

"Me too," Youngmin says loudly.

"Youngmin-ah!" I pull him behind a food cart selling corn dogs, before the girls can register who he is. Even with our disguises, he's still Choi Youngmin of XOXO, easily recognizable if you were to take a closer look. His hair is dyed black again, otherwise he'd really stick out. "We're trying to keep a low profile, remember?"

"Excuse me, can I have a corn dog?" Youngmin's talking to the food cart worker.

We finally make it to the Ferris wheel, after sharing the corn dog between us, dunked in batter and fried until perfectly crispy, then slathered with sweet chili and mustard sauce.

There's a palpable tension in the air, whispers flittering among those standing in line.

I spot Nathaniel and Hyemi, toward the front of the line.

"Youngmin-ah," I say. I don't know what alerts him, but he looks at me, suddenly serious. "I don't want Nathaniel to get into that car with Hyemi."

I wait for him to ask me why, or to laugh, but he just nods.

"Okay."

He jumps forward into the crowd. I lose sight of him immediately. I gape, then scramble to follow. The crowd parts for him, and therefore me, no one willing to stop us and cause a scene even though we're cutting the line.

Nathaniel and Hyemi are next. The Ferris wheel attendants are calling them up. Youngmin pops out of the crowd. Rushing forward, he grabs Hyemi's hand and drags her into one of the cars that's already leaving. The door closes behind them.

Nathaniel stands alone on the platform, in shock.

"Was that Youngmin?" I hear him saying to himself as I rush up. Grabbing his hand, I pull him into the next car.

"Sori?" Nathaniel stares at me as the door shuts and the wheel begins its slow ascent. "What's going on? What are you doing here?"

"I . . . ran into Youngmin at Joah and we . . . decided to come see the Ferris wheel."

As far as explanations go, it's a weak one, but Nathaniel doesn't question it, leaning back in his seat. The car isn't very large, but neither is it small, meant to hold four people. It's enclosed for our safety, with plateglass windows on every side except the floor.

I gaze at Nathaniel. We haven't seen each other—or spoken—since Wednesday.

"You came with Woo Hyemi," I say.

"Hyemi's a nice girl." He has one elbow balanced on the windowsill as he gazes out toward the river. "She's having a hard time right now. It's not just all of the negative attention, she's away from her family, her mother and sister. Her father, a lot of the time. She's a foreigner in a country that should feel like home, but sometimes feels far from it. I can relate to that."

I hadn't thought of the similarities between them. "I'm glad she has you to talk to." Regardless of my own insecurities, I *am* glad. I haven't been able to help Hyemi since the scandal broke. At least, not in any visible ways. But he has. He's given her a shoulder to lean on when she's needed it the most.

"Yeah, well, it's also great that apparently hanging out with her makes you jealous."

"I'm not jealous!"

He laughs. "Whatever you say."

"Was it wise to bring her out here?" I frown. "People might write articles about you and her tomorrow."

"You're one to talk."

I blush.

"The irony." His eyes slide to me. "You escape scandal with me, only to get embroiled in one with Youngmin. A younger man, Min Sori?"

He's teasing, but his smile doesn't reach his eyes.

"Hyemi and I are friends," he says, his gaze moving back toward the window. "They can write an article about that, if they want. I wanted to see the sunset, just like everyone else."

He looks so unhappy. That sadness, I put it there. He'd be happy if it weren't for me.

The sun sets over Seoul, gilding a golden path on the river.

"I want to be honest with you," I say, drawing his gaze.

"You were right. I don't care what people say about me. On the internet or to my face. If it was just me, I could endure it. I could endure most anything . . ." *To be with you.*

I take a deep breath. "But it's not just me. My mother . . . I have to consider how my actions affect her. Two years ago, she asked me to promise her that I'd break it off with you . . .

"It's true that I was afraid of how our scandal might affect any future career that I might want, or how it might affect you and the other XOXO members, but that wasn't why I made that promise.

"I made it for *her*."

Joah means everything to my mother. I've known this since I was a little girl. It gave her purpose after she became pregnant with me; it became her *life* after her marriage fell apart.

"Maybe a scandal of mine won't ruin the company, but there's always that possibility, the fear of being the reason she loses everything."

Nathaniel had dropped his head while I was speaking. He lifts it now. "I can't accept that you'd push me away to protect me . . ." he says slowly, and my heart fills with anguish. "But I can accept that you would for your mother." I catch my breath. "It's always been you and her, hasn't it?" His voice is soft, tender. "Looking out for each other. Protecting each other."

Nathaniel smiles at me, his expression rueful. "This is it, huh? Damn." He rakes his hand through his hair.

Then he edges forward. "I'm sorry that I didn't listen to you before. I didn't understand until now. I won't make you waver any longer. If this is the end, I wanted to tell you, at least once . . ."

We've reached the very top of the Ferris wheel; the sun bathes our carriage in golden light.

"I love you."

Thirty-four

I get ready for the EBC Awards at Soobin and RALA's studio. My black Saint Laurent gown, on loan from the designer, is sleeveless, with a fitted bodice tailored to my exact proportions. It tapers at the waist, flaring slightly at the hips before dropping down to the floor. The long split that ends halfway up my thigh allows for movement, even if it's admittedly a bit . . . scandalous.

I decide not to wear a necklace, leaving my shoulders and décolletage bare. The only jewelry I wear is pearl drop earrings. As for shoes, I choose stilettos.

Soobin has already blown out my hair so that it falls in waves luxuriously over my shoulders, and RALA has executed a sultry nighttime look with winged eyeliner and a matte red lipstick, which leaves only getting dressed. Afterward, Soobin and RALA take photos of me on the balcony, where the lighting, in the hour before sunset, is the best.

My next stop is Joah. Since Nathaniel and I are cohosting the event, we're supposed to arrive together at the venue. On the drive over, my nerves get the better of me. I've never been to an awards ceremony, let alone *hosted* one. Nathaniel hasn't either, not one of this caliber, though he has experience hosting the weekly music shows at EBC. What if I can't read the teleprompter in a natural way or lose my place while reading? Because of the short notice, we hadn't had time for a rehearsal.

The car service drops me off outside the building—tonight, Secretary Park is accompanying my mother—and I hurry through the front doors.

As I enter, I draw up short. All four XOXO members are standing in the lobby, dressed in formal black-tie attire.

They all turn at my entrance.

Collectively, their eyes move from the ground upward, checking me out, and I smile at their appreciation.

"Sori-yah," Sun says, meeting me halfway as I approach them across the lobby. "You look beautiful."

"Min Sori," Jaewoo says with a grin. "Were you always this tall?"

I wrinkle my nose at his teasing. "Shouldn't you be on the way to the airport?" I ask. "Jenny's arriving at any moment."

"I'm thinking of bailing early." He grins. "Do you think anyone will notice?"

"We wanted to support our CEO," Sun explains.

My heart fills with gratitude for all of them. They didn't have to be here. Though invited, they're not actively promoting an album, nominated for an award, or performing. But they're showing up anyway, to support my mother, their CEO, as she accepts this year's Trailblazer Award.

"Thank you," I say softly.

It's Youngmin's turn to greet me next. "Nuna," he says, eyes wide. "You're gorgeous!"

I laugh at the way he keeps his eyes level with mine, staring at me almost fixedly so as not to inadvertently drop his gaze to the *very* deep *V* of my neckline. Poor Youngmin. Maybe I shouldn't have worn this dress and had more consideration for his innocence.

Then it's Nathaniel's turn. And now I'm the one who's stunned. He's dressed entirely in black, even his shirt beneath his jacket, but unlike the others who wear a necktie or a bowtie, the top few buttons of his shirt are undone. Nathaniel in casual wear is heart-fluttering, like your boyfriend who's also a bit of a bad boy, mischievous and too charming for his own good. But Nathaniel in formal wear, with his hair slicked back, his gaze direct, is breathtaking, still a bad boy, but entirely grown up, and quite possibly the most beautiful thing I've ever seen.

I'm vaguely aware that we match almost perfectly, without having coordinated our outfits at all.

"Sori." Nathaniel's eyes are warm as he takes me in. "How are you feeling?"

"Nervous," I confess. "On the way over here, I was thinking of all the things that could go wrong."

"They won't," Nathaniel says confidently. "And if they do, I'll have your back, just like you'll have mine."

He grins. "We're going to kill it. I just know it."

My heart rushes with warmth at his words, and I . . . believe him. I believe him wholeheartedly.

"Limo's here," Sun says, leading the way out the building.

As we're walking out the door, a deliveryman approaches holding a large bouquet of red roses. "Min Sori-ssi?"

I blink at him. "Yes?"

"These are for you."

I gather the bouquet in my arms. Jaewoo and Youngmin tease me as I reach in between the roses to pull out a card. *Congratulations on hosting the EBC Awards. I look forward to seeing you tonight.*

I read the name written at the end of the message. "They're from Cha Donghyun."

"Cha Donghyun, CEO's Cha's nephew?" Sun asks.

Jaewoo frowns. "Was that the guy you were with on Wednesday?"

"Why is Cha Donghyun-ssi sending you flowers, Nuna?"

I stare at them, unsure what to say. Their expressions aren't exactly accusatory—and all of them are careful not to look at Nathaniel, but I can sense their confusion.

"Who wouldn't send Sori flowers?" Nathaniel interjects. "You're just jealous you didn't get some, Youngmin-ah."

Youngmin grins, dispelling whatever tension there might have been. Together, we shuffle into the limo. Sun takes the flowers, putting them to the side, while Jaewoo hands me his suit jacket to cover my legs. As we ride to the venue, I risk glances at Nathaniel. Unlike the others, he hadn't reacted to the bouquet. It's not that I want him to be . . . jealous, but only last night, he'd told me he *loved* me. Though later, after we got off the Ferris wheel, he'd acted as if nothing had changed, laughing and joking with Youngmin, teasing Hyemi, and treating me . . . just like he treated them, as if I were a friend, nothing more.

It's exactly what I asked for, every time I've pushed him away, so then why do I feel so unhappy?

The limo pulls up outside the venue for the awards show at one of the largest arenas in Seoul. Already photographers line the red carpet leading to the front entrance. Even though I'm prepared this time—these photographers are *supposed* to be here; they're doing their jobs in a respectable manner, compared to tabloid reporters—I still feel a bolt of anxiety go through me.

Sun opens the limo door, and a rush of sound pours into the car, high-pitched screams coming from the crowds of fans behind the photographers, separated by a partition. I give Jaewoo back his jacket and he exits after Sun, the screams erupting again. Young-min is next. I shift closer to the door, wincing at a sudden flash of light—a camera, directed at the limousine.

I remember the paparazzi outside the event hall and outside the batting cages, and even before then, those lights from my childhood, following me home from school, reporters yelling for my attention, asking me about my father's affairs, the rumors that my mother was frigid, cold-hearted, that she was the reason they fell apart, because she drove him away.

"Sori." I look down to find Nathaniel holding my hand. His is warm, his grip firm but gentle. He's wearing rings on his fingers. Reaching up, I twist the one on his pointer finger, around and around. He lets me, remaining completely still. He doesn't rush me, though everyone outside is probably wondering why we haven't stepped out yet. He's so patient with me—the one person in the world who has always *seen* me, as I am, flaws and all.

"It's you and me, remember?" he says softly. "We got this."

All those times with the paparazzi, I hadn't been with Nathaniel. I'm with him now. I nod. He lets go of my hand to step out of the car, then he's reaching back to take my hand. There's a roar of sound as I emerge—from the photographers shouting my name, but also the fans, screaming, cheering, for me. *For us.*

Nathaniel draws my hand to his arm, and I grab on to the fabric there, taking strength from him. Together, we face the cameras.

"Nathaniel, look over here!"

"Sori. Nathaniel, over here, please."

"Sori, *Vogue Korea* over here. You look stunning!"

I glance at Nathaniel, who's waving at the photographers, smiling and confident. His confidence, his *presence*, gives *me* confidence.

Taking a deep breath, I turn toward the cameras, pretending the director from Sun's drama is on the carpet, shouting, "Be bold! Be beautiful!" Throwing my shoulders back, placing one hand on my hip, I channel that energy. I direct my sultry gaze at the cameras and pout my lips. The noise on the carpet seems to get even louder, the fans screaming, the photographers clicking at a faster rate.

Nathaniel and I start moving ahead, allowing for more cars to drive up behind us. Every few steps, we stop to pose, and I *know* we look good, standing side by side. At one point, I even drop Nathaniel's arm to take photos alone, showing off my dress and earrings. I've already posted on my SNS that my makeup was done by RALA, my hair by Kim Soobin.

After the red carpet, we head inside the arena. Attendants usher Sun, Jaewoo, and Youngmin to their seats, while Nathaniel and I are shown through a door backstage.

We enter a long, curving hallway, which presumably leads to the stage area. I shiver, the air colder here than it was outside.

Nathaniel notices. Taking off his suit jacket, he places it around my shoulders. It's warm and thick and smells of his cologne.

"Sori-ssi? Nathaniel-ssi?"

A motorized cart pulls up next to us, with Woogi sitting in the front with a driver and Woori sitting in the back next to an empty seat.

"You two . . . Wow . . . ," Woogi says. "I want to take a photograph of you both and frame it on my wall."

"What a silly thing to say, Oppa!" Woori laughs.

Nathaniel steps closer to the cart. "Woori-ssi," he says, "can I ask you for a favor?"

Her eyes widen, blinking rapidly. "Yes, of course."

I stare at Nathaniel, curious what he's up to.

"You're heading to the backstage area, right? That empty seat beside you, can Sori take it?"

"Oh no," I start to protest. "I can walk."

Nathaniel gives my feet—specifically my stilettos—a significant look. "Please, for me." My stomach flutters. Then he adds teasingly, "You're slowing me down."

My feet *are* starting to smart a bit. Woori moves over and I climb into the cart, turning my head to peer at Nathaniel as we pull away.

"I think he's smitten with you," Woori says, drawing my attention to her.

"He was just being considerate." I blush.

"Really? Oppa . . ." She leans forward to shout at her brother. "If I were wearing stilettos, would you think to put me in a passing cart?"

Woogi shouts over the motor, "He said she was slowing him down!"

I feel a little bereft about being parted from Nathaniel, but at least we'll be reunited soon, and he has the attendant with him to keep him company.

In the backstage area, an assistant is waiting to greet me. As we walk toward the hosts' waiting room, I spot Sun Ye and the other ASAP members.

"Sun Ye-yah!" I shout.

"Sori-yah." We air-hug. She's stunning, dressed in a glittering performance outfit. The other members are dressed similarly. They bow to me in greeting. I feel a pang at not seeing Hyemi among them.

"How have you been?" I ask. "I'm sorry I've been absent so much this past week." I was trying to fix the fallout from the scandal with Hyemi, but I was also feeling guilty and sad about my own life.

"It's all very challenging, with ups and downs, but I wouldn't change it for the world. Though I wish Hyemi were promoting with us. Your mother says she's announcing something about that next week."

I frown. "She is?" Did Hyemi's father agree to a deal?

Sun Ye nods. "Whatever it is, she says that she'll take care of everything and not to worry."

Sun Ye says this so matter-of-factly, as if, because my mother told her not to hold on to her worries, she's able to let go of them.

I never asked her why she stayed as a trainee at Joah for so many years when others had left, and I wonder if it's as simple as because she believed in my mother.

"Min Sori?" the assistant calls, having waited patiently this whole time.

"I'll be sure to watch your performance," I tell Sun Ye. "You're opening up the show, aren't you?"

"I am. We've come a long way, haven't we? Since our middle and high school trainee days."

I laugh. "Yes, and still a long way to go."

"I look forward to it!"

Nathaniel's already in the dressing room when I arrive, getting his makeup touched up. Mine has stayed perfectly intact, thanks to my diligence and RALA's superior products. Once Nathaniel is finished, we're whisked away to the staging area. My heart picks up at the rush of sounds coming from behind the curtains, of instruments warming up in the pit below the stage, the mingling voices of thousands of artists, writers, actors, visionaries.

Nathaniel's hand slips over mine, tightening. I look up at him. "Nervous?" I ask.

His Adam's apple bobs. "A little."

"It's you and me, remember?" I repeat his words from earlier. "We got this."

He smiles at me. "We do."

"And now," a voice booms for the speakers, quieting the audience, "introducing our hosts, singer, Nathaniel Lee and model, Min Sori."

Nathaniel and I walk onto the stage to polite applause. The stage lights are bright, making it difficult to see the audience, but I follow Nathaniel's lead as he approaches the markings on the stage, where we're meant to stand behind side-by-side microphones.

As the noise settles, I locate the teleprompter.

"Thank you, everyone, for coming," I read slowly, enunciating my words as clearly as possible. "Tonight we've come together to celebrate the best of music, acting, and variety."

"Speaking of variety, you and I have had our share of guest appearances. How come we weren't nominated for anything?" Nathaniel's reading from the script, but his delivery of his lines is so natural, I can't help laughing as if he *were* ad-libbing.

"That's true. What category do you think we could have been considered for?"

"Best couple?" Nathaniel says cheekily.

The crowd cheers. I hear a loud whistle to the left side of the stage, where I swear I can see Sun and the rest of the XOXO members in the front row.

"Nathaniel-ssi," I say, playfully, "don't be silly." On the screen, that's all it says, but I decide to ad-lib. "That category is for fake couples, not real ones."

Nathaniel's bark of laughter is genuine, joined by the audience.

We continue with the script, which was written by a board of EBC's writers and vetted by Secretary Park beforehand. It's lively and fun, and we ad-lib whenever the opportunity arises.

I can *feel* the chemistry between us; it's electrifying. We joke and laugh and flirt, even. We act as if we share a secret between us, and the secret, which isn't a secret at all, is that we're friends. There's no one else I'd rather be on this stage with, no one who makes me feel as beautiful and confident and clever and safe. I trust him, and he trusts me, and because of that, we make a spectacular team.

"And now for our first performers," Nathaniel reads, "in their awards show debut performance."

"Please welcome," I say. "ASAP."

Thirty-five

Nathaniel and I catch the first half of ASAP's incredible performance before we're hustled backstage to the dressing room. On the way, we're stopped by celebrities—presenters, mostly, but also performers—praising us for our natural presence on stage and our chemistry. After the first few run-ins, I notice that everyone seems to speak to Nathaniel and me as if we are, in fact, a couple. They ask us how *we're* feeling, what performances *we're* looking forward to; Jolly and Heartthrob from *Catch Me If You Can* tease Nathaniel, saying they basically set him up, and Byeol, who's presenting with her costar, tells me that Nathaniel and I look like we're a couple that has been together for years, and that I look happy.

I am happy. It's one of the most exhilarating nights of my life. We have little time to rest, rushing back and forth to the stage. We're walking off after our final skit together when a familiar voice calls out to me. "Sori-ssi?"

My body, which had been warm and relaxed with Nathaniel the whole night, tenses.

I turn. "D-Donghyun-ssi. What are you doing here?"

"I was in the audience enjoying the show," he says, smiling widely. "You were wonderful out there. Both of you." He extends his magnanimity to Nathaniel, before focusing once more on me. "My friend who invited me asked if I wanted to go backstage, and so . . . I hope it's all right. Did I overstep?"

"No, of course not." I attempt to hide my dismay. On our last date, I told him I'd have an answer for him the next time we met. But I'm not ready to give him an answer, especially not here, with Nathaniel looking on. I don't know what to do, what to say. It's one thing to pretend in front of Donghyun, who only knows me as Min Sori, daughter of Min Kyung-mo, model and variety show personality, but not Nathaniel, who knows me inside and out. I can pretend all that I want, I can lie and use people, but not in front of Nathaniel.

"Sori."

I look up. Nathaniel's eyes, when they meet mine, are kind.

"I'll give you two some privacy," he says. "I should get going, anyway." The skit before was our final one. This is the end. With a short bow to Donghyun—who returns it quickly—he starts to walk away.

"Wait!" I catch his arm. "You're not staying?"

He glances down at my hand, then up to my face. "I'll go sit with Jaewoo and the others, then we'll probably head out after your mother's speech." He doesn't explain why, not in front of Donghyun. *To see Jenny.*

He's *leaving*. Without me, this time for good. Before last night, he might have told Donghyun to get lost, dragged me into a stairwell, and kissed me breathless.

But on the Ferris wheel, he promised not to make me waver. He said he was listening to me when I told him I couldn't be with him. This is him, listening to me.

I let go of his sleeve.

"I had fun tonight," he says. Dimples appear in both cheeks as he gives me one last devastating smile. "We make a good team."

Then he turns and walks away.

"Wow," Donghyun says. "So that's the XOXO factor. I think I might have just become a fan."

I laugh outright.

It's such a silly thing to say, and generous too, since I know he picked up on the tension between Nathaniel and me. He'd have to be quite oblivious not to, and Donghyun is not that.

Why did I think it was okay to use Cha Donghyun? Because I didn't know him? That's not the reality now, nor should it have been reason enough to use him in the first place.

He's a sweet person, a *good* person. He's just not *my* person.

Maybe I thought the only way to save Joah was to follow the path my father laid out for me.

But he's not the only parent in my life who's given me a path to follow.

"Donghyun-ssi," I say, "about the question you asked me the other night. I'm afraid that I can't give you the answer you might have hoped for."

Donghyun sighs, then nods. "I understand."

I wonder if he'll mention Nathaniel, that it's clear where my heart lies. But he only smiles. "Even if it was only for a little while, I enjoyed our time together. Let's meet again in the future, as friends."

"I would love that," I say, happy, at last, to speak the truth.

It only takes me a few minutes to find her. She's sequestered in her own private room, with Secretary Park standing on guard outside the door.

"Sori?" My mother stands up from the couch when I enter. "What's wrong?"

"Nothing," I say. "I just wanted to see you. Before your big moment."

She laughs, sitting back down. "I feel like a bride again. I'm even wearing the shoes." She lifts the hem of her pants, showing off her pumps.

"Was your wedding day like today?"

"No. I was a bit of a pariah. A lot of my friends didn't want to associate with me after my scandal. But I had a few guests. Jin-rang, of course, and my group mates. So much has happened since then."

"Was it very hard?" I ask quietly. I don't have to elaborate on what I mean: Was it hard to give up her dream after becoming pregnant with me? Was it hard being stuck in a loveless marriage?

"Yes, but there's not a moment of my life that I regret. Because of it, I have a career that I'm proud of. Because of it, I have you.

"I would walk the same path every lifetime, if I knew that at the end of it, you were waiting for me."

My eyes fill with tears that threaten to spill.

"I was watching you earlier when you were on stage. I'm so proud of you, Sori. When you came to me saying you didn't want to be an idol but wanted to forge your own path, you reminded me so much of myself. And since then, I've watched how hard you've worked to help Hyemi, how much time and energy you've spent with the ASAP girls and Jin-rang's team. You're so smart and strong-willed, everything I hoped you would be."

Reaching out, she takes my hand. "I'm sorry I haven't been

around as much, but I want to change that. I want to be there for you when you need me. You can always rely on me. You know that, right?"

I nod. I do know that. I *had* known that. All my life I've relied on her, even when *she* was the one who needed protection.

Secretary Park knocks on the door before opening it slightly. "It's almost time."

"I'll let you get ready," I say, slipping outside, afraid that if I stay, I'll cry all over her beautiful suit.

Outside, I find Director Ryu waiting backstage. "Are you presenting the Trailblazer Award to my mother?"

"I am," she says, tilting her head to study me, her eyes glinting curiously.

"Would you mind if I—?"

"Oh *yes*," she says. "Please, I despise public speaking. Honestly, I should have thought of that myself. The award will be more meaningful coming from you, anyway."

I bite my lip, nervous now that I've made this impromptu decision.

"Good luck!" Director Ryu says, raising both fists in the air.

I walk onto the stage for the last time. Murmuring sweeps through the crowd at my appearance, Nathaniel and I having already said our goodbyes. I briefly wonder if the show's PD will be upset with the last-minute schedule change but push that thought to the back of my mind.

I reach the podium. Finding the teleprompter, I start to read aloud, "The Trailblazer Award is given to an individual who has changed this industry in a significant way, opening up new pathways for others to follow."

I go on to list my mother's achievements. It takes me five whole minutes to list them all.

"Seo Min Hee isn't just an incredible visionary and business-woman, she's also a mother. *My mother.* I've been with her from the beginning. Well, at least my beginning."

The audience laughs, indulging me.

"I've seen her at her highest highs . . ."—the opening of Joah, the first major award for XOXO—"and her lowest lows . . ." My father's affairs, the night after Hyemi's scandal broke . . .

"No matter the occasion, she rises to the top, with tenacity, with power, with grace. I'm grateful for my mother for many rea-sons. But most importantly, I'm grateful because she shows me, by example, all that I can be, that my pathways are endless. She's a true trailblazer. I am so proud of her, can you tell?"

The crowd laughs.

This whole time I've been worrying about her, but she's *Seo Min Hee.* I don't need to fight my mother's battles; she can fight her own. She always has. Why did I ever think she couldn't?

Everyone believes in her, the ASAP members, the XOXO members, Director Ryu and Secretary Park, but what about me?

When did I lose faith in my mother?

I need to believe in her. I need to trust that she'll find a way, like she has before.

"She's the strongest person I know . . ."

It feels *freeing* to remember that, like letting go of a weight I'd been carrying.

My gaze travels to where the XOXO members are sitting. I

can't see them from here, but I know they're watching, that *he's* watching. "I should be strong as well."

A few people in the crowd shift in their seats, probably wondering what I mean.

"Please join me in honoring tonight's recipient of this year's Trailblazer Award, Founder and CEO of Joah Entertainment, Seo Min Hee."

Everyone rises to their feet as my mother stands and makes her way up the stairs to the podium. As she approaches me, I see that there are actual tears in her eyes. She grabs me in a fierce hug, not caring that she's ruining my makeup and her own.

"Thank you, Sori-yah. You have always given me the most strength. I love you."

My tears match her own. "I love you, Eomma."

There's another award presentation after my mother accepts hers, but I don't stay to watch it, not when I see that Nathaniel and the others have already left their seats.

I race backstage and into the hall that circles the arena.

We make a good team, he'd said. *We do*, I want to tell him, *the very best*. I couldn't see that until tonight. I'd been pushing him away for so many reasons, because I was afraid of what could happen with us being together, scandals and heartbreak and regret, because I thought our lives were too different—he knows how to love and be loved, but for me, love feels like a threat, like something that could be taken away at any moment. Because I thought he was good and I was bad. But I was wrong. We are both bad. He's a flirt and a delinquent, and I'm very much a girl who would risk it all for him.

I catch up with him in the parking lot behind the arena. He's with the other members, walking toward the car service that'll take them back to their dorms.

"Nathaniel!" I call out.

He turns, catching sight of me on the stairs. I quickly walk down them—not too fast, as I'm still wearing stilettos.

He's waiting for me at the bottom. "Did you run in those?" He sounds both afraid for me and a little impressed.

"I need to talk to you," I say, breathless from my run. "Alone."

His eyes meet mine, his expression guarded, giving nothing of his thoughts away.

Finally, turning to the others, he says, "Wait in the car. I'll be right there."

He follows me behind a partitioned wall, out of view.

"Sori," he says. "What's going on? Are you—?"

I cut him off. "You said you've wanted me for half your life, but I think, for me, it's been even longer. I've wanted you my whole life. You, with your sincerity and your teasing and your passion. You, who makes me feel safe and loved and beautiful.

"I was afraid," I confess. "I was afraid of so many things, but mostly I was afraid of how much I wanted you."

The mask he'd worn to hide his emotions falls; he looks vulnerable, his cheeks flushed, his lips parted. "I've only ever loved one girl," he says, "since I was fourteen. Maybe I could love someone else in in the future . . ."

I draw his mouth to mine, pressing my body to his, making him take back the words. I only release him when I'm satisfied. "I didn't like what you said, about loving someone else in the future. The only girl you love, who you will *ever* love, is me."

He laughs unsteadily. "I've never seen this selfish side of you."

"When it comes to you, I'm entirely selfish. I want all your attention." I press another kiss to the corner of his lips, the edge of his cheeks. When I draw away, his eyes flutter open. "I crave it. I want you to look only at me."

"Now that you're being forthright," he says, "you're making me blush."

I circle my arms around his neck and bring my lips to his ear. "Come home with me. I want to be alone with you."

He holds me close a moment longer, his hands tightening around my waist before letting go. Taking my hand, he leads me from behind the partition to a different car in the long line of them. We climb inside and he gives the driver my address.

"Aren't the others waiting for you?" I ask as we pull out of the parking lot.

He takes out his phone with one hand—never letting go of mine with the other—presumably to text them. But he only looks down at the screen for a few seconds before pocketing it again. "No," he says, color in his cheeks. "They're not."

I arch my brow, wondering what sort of texts they're sending him.

Neither of us speaks on the long drive to my house, conscious of the driver in the front. When we pull up outside, Nathaniel pays the driver while I key in the code to the gate. The garden lights blink on as we walk up the steps, as if welcoming us home.

We pause briefly in the foyer to remove our shoes. I sigh in relief as my stilettos drop to the ground, and then we're stumbling up the steps, laughing.

Nathaniel shuts my bedroom door behind us. I fall backward onto the bed, spreading my arms wide on either side of me. I look up to find Nathaniel standing at the foot of the bed, looking incredibly pleased with himself. "That's one of your rules broken." *You're not allowed to come into my room.*

I lift a brow. "And the other?"

He'd already discarded his jacket. Reaching up, he unbuttons more of his obscenely buttoned shirt, pulling it over his head. My mouth goes dry at the sight of his lean muscles and taut stomach. Circling his hand around my ankle, he bends my leg. He lowers his head, kissing the Band-Aid over my scraped knee, then he wraps my leg around his waist, climbing over me.

We kiss, more passionately than before, every touch of our lips a promise of love, of belief, of trust. I want, *need*, to be closer to him, the fabric of my dress catching around my legs. He finds the zipper at my back, sliding it down. I gasp at the touch of his rings against my skin.

I draw him up to me, so that I can look into his eyes.

"I mean it," I say, breathless. "Do you doubt me?"

His dusky eyelashes lower. "After the Ferris wheel, I thought it was over between us." His voice is unsteady, an echo of his anguish. "I was prepared to live my life without you. It felt like my heart was being torn from my body."

"Not without me," I breathe, "never without me."

I raise my hand to his cheek, and he lifts his to cover mine. Our eyes meet and my heart feels like it could burst with love for him.

Ever since he first teased me, I think I knew, and even as the years have gone by, and we've been pulled apart and pushed together again, my heart has always been drawn to him.

"I love you," I say.

His eyes are bright. And then we're kissing, falling into each other, in a night of endless bliss.

Thirty-six

I wake the next morning with the blankets kicked to my feet and my arms outstretched above my head. Abruptly I sit up, grabbing a pillow and bringing it to my chest. When I turn, I find Nathaniel still asleep. He's lying on his stomach, his head turned toward me, strands of his hair falling across his bow. He's so handsome, with the sunlight streaming over his face, that I forget my embarrassment entirely. I reach out to push the hair from his eyes.

My stomach growls. I haven't had a proper meal since an early dinner the day before, and I'm *starving*. But I don't want to wake Nathaniel, not when he's sleeping so peacefully.

I edge toward the side of the bed.

"Sori?"

I peek over my shoulder to see Nathaniel sit up groggily. The muscles in his arms flex as he pushes himself up off the bed. Catching me admiring him, he smiles, which turns to a frown as he reaches beneath him to pull out a Pikachu.

"Sori, how can you sleep like this? I feel like I'm being watched." He tosses Pikachu off the bed. I follow its trajectory until it hits the floor, joining dozens of my stuffed animals that Nathaniel had presumably chucked off the bed while I was asleep.

I meet his eyes. "How could you?" I whisper accusatorially.

He's unrepentant. "They'll live."

"This is *their* bed. *You're* the intruder."

"I'm sorry if I've disturbed their freeloading existence and probably scarred them to boot." He grins, dimples showing.

He looks confident, *too* confident—which makes *me* feel vulnerable—so I pout, biting my lip.

He immediately turns conciliatory, shifting closer to me. "I'll apologize to each and every one of your stuffed animals if that'll make you happy."

I nod.

He kisses me, dragging the pillow away.

It's midmorning by the time we finally break apart and emerge from my room. I give him one of his shirts, which I'd discovered the day after he left.

"I cleaned and pressed it myself." I hand it over to him and he immediately draws it over his head. "Ajumma was on a spa vacation with her girlfriends."

Nathaniel frowns. "You were here by yourself all week?"

"Yes, don't you feel awful for leaving me?" I don't point out that *I* was the reason he left. He doesn't either. Because he's smart.

"Yes." He nods seriously. "It won't happen again."

We head downstairs, raiding the kitchen. While Nathaniel makes toast and sets the dining table, I cook eggs and bacon in a pan.

It takes us longer to make breakfast because we keep on stopping to kiss, but only fifteen minutes to eat it, both of us starving.

"I'm going to run down and get iced coffee from the convenience store," Nathaniel says. "You want anything?"

"I'm okay," I say, taking the dishes to the kitchen. I'm loading them into the dishwasher when I hear Nathaniel come back into the house.

"That was fast," I stay, stepping out of the dining room.

My father stands in the middle of the foyer.

"Abeoji," I say, a sudden coldness in my stomach.

He doesn't say anything, just looks at me, and *I know* he knows that Nathaniel spent the night. He must also suspect that I'd broken it off with Cha Donghyun.

The door opens and I have the second shock of the morning when my mother walks through the door. She doesn't look surprised to see my father. She must have known he'd be here. Did he tell her to come?

"Wh-where's Nathaniel?" I ask her. There isn't any way they didn't see him; he'd only been gone for a few minutes.

"I sent him home," she says, her gaze averted from my face. Only last night, she'd accepted her award from my hands, pride in her eyes. Now she can't even look at me.

"He doesn't have his things," I say. His wallet and phone are still in my room, along with his suit jacket.

"He'll be fine," my mother says curtly. "Secretary Park is taking him back to his apartment. We'll return his things to him later."

I stare at them both. "Why are you here?" It's a reasonable question. My mother hasn't been at the house in weeks, my father in *years*.

"This is *my* house," my father says. "Why shouldn't I be here?" I flinch at his tone of voice, which he's never used with me. Though I've heard him use it with his aides, Secretary Lee, and even with my mother, when we lived together. "I wanted to see for myself if my daughter was truly lying to me behind my back."

It's because your back is turned from me, that I lie to you, I want to say, but I've never spoken like that to my father.

"Sori-abeoji," my mother chides. "What is this all about? So our daughter had a boy over to the house. This is the twenty-first century. Do your constituents know you're so close-minded?"

My stomach sinks. She doesn't know that Nathaniel's been living here. My father's face hardens. Does he know?

"Follow me."

Without explanation, he heads into the media room, turning on the television. He presses a button, and the feed from the external video surveillance cameras around the house appear on the screen. He highlights one of the cameras labeled "Front Gate." Rewinding to last night, he plays it backward.

I watch, numb, as on the screen the car service pulls up outside the gate. I see myself climb out and hurry to open the door while Nathaniel pays, then we're passing through the gate together.

My father rewinds it to earlier this week, and I feel a sharp pain at the memory of that night. I see myself stop outside the gate by the vine-covered wall. When I start to cry, Nathaniel rushes back to embrace me. He leaves a few minutes later, and I drop to the ground, breaking down in tears.

My father clicks his tongue in disgust, pressing the button to rewind. I glance at my mother, wondering what she thinks of all this, but her expression is carefully blank, the only evidence that she feels *something* is the slight trembling of her hands.

On and on my father rewinds, showing with irrefutable proof that Nathaniel had been living at the house with me.

Nearly every day for two weeks we're shown walking up to the house, usually at the same time.

And in every video, we're laughing.

I don't know what my father expects me to see watching all this back, but it only serves to remind me of how happy I was those weeks with Nathaniel. Not only were my days filled with hard, satisfying work—training with Hyemi, being a part of ASAP's team under Director Ryu's leadership—but my nights were filled with laughter and love.

My father turns off the television.

"You were living with a boy," he seethes, "under *my* roof. One you specifically told me you weren't seeing. Was meeting with CEO Cha's nephew a lie as well? How am I supposed to believe anything you say?" He swipes his hand down his face. "Do you think, after you've shown how irresponsible you are, that I'll give my shares to you?"

"What do you mean?" my mother asks sharply.

My father blinks, having apparently forgotten she's in the room.

"Sori," my mother says, frowning, "were you meeting with CEO Cha's nephew in exchange for your father's shares of Joah?"

"Never mind that," my father interrupts before I can answer. "I'm disappointed in you, Sori. I thought you were like me, but you're not. You're weak-minded and lack discipline. You betrayed my trust. But you can make up for it, prove to me that you're serious, by breaking up with that boy. Maybe then I'll consider giving you the shares."

He's giving me an ultimatum: either choose Nathaniel or save the company.

"Don't," my mother says.

There's a sharp silence.

"Don't break up with Nathaniel."

I gape at my mother. "That is," she says, "you don't have to break up with him, if you don't want to."

She turns to my father, her eyes flashing. "I can endure you speaking down to me—I care so little of your opinion, it hardly matters—but not to my daughter, *never* to Sori."

I've never seen her stand up to him, not like this. "Get out of my house."

My father's face turns a curious shade of red. "You're both ungrateful, after all I've done for you . . . Let's see if you can survive on your own."

He begins to walk from the room, stopping in front of me. "It's not too late, Sori. Come with me now and I'll forgive you. I might even forgive your mother, in time."

I take a deep breath, meeting his gaze. "You say I betrayed your trust, but I think it's the other way around."

He bristles. "How dare you speak to me like that. You're my daughter."

"I don't feel like I am. If love is conditional between us, mine is that you respect and love me without conditions."

My father watches me for a second, his gaze never leaving

mine, and then he stomps from the room, slamming the door on the way out.

I sink to the floor. What have I done? Have I doomed Joah? My plan was getting my father's shares. Without them, my mother will have to sell the company.

She starts to speak but stops when her phone chirps. Mine does as well, vibrating in my pocket. It's a message, from Secretary Park, sent to both of us:

Woo Hyemi's been in an accident.

Thirty-seven

I burst into the hospital room, my mother right behind me. Hyemi's sitting up in bed with her arm in a cast, eating ice cream from a tub. In an impressive show of ambidexterity, she's balancing the tub against her chest with the cast, holding the spoon with her left hand.

"What happened?" I hurry over.

"It was like I was in a scene from a drama," Hyemi says. "I was at a crosswalk and a motorcyclist ran a red light, almost bowling me over. I landed on my arm, pretty hard. Too bad there wasn't a cute boy to catch me!"

I stare at her face. Is she masking her pain with cheerfulness? Except that she really does look okay. She doesn't appear to have any wounds, besides her arm.

"Your father's in Hong Kong, isn't he?" my mother says, coming to stand next to me. "Has anyone checked you in?"

"I don't think so. I called Secretary Park when I got here, after I called my mom and dad."

"I'll go check with the doctor," my mother says, leaving the room.

"Sun Ye-eonni and the others were here," Hyemi says. "You just missed them. They brought the ice cream. Also snacks and toys and stuffed animals. Ruby brought her Tamagotchi, which is actually kind of stressful." I look behind her to a box of items stuffed with colorful bags of chips, Pepero, and Choco Pies, as well as a Switch; on the top of the box is a crocheted carrot with a face.

"They had to leave for a recording," she explains.

Her words are followed by a brief lull.

"I'm sorry I haven't been around this past week," I say into the silence.

"After the news article . . ."—I don't have to explain the one— "I became obsessed with saving the company, as if it was something *I* could do, on my own. I was so caught up with everything going on in my own life, that I'd forgotten the person who was struggling the most. I'm sorry, Hyemi."

"You know, since you brought it up, I *was* hurt." My chest tightens. "I thought, when you didn't come to see me, that you *were* only helping me because of my father's money."

"Hyemi . . ." My heart constricts.

"But then Nathaniel said something that made me realize that I was wrong to think that of you. He asked me if I thought you were someone who'd help me *just* for my father's money, and not because maybe you liked me, just a little."

"I like you *a lot*."

She giggles. "And I realized . . . I didn't. I don't. You helped me because you genuinely wanted to. I could feel that. Every hour you spent with me in that practice room, every time you listened to me, I felt your sincerity.

"Nathaniel and I . . . we talked a lot about you." She scratches her chin. "Actually, most of our conversations were about you. He was the one who guessed you were dating CEO Cha's nephew because you were trying to save Joah . . ."

Nathaniel.

"Hyemi." I take a deep breath. "There's something I have to tell you."

She looks at me, her expression open.

"I'm in love with Nathaniel."

"I know," she says, deadpan. "I saw all your appearances together. You can't fake that kind of chemistry. And I know you're not an actress. I watched your cameo."

I gape at her, then laugh. "Hyemi-yah!"

"I'm happy loving Nathaniel from afar, like a fan. My heart isn't broken, so don't worry about me. Honestly, I like *you* more than I like Nathaniel. I'm cheering for *you*, Eonni."

She's so sweet. I wipe the tears gathering at the corners of my eyes. "What about ASAP? Have you thought about whether you want to stay?"

"I don't know . . ." She tucks a strand of her hair behind her ear. "I miss performing. This whole week, I've wanted to be on stage with the other members, but I don't want to be a burden to them either."

I frown, remembering something that Sun Ye said last night. "When Sun Ye and the others were here, did she talk about an announcement regarding ASAP?"

"She did, though she was pretty cryptic about it."

"If you want to stay in the group, you should stay. The other members also want that. Let's trust in our CEO, Hyemi. She'll make things right."

She beams. "Okay, Eonni."

"Hyemi-yah!" Youngmin stands in the doorway holding a humongous bouquet of pink roses.

"Youngmin-ah! Are those for me?"

"Oh, these? They're for the halmeoni two doors down. Of course they're for you!"

He flounces over and she laughs.

I leave the two of them, stepping outside the door. My mother waits on one of the benches opposite the room.

I take a seat beside her. I'm still shocked about what happened at the house with my father. "Did you really mean it?" I ask quietly. "About not breaking up with Nathaniel."

She leans back in her chair, crossing one leg over the other. "Whatever your father says, I always want to do the opposite. It worked out for you, in this case."

"Eomma . . . are you making a joke?"

She laughs, a bright sound. "It's been a while, hasn't it? Don't worry. I will support you. Looking at the security camera footage—which, by the way, I'm going to cut your father's access to—from these past weeks really helped me to see. I mean, I'm not pleased that you lied to me and invited Nathaniel to stay with you, even with Ajumma around. But watching those videos made me remember what matters most, what has always mattered most. Your happiness."

She sighs, but not with distress. With relief. "I'm going to divorce your father."

"But . . ." I'm so shocked that I say the first thing that comes to mind. "What about the shares?"

Her eyes widen. "You thought I was staying with your father because of the shares?"

"Yes?"

332

"No, Sori-yah, I stayed with him *for you*. I wanted you to have a family, something I, as an orphan, couldn't give you. But then I realized, you already have a family. Me. And Ajumma. But also Nathaniel and the other XOXO members. Joah is your family."

"But the house."

"Sori-yah, it's *my* house."

"Yes, but Abeoji bought it for you."

"Exactly. He bought me the house as a condition that I didn't leave him after his first affair went public. It's not a gift unless the receiver *owns* the house. I made him buy it in my name."

The house doesn't belong to my father. *It belongs to my mother.*

"It's true that I signed a prenuptial agreement, but I don't want your father's money. I don't need it."

"And—and the company?" I'm a little breathless with all the revelations. "I saw the papers in your drawer, that you were selling the company to KS."

"Oh, Sori. You must have been so stressed. Is that why you were dating CEO Cha's nephew?"

She shakes her head. "I'll admit, I did . . . waver, but I never truly considered the offer. The papers were drawn up by KS's lawyers.

"Since it's worrying you, I can tell you I took out a loan. The company will be fine. Every day presents new challenges, but I'll work together with my team to face them. I toed the line before, bringing Hyemi into ASAP in exchange for her father's money, but I've decided to stick to my principles from now on.

"Even if Hyemi's father should offer the money tomorrow, I won't accept it. Hyemi is talented and hardworking, so she'll remain in the group. I want to *protect* Hyemi. I want to pave a path for her with lots of beautiful things for her to see along the way. That's my dream for her. That's my dream of Joah."

"Eomma," I say, tears in my eyes, "I'm so proud of you."

"And I'm so proud of *you*, my darling girl." She takes me into her arms, holding me close. After a few minutes, she gently releases me, her own eyes a little damp. "What do you think about finally having that meal?"

Thirty-eight

"Jenny-nuna!"

"Youngmin-ah!"

Jenny and Youngmin run from opposite ends of my front lawn like they're in the penultimate scene of a drama. In fact, this is exactly how the latest episode of Sun's drama ended, with Sun and the heroine running toward each other across a beach. I'd watched the episode with Hyemi in the hospital before my mother and I had left to grab lunch.

When they reach each other, Youngmin picks Jenny up and spins her around.

It's a little last minute, but with Jenny, Gi Taek, and Angela's help, as well as Ajumma and my mother's, we've managed to turn my front lawn into the setting for a party. We've put out tables and chairs, Angela and Gi Taek brought decorations—party balloons and a congratulatory banner—and Nadine is bringing a cake from a bakery near her university. We're catering sandwiches from a local delicatessen, and Sun said he'll bring alcohol "for the adults." As for entertainment, I glance nervously at the microphone in its stand.

When I came up with this plan, I thought of doing something that would please Nathaniel, and bearing my feelings for him in front of our friends and family, while mortifying for me, *would* make him ridiculously happy.

There's still a chance to back out. . . .

No, I'm determined. I *want* to do this.

I want to celebrate him, for the launch of his song, and for completing his class—Nadine informed me that he passed his final exam—but also, I want to show him how much these past two weeks have meant to me, and the years before, when he first stood up for me against my bullies. We hadn't even been friends then, but Nathaniel could never tolerate injustice. I used to envy his fearlessness, because I knew that it came from having his family to lean on, but now all I feel is gratitude, for them, *for him*.

I love how confident he is. He always thinks the best of people, which makes me want to be better. He gives *me* strength. And he's become *my* family, like Sun and the others, like Jenny, and Ajumma, and my mother, family I *choose*, and who've chosen me.

I'm still sad about what happened with my father, but I've left the door open. He can take the final steps to walk through. It's up to him.

After Youngmin, the guests start arriving. Sun pulls up in a Porsche, bearing flowers for my mother, who hands them to Ajumma and goes to help with the drinks.

"I *told* you she lives in a mansion." I hear Hyemi's bright voice outside the gate.

I hurry down to let her and the ASAP members inside.

"Daebak," Jiyoo says, her eyes wide as she takes in the front garden and house. "You're so cool, CEO Seo!"

My mother just shakes her head with a smile. She hasn't told them yet, but Joah is releasing a statement tomorrow morning to clear up the situation surrounding Hyemi's scandal. Since Joah *won't* be accepting money from her father, she can join ASAP with a clear conscience. Once Hyemi's arm heals, she'll be able to start promotions as early as next week.

Director Ryu is next to arrive, sweeping through the gate in a stylish brown blazer and slacks. She joins the ASAP members at their table, where Youngmin is trying to resurrect Jiyoo's Tamagotchi.

I pull my mother aside. "Remember, back when you asked me to help Hyemi, after I told you I no longer wished to be an idol, you said you'd support me on whatever career path I did end up choosing?"

My mother nods. "I remember."

"I know what that is now. I want to work with Director Ryu. I want to continue helping her with developing ASAP's brand, but I also want to help envision and launch new groups. And maybe one day, I can become a creative designer with a team of my own."

"I think . . . ," my mother says slowly, "that's a great idea. It might not have seemed like it, but I was observing you, and I couldn't have chosen a better career for you myself. Jin-rang has already praised you to me, so I know she'd be happy to have you on her team."

My mother turns contemplative. "It's more of a behind-the-scenes role, and it won't get you as much recognition."

"I'll have appreciation from the people who *I* care about, who matter to me, that's enough."

My mother smiles, pleased for me.

Nadine arrives, bearing a rather large cake in a box that a few of the ASAP members help her carry inside, and then Jenny's running up to me.

"Jaewoo texted! They just pulled up in front of the house."

I hurry over to the mic stand, with Youngmin grabbing his guitar to join me.

Nathaniel walks through the gate, his eyes locking on to me.

Youngmin plays the opening chords, and I bring the microphone to my lips. The song is Nathaniel's, the one he wrote with Naseol, arranged for acoustic guitar. I block out the eyes of everyone watching and focus on Nathaniel. I don't have the most beautiful voice, but I *do* have years of voice training, and anyway, I'm not trying to demonstrate my skills, I'm singing to show Nathaniel that I'm willing to be vulnerable, in front of him, in front of our friends and family. That, to me, he's worth every small and big gesture, he's worth *everything*.

When the song is over, there's a brief silence. Then he's walking across the grass, and I'm standing up to meet him. I launch myself into his arms, and it's like we're in a drama of our own, except that it's real.

Afterward, Nathaniel and I sneak up to my room so that I can give him back his wallet and phone that he left the morning after the awards show.

"Wait," I say, when he starts to slide his phone into his back pocket.

I take out mine and pull up his contact, clicking the Call button. "I couldn't find your phone, so I called it."

On his screen, my incoming call lights up with the name *Songbird*. It was his nickname for me while we were dating.

"Did you change it back or did you . . . ?"

"I never changed it."

Feeling overwhelmed, I look away. "I changed yours back." I pull up his contact and show him the screen where it says *Boyfriend*.

"Back?" He lifts a brow. "Which means you changed it *from* 'Boyfriend' to something else. Was it 'The One Who Got Away'?" He grins.

"'The One Who Annoys Me Endlessly.'"

"I'll take it," Nathaniel says.

I shake my head, amused.

I move behind him toward the door, then stop when I feel his hand slide along my waist. "I like your skirt. Where did you get it?"

I turn in his arms, peering up to study his face. "You're stalling, aren't you?"

"I just want to spend a little longer with you," he says, his fingers fiddling with the band of the skirt. "They can wait." His eyes lift, meeting mine. "I can't."

My heart fills with love for him. We've been through so much and waited so long.

"Neither can I," I say, and bring my mouth to his for a kiss.

Dear Jenny,

Nathaniel and I arrived in New York safely. We're staying at a hotel in Manhattan. I wanted to stay at his parents' house— his mother makes the most delicious meals, and his father treats me like his fifth daughter, which is to say, he adores me— but Nathaniel wanted to "have me to himself" or whatever ridiculous things he likes to say. I think he says stuff like that just to get a reaction out of me, and it works every time! Ugh!

I know I'm talking to you over video chat later today, but I wanted to send you a postcard. Isn't the photo on the front gorgeous? Remember when you accidentally read the postcard Nathaniel sent me, and we had that whole misunderstanding? Ha ha. Well, this one's for you. You can read this one.

I'm so happy, Jenny, happier than I've ever been, and the best part about it? I know this happiness will last. Because of Nathaniel, but also because of you and all our friends. Nathaniel and I are going to Paris next, then Milan, but we'll be back in Seoul by the end of the year. Let's celebrate together.

XOXO,
Sori

Acknowledgments

First and foremost, thank you to all the readers who showered *XOXO* with so much love and support. This book would not be possible without you. 감사합니다.

To my editor, Carolina Ortiz, thank you for your gentle guidance and wonderful edits. *ASAP* is the book it is today because of you. To my agent, Patricia Nelson, this is our fifth book together! We've come such a long way—thank you for everything.

I was ecstatic when I found out I'd get to work with designer Jessie Gang and illustrator Zipcy again: thank you for the most beautiful, dreamy cover! You always hit it out of the ballpark.

To everyone working behind the scenes: copyeditor Jill Freshney, proofreader Genevieve Kim, production editors Mikayla Lawrence and Gweneth Morton, production managers Annabelle Sinoff and Nicole Moulaison, you give me so much confidence, and for that I will forever be grateful.

To the team at HarperTeen and Epic Reads, including Lisa Calcasola and Kelly Haberstroh, I'm so proud to have you on Team *ASAP*. And to my wonderful audiobook narrators, Greta Jung, a.k.a. Jenny from *XOXO*, and Joy Osmanski, a.k.a. Sori from *ASAP*—thank you for bringing my characters to life!

Special thanks to Nadia Kim for your invaluable insights and to Anissa from FairyLoot, whose dedication to and passion for books inspires me!

My Korean author friends grow every year—I treasure all of you: Kat Cho, Sarah Suk, Susan Lee, Grace K. Shim, Lyla Lee, Stephan Lee, and Ellen Oh. Thanks for all the laughs and real talk!

To the Tree chat, I honestly don't know how I'd even write a novel without all of you: Akshaya Raman, a.k.a. ATEEZ's #1 fan (special shout-out to Wooyoung); Katy Rose Pool, CRJ's and Sufjan's group chat representative; and Madeleine Colis and Erin Rose Kim, my favorite Swifties.

Thank you to my critique partners: Meg Kohlmann, Amanda Foody, Amanda Haas, Alexis Castellanos, Ashley Burdin, C. L. Herman, Mara Fitzgerald, Melody Simpson, Tara Sim, and Janella Angeles—you're more than critique partners; you're friends for life.

To all my friends, old and new, thank you: Karuna Riazi, Nafiza Azad, Lauren Hennessy, Ashley Kim, Michelle Kim, Kristin Dwyer, Adalyn Grace, Stephanie Willing, Candice Iloh, Devon Van Essen, Michelle Calero, Gaby Brabazon, Cynthia Mun, Cindy Pon, Judy I. Lin, Swati Teerdhala, Hannah Bahn, Veeda Bybee, and June CL Tan.

To the wonderful owners of the Writer's Block, Drew and Scott—thank you for providing a home for the Las Vegas book-loving community!

To the foreign publishers of *XOXO* and *ASAP*—thank you for sharing my stories with readers all around the world! And to *XOXO*'s international fans, thank you! I'm honored to have such fantastic readers.

Thank you to all the bloggers and booklovers who've supported me and my stories; special shout-outs to Alexa from

@alexalovesbooks, Lili from @utopia.state.of.mind, Cori from @coristoryreads, Michelle from @magicalreads7, and Tiffany from @readbytiffany.

To my very large extended family: I love you all so much!! Special shout-out to Rhys and Nora, our newest members <3

To Toro and Leila: I love you, mong mong!

And last, but never least, to my family, who have always given me the most strength: Mom and Dad, Camille, and Jason.